Trails

&

Blades

by
Amanda Kaye

To hear about the next exciting release from Amanda Kaye, sign up for her newsletter at:

www.amandakayebooks.com/subscribe-now/

Cristoph would have a heart attack if he knew I was here.

Why my brother's convinced a noblewoman can't do anything more strenuous than lifting a teacup when I spent our childhood falling out of trees and roaming the countryside is one of life's great mysteries. But even I have to admit I might've pushed things too far this time.

I study the hastily scrawled directions on the stained parchment, then frown at the building. The collection of leaning walls and the sagging thatched roof look more like an abandoned cottage than the common house where I'm supposed to meet my contact. Any business sign or mark is long gone, and the blank stone wall with its warped, narrow door doesn't give any hints to what lurks behind it. The other buildings on the street are even less reassuring, with their collapsed walls and air of desolation. Squeaks come from the shadows and I gulp, my stomach twisting.

If this wasn't my best chance to track down my prey, I'd turn around and never look back. But in the years that I've been hiring any half-competent investigators—and far too many incompetent ones—this is the first hint of a real lead. I can't let it go to waste.

At least my height will help me blend in with the men. I check that my long black braid's firmly tucked under my shapeless cap and that my oversized black coat is buttoned up to hide my figure, then square my shoulders and squeeze through the misshapen door.

It takes a moment for my eyes to adjust to the faint flickering light from the fireplace on the back wall. A few long tables are shoved haphazardly around the narrow room, a smattering of dark silhouettes scattered around them. Nobody so much as twitches, but I feel their eyes watching, judging. I suppress a shiver and thrust out my chin as I peer through the smoky air.

A small tip of a tankard draws my eye. I force myself to walk purposefully over to the corner where my contact is slouched at a small table. Hartwin's wearing the same patched gray coat and dung-colored shirt he had on at our first and only meeting a year ago. In that time, his curly, reddish-brown hair has faded to iron gray around his temples, and his unruly beard has acquired a few new white patches. At least Hartwin looks like he knows what soap is, which makes him a huge improvement over the last charlatan.

He kicks the spare chair toward me. I perch on the edge of the seat and force my shoulders to relax. The man who recommended Hartwin swore he used to work for the Spymaster, but it's likely a tale used to inflate his fee. Hartwin takes a long draw on the tankard, watching me with his one bright brown eye. I stare right back, ready to bet a sizable sum he doesn't cover the milky white eye to make people uncomfortable, giving him an advantage. He'll use every dirty trick in the book to get results, which is why I happily paid his ridiculous price.

Hartwin finishes his drink while I bite the tip of my tongue to keep silent. I've dealt with enough of these scoundrels to know speaking first would be a mistake.

I'd like to imagine there's a flicker of respect in his working eye. "Good news, Lady Carina." He reaches inside his coat and tosses a scorched parchment on the table. "The Bane fled Balut before I could catch them, but I did find this."

My heart speeds up, my breath catching as I snatch it up. *Is this it? Will I finally get answers?* My excitement quickly turns to confusion, then annoyance. There's nothing on the page except a few smudged words and a half-done sketch in the corner. "What's this? It's nothing."

Hartwin leans back in his chair with a smug look. "Look closer."

I grit my teeth and squint at the page. "Sunselt… Merc… Kag….?" Sunselt marks the middle of summer, but what could the other two mean?

"*Kangan* Brecht's annual Sunselt party at Merchwood is coming up in three weeks." He nods at my gasp of recognition. "The Bane will be there to hunt their new target."

Yes! I lean forward, gripping the edge of the table, barely staying in my seat. "Who are they? What do they look like?"

The former spy shrugs. "No idea."

"Nothing?" My chest tightens as my fists clench, crumpling the note. "A name? Are they a man? Woman? Wood elf?"

"They're a ghost. Been after them for almost fifteen years, and this is the first whiff I've had. Never uses the same poison twice, and never the same delivery method. Clothing, food, coating objects." Hartwin picks up his tankard, then glowers at the empty cup. "Means we can't even be sure most times that the Bane was the culprit. And they always hide in a crowd, so we can't narrow down their identity. Take this wingding at the noble's house. It'll have over two hundred people between guests and staff, not to mention the nearby town. But I'll suss them out. I've got their scent now."

I narrow my brown eyes, annoyance flashing through me. "That's what you said when you went to Balut, but you still don't know who you're hunting."

He glares at me. "Oy, I found out where they'll be, didn't I? That's more than anyone else has done."

Fair, but it doesn't make me feel better. "What if they get away again? They might disappear forever." Heads swivel our way and I lower my voice. "They can't escape." I touch my coat, feeling my mother's gold locket hidden under the fabric.

Hartwin nods. "Which is why I want to hire more men."

It's my turn to lean back in the chair. I cross my arms and lift an eyebrow. "And you want me to pay for it."

He smirks. "I don't work for free."

Don't I know it. I mull it over for a moment. It's possible Hartwin's only trying to wring more money from me, but the need for answers overrides any caution.

"Fine." I pull a bag of coins from my pocket and set it on the table, keeping my hand firmly clamped on the pouch. "But you'll need more than that. Nobles have their own spaces where the staff aren't welcome, and they can sniff out an imposter in minutes. You need someone in their circles to be your eyes and ears."

I smile sweetly at the sudden wariness on his face. "Which is why I'm coming with you."

The spectacular descriptions of Merchwood fail to live up to
the reality as my hired carriage rolls down the long road to
the estate. A winding drive offers tantalizing views of the
hundreds of acres of woodlands, including glimpses of the
estate's famous jumping course. The golden stone building's
at least seven stories tall, with sweeping east and west wings,
complete with turrets. Off to the left side of the palace are
gardens overflowing with flowers, fountains, and mazes that
are redesigned every season. *If this is the* Kangan*'s summer
palace, I can only imagine what the High King's palace is
like.*

The carriage rumbles across the small bridge and I lean
back into my seat with a happy sigh. If I have to be around a
bunch of stuffy lords and ladies for the next few weeks, at
least I'll have an easy escape to nature.

I glance at my traveling companion, amused that
Hartwin's pretending to be asleep again. "How will you
contact me when you have an update? When will I hear from
you?"

He shifts lower in the seat, pulling his cap over his eyes. "When I feel like it."

I eye him for a moment, then kick his shin.

"Oy, no need to get violent." He glares at me, rubbing his leg. "I'll send you a message when I hear anything. And if you learn something, put a kerchief in the corner of your window." Hartwin scratches his beard, giving me an appraising look. "Make sure you listen to the gossip. Most of it's rubbish, but there's usually a gold kernel buried under all the dung."

I make a face. "Can't I search their rooms, or slip them a truth tonic and interrogate them?"

"That's my job. You keep your ears open and use your head."

My stomach tenses. I shift on my seat, biting my bottom lip. "It might take me a while to get any good tidbits. It'll take some time before they trust a stranger." I haven't been home since Mother and I went to the Anglish countryside five years ago. Everyone thinks it was to recover from a long illness, but Hartwin's one of the few people outside our family that knows the truth.

"Slow's fine. Don't push or you'll give away the game. The party lasts weeks, after all." He raps on the roof of the carriage and we rattle to a stop. "Make sure you don't alert anyone why you're here. If the Bane gets a whiff of you snooping around, they'll go to ground and we'll never find them." Hartwin jumps out the door without a farewell and disappears into the woods.

His warning sits heavy in my heart as the carriage approaches the palace. I've been so focused on helping capture the Bane that I hadn't considered I could be a liability. I square my shoulders. *That just means I'll have to be careful and make sure everyone believes I'm just a flighty, silly lady who's only here to enjoy the party and mingle with the rest of the local nobility.*

I take out the frustratingly small list of the Bane's suspected victims and review them again, though I long ago memorized it:

> *3 mos - Lady Neff - Asdine, Balut - nightshade*
> *13 mos - Lord Schnoebelen - Deval, Irelin - poison extracted from peach pits*

My eyes automatically skip the next entry, though it doesn't stop the knot from forming in my stomach.

> *6 years - Mr Riemenschneider - Donaj, Germania - unknown*
> *7 years - Mr Tolkien - Norger, Irelin - Sunslit (common Maccar plant)*
> *12 years - Lady Jahns - Tescir, Macco - unknown*
> *15 years - Lord Altmont – Landsheer - Fate's Tears (rare Rus plant)*

Hartwin didn't provide the Bane's full history, since it's a lot of speculation and assumptions—and he's probably paranoid that I'd shout it out to everyone I meet. If Hartwin's obsession with catching the Bane didn't rival mine, I'd be insulted that he thinks so little of me. But I agree that focusing on the few mostly-confirmed cases will make it easier to narrow down our suspects while keeping the Bane unaware of our inquiries.

The carriage stops and I quickly tuck the parchment into my pocket, then take the footman's hand to climb out. A lovely blonde woman glides forward to greet me, her pale green gown a beautiful complement to her bright blue eyes that tilt up at the corners. I'd guess she's close to my age, though her effortless poise makes me feel like a grubby child covered in road dust.

She holds out her hand with a serene smile. "Lady Carina, I'm so glad you could join us for Sunselt. I'm *Rirzan Aliz*."

*T*he Kangan*'s sister. She must be helping him host.* I take her hand and dip into a curtsy. "The pleasure's mine. Merchwood parties are famous, and I was flattered you invited me." The polite exchange scripted by society is painfully bland, but I'd better get used to it if I want to fit in here.

"Will your brother be joining us?"

I hope not—he'd have a fit if he knew I was here. "No, Cristoph has business keeping him in Wittrow. He asked me to pass on his apologies." A kaleidoscope of blue butterflies bursts from the nearby bush and swirls around us. *So pretty!* I watch them ribbon through the air in a fantastic pattern, absentmindedly saying, "He has hay fever, and he's afraid of bees, so he'd probably be blowing his nose and miserable the whole time. You're better off meeting him in winter when he's more fun." My jaw snaps shut and my stomach twists as heat rushes into my cheeks. I stare at Aliz in horror. *What did I just say? Cristoph will kill me when he finds out. She must think I'm a dolt!*

Aliz's face scrunches. I pray to the Fortunes for the ground to open up and swallow me so I can die of embarrassment in peace. A strangled giggle escapes her. Then another. She bursts into loud laughter and my shoulders relax, my giggles joining hers.

She wipes the corner of her eyes. "I'll keep that in mind. But unfortunately, you won't be able to escape my brother. The Sunselt party's his favorite, and he can be a bit…much the first time you meet him."

I grin. "I consider myself warned."

Aliz links her arm through mine and leads me inside, chatting easily about the upcoming party events. The air's cooler in the palace, sending a shiver over my skin. The beautiful elegance of Merchwood continues inside, with a spacious plastered entryway decorated in warm yellows and tans. Large hallways branch out on either side of the space, and in front of us is an enormous marble stairway leading to the next floor. A few small tables are scattered by the doorway with large landscape paintings on the wall, completing the welcoming atmosphere.

She pauses at the foot of the stairs, where a maid in a crisp uniform is waiting. "Felice will show you to your room. You can rest, or feel free to explore Merchwood until supper. I wish I could give you a tour now, but Lord von Bron should be arriving at any moment and I need to greet him. I hope we can spend more time together this evening?" Her smile has an endearing touch of shyness.

My pulse skitters to a stop, and a painful roar fills my ears. *Alexander?*

I'd been so worried about my brother showing up unexpectedly, I never even considered that Alexander would be here. *How could I be so foolish? He gets the same invites Cristoph and I do.* A sour taste floods my mouth as my chest tightens. *Mayhap coming here wasn't a good idea. In fact, it's a terrible, horrible, dreadful idea. Can I leave? Is the carriage still here?*

Aliz's still happily talking away. "—him?"

I blink at her. "What?"

She tilts her head to the side. "I was asking if you knew Lord von Bron. You're from the same providence, aren't you?"

I swallow hard, keeping my face pleasant despite the icy hand squeezing my heart. "Yes." She seems to expect more, so I force out. "We're neighbors. But I haven't seen him in many years."

Her brow furrows and a sympathetic look comes over her face as she probably recalls my long illness and exile to Angland. "Oh, of course. Well, I'll see you tonight."

I mumble something that I hope's a polite goodbye, then blindly follow the maid, my mind reeling.

Stupid. Stupid. Stupid. How could I forget about Alexander? Probably because I've spent every moment since I left home trying not to think of him. My best friend and childhood love—and the boy who broke me. *I can't face him. Not now. But I can't leave when I'm so close to finally catching the Bane...* I struggle to breathe. Every nerve's stretched, my skin clammy. A wave of dizziness washes over me.

I lurch to a stop. "I need some fresh air."

Leaving the startled maid behind, I flee down the hallway and down the stairs, my feet tripping over each other in my haste. I curse my yellow traveling dress, tugging at the neckline. I break into a run when I spot the front doors. At the last second, I remember Alexander might be out there, and veer down a random hallway, frantically searching for a way out.

Room after room without a door to the outside, my swearing growing more creative as I'm blocked at every turn. Every creak makes me flinch, convinced I'll find him standing behind me. My palms are slick with sweat. I finally shove open a window and crawl through it, landing ungracefully on a gravel path.

I pick up my skirt and race to the forest, uncaring of who might see me. All I know is I need to get away and think. I don't stop when I reach the tree line, plunging into its shadowy depths, thankful for its protection. I weave between the trunks, moving further into the forest, until I reach a great oak with low branches.

With practiced ease, I tuck my skirt up out of the way, then I grasp the closest branch and climb to a wide fork in the tree. I rest my head on my knees, gripping my locket in both hands, and force myself to breathe deeply until my pulse slows and the lightheadedness passes. Once the knots in my chest loosen to something manageable, I turn my mind to the source of my panic.

Alexander von Bron. The boy I hoped to never see again. The reason my mother is dead.

3

From the moment we met, Alexander and I were inseparable. Every day with him was an adventure as we tromped around the providence, always side by side. He was my closest and truest friend until I was fourteen. Until my life fell apart.

Nobody thought it was odd when the box of fancy bonbons arrived at Alexander's house from a specialty shop in Lonnheim. His father did a lot of business there, and it wasn't unusual for people to send samples or gifts, hoping for an investment.

Alexander knew chocolate was my obsession, so he begged his parents to give them to me. I was so touched by his thoughtfulness that I kissed him on the cheek—very daring of me—before running home to share them with my mother.

The poison was from a common wildflower that grows around our homes. We didn't know what was happening until that night, when the first pains started. Then the weeks in bed, tossing and sweating, feeling like my insides were trying to crawl out. Unable to keep anything down, but dying of thirst. Fever dreams and hallucinations. Screaming and crying and saying Fortunes-know-what through waves of delirium.

Once I was in my right mind again, it would've been easy to direct all my rage at Alexander. I was in tremendous pain, more terrified than I'd ever been in my life, and wrestling with the guilt that I'd poisoned my mother. It would've been a relief to say it was his fault this happened. But I always knew it wasn't, just like I knew I shouldn't blame myself for sharing the chocolates with Mother.

What I can't forgive is that Alexander refused to see me, no matter how many times I asked for him or wrote him. I spent weeks waiting for the moment he'd slip inside my room, take my hand, and tell me everything would be all right. Every day, when someone came through my door that wasn't him, a little piece of my heart died. It took far too long for me to accept that my best friend had abandoned me when I needed him the most.

Thank the Fortunes I had my brother, since Father was busy taking care of our mother. The menders thought going to the Anglish coast would help us both recover. Perhaps it did help, a little. Father and Cristoph had to stay behind to manage the estate, but they visited as much as they could.

It took me years to regain most of my health, but Mother never fully recovered. She was always weak and she tired easily. The news of Father's accidental death was the last blow. I know she tried to stay for me and Cristoph, but it was too much for her. In the twilight hours before dawn when I can be honest with myself, I'm relieved she's no longer in pain, even though I miss her every day.

It was only after we'd left for Angland that rumors of a mysterious assassin called the Bane reached us. Alexander's family and mine did everything they could to find out who the Bane was, but they never got anywhere with their inquiries.

And now Alexander's here, complicating my life again when I'm finally on the brink of catching the Bane. The Fortunes have a cruel sense of humor.

Alexander can't find out what I'm really doing at Merchwood. I can't risk him messing things up or tattling to Cristoph out of some sense of duty. My brother would sew me in a sack and ship me to Rus if he knew I was trying to catch the Bane.

My jaw clenches and I narrow my eyes. I'll just have to avoid Alexander as much as possible. It's a large party. There's really no reason for us to spend time together. And it's been years. He's probably forgotten about me the same way I've forgotten him. A nagging little voice whispers that I never forgot him, but I ignore it. All I have to do is keep out of his way. No—he should keep out of my way. He's the one who didn't want to be my friend, after all.

Satisfied, I lean back against the trunk of the tree and watch the birds flittering from branch to branch. Errant leaves drift by, floating on invisible currents while sunbeams dance through the air. I idly rub my thumb over the locket's engraved rose pattern, letting my mind wander on the wind. There are few things as soothing as being alone in the forest. No matter where I go, I always know I can climb a tree and find a few hours of peace.

There's a rustle below me, then another. *A fox?* I lazily lean over and glance down, trying to spot the sly creature, keeping my hand on the branch for balance. A crow dives at me, screeching, madly flapping its wings in my face. I startle back—and overbalance.

With a shriek, I slip off the limb. My stomach leaps into my throat as I plunge through the air, bouncing off a branch, then another. Every hit rattles my teeth, forcing the breath from my lungs. I instinctively twist to get my feet below me—then slam into something that staggers sideways, and we tumble to the ground.

Dazed, I shake my head, trying to orient myself. A pair of arms is wrapped around my waist, something soft beneath me. It takes a moment to realize someone caught me. I tilt my head back to thank my rescuer and the words die in my throat.

Alexander's staring down at me in astonishment.

4

This cannot be happening. I close my eyes and silently groan. No, no, no. Not him. Anyone but him. The Fortunes wouldn't do this to me. This is just a nightmare. I need to wake up. Any moment now, I'll be back in bed and relieved it was only a dream.

"Carina? Do you—what are—are you hurt? What happened?"

So much for avoiding him. With a sigh, I open my eyes. Alexander's even more beautiful than I remember—and I hate him for it. If I'm going to be forced to see him again, at least he could have the decency to look ugly and surly.

Instead, the features that captured my fancy when we were young have matured into something far more appealing. The wavy brown hair that curls at his collar, the dark moss-green eyes, the jaw line lightly sprinkled with stubble. The softness of childhood has melted away to make his straight nose and high cheekbones more defined. Even the bottom tooth that's slightly crooked is charming. But there's an edge to his gaze and a tenseness to his jaw that warns me life has sharpened the easygoing boy I knew.

I scramble off his lap and jump back, blurting out, "What are you doing here?"

Alexander's brow furrows. "I was invited."

"No, I mean *here*." I gesture at the trees.

"Oh. I wanted to walk after that long carriage ride." His expression darkens as he stands. "What were you doing up there? Are you trying to break your neck?"

"It's your fault I fell! Well, yours, and that burning bird." I busy myself brushing the twigs and leaves off my dress, hiding my flaming cheeks and avoiding his gaze. "I'm fine, so you can go on and finish your walk."

Alexander doesn't budge. After a few moments that feel like an eternity, he clears his throat. "I didn't know you'd be here."

I'm dying to know if he meant he didn't expect me at the party, or to find me in the woods. "Neither did I. That you'd be here, I mean. I should've guessed since you would be invited, and most of the nobility in this region came. But for some reason, I didn't think you would. Not that it matters. Whether you came here or not, I mean. I was just surprised."

I snap my jaw shut, cursing the nerves that have turned me into a babbling fool. Being this close to him after all these years has shoved every bit of common sense out of my mind. If I had to run into him, I should've been polite and aloof. Instead, I'm a rambling mess.

The silence stretches between us. I finished dusting off my dress two minutes ago and now I'm just uselessly going through the motions. *Why is he still here? He's the one who cut off our friendship. Why doesn't he leave already?*

I should be the one that walks away. Show him he means as little to me as I do to him. It would be the smart thing to do. But my heart has never been very good at protecting itself. It insists on drinking in every moment with him, even as it reopens every crack and fracture that I thought had healed long ago.

Finally, I sigh in defeat, grudgingly meeting his eyes. Alexander's watching me with the strangest expression that I can't quite decipher. I'm used to knowing his every mood, but time has brought changes to both of us. If I didn't know better, I'd think he's as reluctant to leave as I am.

I wrap my arms around my waist, shifting from foot to foot. A sharp pinch flares in my right side and I wince. *Burning tree branch.* I'm going to be a giant bruise for a few days.

A line appears between Alexander's eyebrows. "Do you need help getting back to the palace?"

"No. It's nothing." I lift my chin. "It's not the first time I've fallen out of a tree."

"And probably not the last." A ghost of a smile dances on his lips and my pulse jumps.

I shouldn't be this jittery around him. It's just because he caught me off guard. If he hadn't surprised me, I would be calmer. I seize on to the annoyance, using it to steady my nerves as I take a deep breath. I can do this. Calm. Detached. Sophisticated. "How was your trip?"

"Not as long as yours." Alexander steps closer.

My heart speeds up, my body humming. I refuse to move and show him how much his nearness affects me. "I didn't mind. The countryside's so pretty and I made good time." *Burn it, what else are we supposed to talk about?* This is the perfect opportunity to use the dreary society script to my advantage, but it's all flown out of my head. "I hope your mother and father are doing well." I clamp my lips shut, wanting to snatch the words back, but it's too late.

"Carina." He hesitates, his brow furrowing, then says, "I'm sorry about your parents. They were wonderful people."

My chest tightens. "Yes, they were." I touch my mother's locket.

His eyes follow my movement. "Why did you stay in Angland?" There's a hint of accusation in his voice.

Because you weren't there. I glare at him. "Keeping track of me? I don't know why you care now."

Alexander tilts his head to the side, his gaze sharpening. "I've always cared."

"You have a funny way of showing it." I look away, pressing my lips together. *Calm. Detached. Sophisticated.* "This is my first Sunselt party at Merchwood. Is it yours?"

"No, I've been coming for the past few years. Carina, about your mother. I—"

"There's supposed to be a different event every day. Can you imagine? At least we'll never be bored." Tears sting my eyes as a lump grows in my throat. The grief from my mother's death is always hovering just under the surface. I can't manage it and Alexander without something breaking. A dull throb pulses in my head and I swallow hard. *I can't cry in front of him. I won't.*

Alexander stiffens, then runs a hand through his hair. "She was—"

"Don't talk about her," I snap, the heaviness in my chest making it hard to breathe. *Calm. Detat—burn it, burn it, burn it!* A tear escapes. I pretend to brush a strand of hair back, using the movement to wipe away the traitorous drop.

His shoulders slump. "I'm sorry."

I don't know if he's apologizing for now or his actions

back then, but it doesn't matter. This is getting too close to wounds I don't want to reopen. I desperately search for some way to get his gaze off me before he sees too much. "Did *Rirzan* Aliz greet you?"

He finally looks away, and I breathe a silent sigh of relief. "Yes. The *Kangan*'s sister is acting as the hostess for the Sunselt party."

Obviously. Why is he telling me things I already know? "She seems nice."

"Indeed. Well, I should prepare for supper." He gives me a hasty bow, then turns toward the palace. Alexander pauses. "I'm glad you're not hurt." He strides away. He doesn't look back.

I open my mouth to say—what, I have no idea. Instead, I watch him disappear into the trees. I should be happy he left, so why does it feel like he's abandoning me all over again?

But mostly, I'm…confused. I thought he'd be eager to ignore me and leave as soon as he knew I was all right. So why did he stay?

He was probably worried I was going to faint. I did just fall out of a tree. And a gentleman like Alexander wouldn't leave anyone alone if he thought they needed help. Not even his worst enemy. So, he had to wait until he was convinced that I'm really fine. That's all.

The explanation's logical, plausible, and all wrong. And he didn't seem angry. Well, he was angry that I fell out of a tree and landed on top of him, but that's understandable. Mostly, he seemed concerned. About me.

No. I grit my teeth. He's not my friend, not anymore. I need to remember that. All that matters is catching the Bane, and nothing's going to stop me, including Alexander.

A growing pit in my stomach says this was my first

encounter with Alexander, but it won't be the last. If I'm going to end up in knots every time I see him, I need to figure out a way to stay away from him. Fast.

This party is off to a spectacular start.

5

When I return to the palace in my stained and torn dress, the maid I met earlier gives a dismayed cry. "Milady, were you attacked?"

"No, just an unfortunate incident with some branches." I run a hand over my hair, sending bits of twigs falling to the floor. "Could you please show me to my room?"

She gives me curious looks over her shoulder as she guides me through the palace to the fourth floor, lingering in the doorway before I shoo her out, assuring her I don't need any help dressing for supper. After I shut the door firmly behind her, I glance around my new home for the next few weeks.

It's a tidy little room with a bed, a small vanity, and a nook near the window for reading. Someone has already hung my clothes in the wardrobe with sprigs of lavender and stored the luggage under the bed. There's a vase with blooming pink roses next to the washbasin that matches the cheery curtains, while a bowl of fresh fruit sits on a low stool by the nook.

Pleased with my accommodations, I inspect my face in the mirror. No scratches—whew. That's the first bit of luck I've had today. There's a faint shadow of a bruise on my jaw, but that's easy enough to cover with some light powder.

The yellow traveling dress looks like it held up surprisingly well from my tumble, only needing a thorough cleaning and a little mending to restore it. I undress slowly, wincing at the aches and twinges from my spontaneous descent from the tree. Because there's not much time before the supper bell rings, I wash up with the water in the basin, promising my sore muscles a long soak in a hot bath later tonight.

The evening dress selection takes longer. It's a good thing I updated my wardrobe before the party so I'll blend in with the rest of the gentry. I survey the garments, considering all my options carefully. I need to present myself as an unassuming guest that's only here to enjoy the party. Just another face in the crowd, that fades into the scenery, letting me eavesdrop on their gossip without being noticed.

I finally select a plum silk dress with long sleeves and gold lace embellishments. It feels overly formal after years of sturdy country dresses, but I remember my mother wearing similar gowns whenever my parents would go out for supper parties or dine with neighbors. I don't have the patience to curl my hair right now, so I settle for twisting it up into a simple knot anchored with jeweled pins that match my gold and ruby earrings. I fasten the final pin as the supper bell rings. One last glance in the mirror confirms the bruise is covered, then I fix a pleasant smile on my face and hurry to the first floor to join the queue for our meal.

The dining room's nothing short of spectacular. It's hard

not to gape as I follow my escort to my seat, trying to see everything at once. The two long tables for the guests are dwarfed by the expansive room that could seat five hundred comfortably. Each table is covered in a deep blue cloth, with huge candelabras and towering vases of ivy, edelweiss, and a blue flower I don't recognize. Enormous fireplaces sit empty at both ends of the room since the stone walls and the summer heat keep the room a comfortable temperature. Ancient tapestries depicting whimsical forest scenes cover three of the walls, while the fourth wall has a series of double doors opened to the gardens and the fading sunlight.

Aliz is at the head of one table, making it good odds that the stern man at the second table is her brother, the *Kangan* of Merchwood. The guests are all dressed in their evening best, with jewels and silks on display. I knew there were over a hundred guests, but seeing them gathered in one room is overwhelming after years of isolation and small gatherings. I'm sure to most of the nobles think this is an intimate party, but it feels like I've been tossed into an endless sea of people.

And somewhere around here is the Bane.

I'm so busy ogling the decorations, I don't notice my seatmate until the footman pulls out my chair. In his formal black dinner clothes, Alexander's elegant and somehow even more handsome. The candlelight brings out the gold highlights in his brown hair, and the stubble from earlier has disappeared, enhancing his sharp jawline. We lock eyes and my heart flutters before I sternly remind it that we don't like him anymore.

Alexander has the grace to wince as he stands and bows. "This wasn't my doing."

Aliz. I'm touched that she seated me next to someone I

know, but I wish she'd been a little less thoughtful. I give Alexander a tight smile and nod as I sit, aware of the curious eyes on us. "Lord von Bron." I quickly turn to the neighbor on my left and introduce myself.

The man's probably approaching seventy, with wide shoulders and a sour expression. But it's the absurdly long mustache that dangles past his chin and his stout stomach that clinches the impression of a grumpy walrus. He frowns at me. "These girls today, always putting themselves forward. I'd wager you don't have a chaperone either. No sense of propriety."

I flinch, my cheeks heating. Is there a way to start today over?

The woman across from me leans forward, her lime green dress a spot of brightness in a sea of somber colors. Her black hair is streaked with silver, and there are laugh lines at the corner of her gray eyes. "Don't listen to Lord Marx, dear. He's stuck in the old ways and refuses to be modern. I'm Lady Goethe, but please call me Dorthea." Her eyes narrow at Lord Marx as he opens his mouth. "Not you."

I smother my giggle as he sniffs loudly.

"I would never be so indelicate as so to call a Lady by her first name," Lord Marx declares loudly, mopping his forehead with his napkin. "And you shouldn't encourage her, Lady Goethe. There's enough talk of modernizing these days, which is just an excuse for women to run amok. But it's no matter to me what the young people are up to."

She raises an eyebrow. "Of course not. You don't know any."

Lord Marx grumbles into his wineglass, then focuses on Alexander. "Lord von Bron, are you joining the rowing competition tomorrow? *Kangan* Brecht says he added a few surprises to the race."

Alexander chuckles and shakes his head. "I've learned to avoid the *Kangan*'s surprises at any cost. Last time, he set up a group of trumpet players in the middle of the jumping course. When we came around the corner, they started playing a charge and startled all the horses. I got thrown and broke my arm in two places."

My chest tightens. *He did? Which arm?* I hide my clenched fists in my lap, forcing my shoulders to relax. It's silly to be worried about something that happened to someone I don't even care about.

Lord Marx nods condescendingly, his voice full of false sympathy. "Yes, it's best not to enter if you're not up to the challenge. I'd join the games tomorrow, but unfortunately my old war wound makes rowing impossible."

His smug air as he sips his wine sets my teeth on edge. Lord Marx may like to play the gentleman, but he's little more than a bully. I narrow my eyes, then look across the table with a grin. "Lady Goethe—"

"Dorthea, dear."

"Dorthea." I widen my eyes innocently. "Are you going to enter *Kangan* Brecht's competition?"

Her smile's full of mischief as Lord Marx splutters. "I'm tempted, but it's too early for me. It would take something a lot more interesting to get me out of bed at dawn. Are you?"

"Oh, no. Like you, I can't be bothered to wake up that early to row a boat. Now, if *Kangan* Brecht wants to have a horse race, I might be persuaded. I'd have to dig up some trousers, though. After all, it's never safe to ride sidesaddle on a new course."

Lord Marx's face turns an interesting shade of purple. "*Kangan* Brecht would never allow such a thing! It would be a scandal!"

Dorthea smirks. "You haven't spent enough time in the countryside if you think women don't wear trousers or ride astride. In Eaglan, the boutiques probably sell more trousers than dresses."

He makes a face. "Eaglan's hardly the measure for what society considers acceptable."

"It may not be as cosmopolitan as Lonnheim or Gretzberg, but there's plenty of society up there if one desires. And as Lady Lux knows, the countryside has its own charms, which is why I hardly ever leave my estate."

Lord Marx motions to a footman to refill his wineglass. "I thought it was because it takes you a month to get to the next town."

"That too." She laughs as she winks at me.

Alexander leans forward with a friendly smile. "The beauty of Eaglan is legendary. I'd love to see the fjords."

Dorthea looks off to the side and says coolly, "Yes, they're quite something."

My eyebrows rise and I can't help being a tiny bit pleased that someone at the house party's immune to Alexander's charms.

As servers sweep into the rooms pushing loaded carts, Lord Marx pats his bulging stomach. "Ah, finally. I heard Chef Kloss has outdone himself for tonight's feast."

Bowls of cold cucumber soup garnished with a tangy cream sauce are placed in front of us. Lord Marx leans forward and sniffs loudly, his eyes closed. I watch in horrified fascination as the tips of his long mustache dangle a whisker's breadth above the surface of the green liquid. He sits back in his chair and I relax—then tense as he leans forward again, the ends of his mustache dancing above the soup as he talks.

"Every course Chef Kloss makes is superb, but he's famous for his desserts. I heard Rus spies have tried to infiltrate his kitchen to steal his secrets." He dips his spoon into the creamy green soup, then slowly brings it to his mouth, closing his eyes as he takes his first taste.

The chef certainly has a fan in Lord Marx. Intrigued, I turn my attention to my own bowl while the conversation flows around me. The cucumber soup has a light, refreshing taste, making me think of spring. There's the tiniest hint of dill in the cream, enough to enhance the flavor without overpowering it. The cold dish is welcome after the heat of the day and makes me eager for the next course.

As the bowls are removed from the table, Dorthea turns to me, fiddling with the wooden luck bead dangling from her gold bracelet. "Carina, did those fires in Wittrow last year reach your estate?"

Cristoph never said anything in his letters about that. Then again, my brother wouldn't tell me if a bagpipe-playing dragon showed up in our parlor because it could 'upset me.' "I'm not sure. I've been in the Anglish countryside for the past several years."

Alexander says, "There was a fire in the hillsides, but it never spread to town or any homes."

A knot forms in my stomach. "Did it reach the lake?"

"No, it was higher up." The softness in his eyes is probably a trick of the light.

Dorthea nods at him curtly, then her expression clears as she looks at me. "I knew we were kindred spirits. This is the first time in six years I've left Eaglan, but I couldn't resist attending. A lunar eclipse on Sunselt is a once-in-a-lifetime occurrence and a very lucky time for relationships. I've been speaking with *Rirzan* Aliz about adding a lunar party to the events. If she does, I hope you'll join me."

A warmth grows in my chest. "I'd be delighted."

Lord Marx scoffs and dabs at his forehead with his napkin. "You speak of being modern, but believe in those old witch's tales."

She narrows her gray eyes. "It doesn't have to be one or the other. There's a lot of wisdom in the old ways, but I don't cling to them out of tradition."

"Nonsense. Believing the Fortunes direct the moon, or stars, or weather is foolish."

While they bicker, Alexander leans toward me. "Lady Goethe has certainly taken a shine to you."

I shrug a shoulder, ignoring the way his breath tickles my ear and sends a warm shiver down my back. The spicy scent of his shaving cream drifts over me, and I close my eyes, fighting the urge to breathe deeply before giving in. *Just because I think he smells nice doesn't mean I forgive him for abandoning me. Someone smelling nice is an objective fact and nothing else. It doesn't mean anything.*

The soup course is followed by a cup of tiny mint-flavored ice that leaves a refreshing aftertaste, then small puff pastries stuffed with a creamy cheese, tart cranberries, and smoked chicken. Lord Marx exclaims over each course, praising Chef Kloss's skill and ingenuity, while Dorthea and I chat about Merchwood and the upcoming events.

As Alexander exchanges jokes with the man next to him, he moves a fork from the right side of his plate to the left, bringing a smile to my lips. When our families dined together, we would bet on how long it would take our parents to notice we moved our forks to the wrong side. I think his father always knew, but he would wait for someone else to catch it, then tease that we must be mischievous changelings sent by the witch of the woods. He always had us in giggles by the time dessert was served.

I pick up my fork—then set it down. *That was a lifetime ago.* Alexander frowns at me. To cover my movement, I grab my cup and sip the crisp white punch, but he's focused on my wrist.

"You're hurt."

I twist my arm, nearly upending my glass on the table. A faint bruise peeks out from the bottom of my sleeve. "Oh, that's nothing."

A line forms between his eyebrows as he leans closer. "Do you need ice for it? I'm sure the kitchen has some."

Why is he pretending to care now? I glare at him. "You're worse than Cristoph. It's just a bruise. It doesn't even hurt."

Dorthea says, "You should wash it with a tisane before you go to bed."

Lord Marx snorts. "Everyone knows you need a good beefsteak for bruises."

My cheeks heat. "I appreciate everyone's concern, but it's fine. Really."

Alexander reaches for my hand. "But you—"

I jerk away, nearly spilling my drink. "I'm fine. I don't need anyone's help."

Everyone around us has fallen silent. I stare down at my plate, the back of my neck hot.

Dorthea says, "Parasols are so fashionable these days. I heard *Rirzan* Aliz will be handing them out at the Sunselt party."

I give her a grateful smile. "Parasols? How wonderful!" I prattle on mindlessly about colors and patterns, barely paying attention to what I'm saying.

I do my best to ignore Alexander for the rest of the meal, speaking to Dorthea about trivial things, or politely asking Lord Marx a question when the conversation stalls. I feel Alexander's gaze on me throughout the evening, but I studiously avoid it, keeping my focus on my plate. The food looks delicious, but everything tastes like ash.

After the last course of berry compote topped with fluffy dollops of cream, the guests begin to drift out of the dining room. I take the opportunity to flee, sneering at myself for being a coward, but I can't sit there another minute while Alexander broods. *He doesn't get to act hurt and try to make me feel guilty. He made his choice years ago, and now he has to live with it.*

I stumble to a stop and look around. In my haste, I made a wrong turn and now I'm stranded in a strange corridor with nobody in sight.

Burning palace with its burning confusing hallways. Who needs this many burning rooms, anyway? Waste of burning space that's built just to confuse people and make sure they get lost.

I finally find a hallway that looks familiar and make my way back to the main part of the palace. When I hear Alexander's laugh, my stomach twists and I duck behind a column, frantically trying to spot him. He's standing by the stairs, talking with an older woman and blocking the path to my room. *Is there no escaping him?*

Aliz glides down the hallway, looking like she stepped out of a painting with her upswept hair and flowing, ice-blue silk gown. She seems lost in thought until her gaze falls on Alexander. She freezes, then spins away and darts through the nearest doorway before he notices her.

Interesting. Why's she avoiding him? She didn't say anything about knowing him earlier… And now that I think of it, Alexander had an odd reaction when I mentioned her in the forest.

I frown, an unpleasant sensation growing in my stomach. *Did something happen between them?* I hurry after Aliz, determined to find out what's going on.

The huge crowd packed into the parlor almost sends me running in the other direction. Groups of women are gathered around the card tables, sofas, and clustered around the room. It feels like every pair of eyes is glued to me. I pause in the doorway, my mouth dry. Then I blink, and they're all absorbed in their own conversations with only a few curious glances directed my way.

There's no sign of Aliz, but I came to Merchwood to hear gossip and investigate the nobles. *There's no time like the present.* I move toward a small group of women who appear near my age, wearing empire-waist dresses in bright pastels and using light sandalwood hand fans to chase away the heat in the stuffy room.

When I near the group, I hear my name and my feet stumble to a stop.

The tall blond says, "I heard her brother refused to let her come home after their mother died."

Her friend loudly whispers, "That's because Lord von Bron threatened to ruin him if he did. Von Bron hates her."

"As he should," a third one pipes up. "I can't believe she came when nobody wants her here. How humiliating."

They all giggle loudly, their eyes darting my direction, confirming they meant for me to hear everything.

They may be right about Alexander hating me, but I'd never let jackals see me hurt. It only encourages them. I keep my head up and raise an eyebrow as I smile smugly. "And yet, I'm all that everyone seems to be talking about. I'm glad I could add some excitement to your lives. I'll be sure to mention your kind words to Lord von Bron when I see him at supper tomorrow."

Their fans go into double speed, the tall blonde's face furious.

An arm slips into mine.

Aliz smiles at me. "Carina, dear, could you please come with me? Luther has been begging me to introduce you to him. I don't think I can hold him off much longer. The poor man's desperate."

It's hard not to grin at her cleverness. *She knows how to hit them where it hurts.* I sigh dramatically. "I know you did your best, but we can't put it off forever." Then I nod cooly to the women. "Another time, ladies. The *Kangan*'s waiting."

When we're safely out of earshot, I whisper, "Thanks. I didn't realize I was walking into a pit of vipers."

She smirks. "Gisele thinks far too highly of herself. She's convinced Lord von Bron's going to propose to her any day now. No matter that he hasn't said two words to her and probably doesn't know she exists. But she normally hides her claws better. She must think you're a threat."

Is everything this week going to be about Alexander? "She's welcome to him. But it's been a long day, and I'd rather save the verbal sparring for another time."

Aliz laughs. "You must not like him very much if you're willing to throw him to those snakes."

"I don't know him well enough anymore to like him or dislike him." The lie sits heavy, so I quickly add, "But I'd very much like to know why you were avoiding him a few minutes ago."

She winces. "I hope nobody else saw that." Aliz folds her arms and leans against the wall, her cheeks pink. "He's considering courting me. An idea I don't want to encourage."

My brow wrinkles as a knot forms in my stomach. "Why? He's handsome, almost as wealthy as your brother, and probably not obnoxious. Every woman's dream."

"And very interested in a business venture with my brother. I'd like my husband to like me, and not what I can do to increase his wealth." She sighs. "Silly schoolgirl dreams, I know. But I'm stubborn."

I wrestle with my conscious for a moment, before grudgingly saying, "From what I know of him, his intentions are likely honorable. If Alexan—Lord von Bron's courting you, it's because he wants to. He wouldn't pursue you for a business deal." It's annoying defending the man who hurt me so badly, but Aliz deserves the truth.

Her brow crinkles. "He certainly doesn't give that impression. Oh, he's always polite and listens to me, but there's an indifference I wouldn't expect from a suitor."

I shrug a shoulder. "He might just be trying to be respectful."

"Hmm, perhaps." Her smile turns mischievous. "Or mayhap he's in love with you. He certainly didn't take his eyes off of you during supper."

My cheeks heat and I lie, "Just nostalgia. We were practically brother and sister growing up, and we had a lot to catch up on." I smirk at her. "And perhaps you're not as indifferent as you pretend if you were watching him that closely."

She laughs. "I'll admit it's flattering to have a

handsome, almost-as-wealthy-as-my-brother, and probably-not-obnoxious man interested in me. Better than the fortune hunters that usually come sniffing around. But it wouldn't break my heart if he moved on to someone else."

Someone calls out to Aliz, and she waves back.

I suddenly realize Aliz must have a thousand other more important things to deal with than saving me from snotty upstart girls. "Please don't let me keep you if you need to entertain your guests."

"I have weeks to talk with them, and it's my brother's turn to take up some hosting duties." Aliz brushes a loose strand of her blond hair back and grins. "You're actually saving me from being trapped in a three-hour discussion with Lady Frank about why the waltz is too modern, and how her son would make the perfect husband for me. No matter that he's already engaged to a lovely seamstress from Floren."

Her smile turns mischievous. "Now, if you hate meaningless chitchat as much as I do, there's a little nook in the library where I hide my romance novels. It's the perfect place to have a proper conversation, and I have snacks stashed in one of the cubbies if we get hungry. Care to join me?"

"Done and done." Giggling, I follow her as we sneak out of the room, my steps light. If the Fortunes are kind, I might make a new friend before I capture the Bane.

The day's off to a glorious start when a maid delivers an enormous sticky bun and steaming pot of cinnamon tea to my room. I'm impressed again by Aliz's extraordinary hostess skills. How she discovered my favorite breakfast is beyond me, but it instantly lightens my spirit.

I pick out today's dress between bites of sticky bun, settling on a pale pink dress, with sprigs of bluebells sewn on the skirt, and matching sapphire earrings. My black hair's swept up into a simple twist with loose strands hanging around my face, adding to my innocent-girl facade. *Nothing to make the Bane suspicious here. Just a feather-wit enjoying the party.*

As I'm licking the last bits of icing off my fingers, a staff member knocks on my door with a coded message from Hartwin with instructions to meet him. I kiss the locket around my neck. "Grant me luck today, Mamma."

The ground's damp with dew, and I enjoy the way my slippers squish against the grass as I cross the lawn. I slip into the greenhouse, wrinkling my nose at the heavy moisture hanging in the air, and quickly make my way to the potting table in the back. My dress clings to my damp skin and I fan myself to keep from overheating. "Hartwin? Where are you?"

"Oy, lassie." He appears from the shadows, removing a pair of large leather gloves. He's dressed like one of the gardeners, with a lumpy hat pulled low on this head, his shirt sleeves rolled up, and his coarse trousers stained at the knees. The milky eye's covered with a patch today. "I think the Bane's next target is Lord Marx."

My eyes widen and a thrill runs through me. *That's the angry walrus with the ridiculous mustache.* "I sat by him at supper. What makes you think he'll be next?"

Hartwin leans against the potting table, slapping his gloves against his thigh. "He's amassed quite a bit of gambling debt. Word is there's nothing left in the estate to pay it off. But if Lord Marx dies, his heir has plenty of money and would have to pay off the debt in order to inherit the title."

Killing a man over some debts seems extreme, but Hartwin has more experience with these matters than I do. "Should we warn him?"

"Nah, I've got people watching his rooms and keeping an eye on him. If the Bane tries to make a move, we'll catch them." He tilts his cap back. "Have you heard anything from your flock of peacocks?"

"Not much." I fill him in on the few tidbits of gossip Aliz shared that seem relevant. "But I'll be able to talk to more guests at the water party today, and at tonight's ball." I fiddle with my locket for a moment. "There's another thing I'd like you to look into on the side. Lord Alexander von Bron." My stomach knots, and I almost stop, but years of anger spurs me on. "I'd like you to find something on him, or his family. Something I can use against him."

He raises an eyebrow at me. "Poisoning you and yer mother isn't enough?"

My jaw clenches. "Something that wouldn't drag my family into the scandal."

"It'll cost you."

"I wouldn't expect anything less."

Hartwin and I haggle, but my heart isn't in it, and I give in after a few token counteroffers. I stand firm on him actually finding something that can be verified before getting payment—I'm not fool enough to pay for half-truths and rumors. And Alexander wouldn't be put off by gossip, anyway.

Stepping out of the swampy greenhouse into the fresh air brings a rush of relief. A little nagging voice tells me I should call Hartwin back and cancel the new deal, but I shush it by reassuring myself it's only in case I need to make him keep his distance. Our encounters at Merchwood are too unsettling to continue, and I can't risk him distracting me from finding the Bane.

It's late morning as I head toward the small lake for the water party. Instead of riding in one of the provided horse-drawn carts, I opt to walk down the wide trail, enjoying the chance to stretch my legs and drink in the meadows filled with flowers. Bees buzz lazily in the sun, and a gentle breeze follows me along the path until I reach my destination.

It looks like one of the landscape paintings hanging in Merchwood. The lake's nestled among gentle rolling hills, sunlight glinting off the blue water. A half-dozen boats are out on the lake, while another dozen rest on the shoreline, ready to be put to use. Some guests are settled on blankets on the bright green grass or milling around and chatting, while others are browsing the tables stacked with plates of flatcakes, bowls of fruit, and assorted delicacies.

I was hoping to spy on Lord Marx now that I know he's the Bane's target, but I don't see him anywhere, so he's probably sleeping in. My stomach grumbles, the sticky bun a long-forgotten memory, and I make my way to the tables to pile a plate high with crispy sausages, fresh raspberries, and golden flatcakes lathered in butter and honey. I try to convince myself to join one of the groups, then settle on an empty blanket. It's too early for mindless chatter. There's plenty of time to talk to people after I've enjoyed my feast.

The first bite of flatcakes and raspberries makes me groan with happiness. There's a giggle behind me, then Aliz joins me on the blanket. Her blue-green dress makes her eyes look even bluer, and her wide straw hat shades her delicate features.

She steals a berry from my plate and pops it into her mouth. "There's nothing better than fresh raspberries on flatcakes. Except chocolate."

My stomach lurches, but I manage a smile. Ever since that box of poisoned bonbons, I haven't been able to eat chocolate without getting sick. Even the smell makes me nauseous. *Another thing I can curse the Bane for.* "I don't care for chocolate, but you're right about the raspberries and flatcakes. Or raspberries and cream cake. Or raspberries and lemon cake."

"Or raspberries and chocolate," she teases.

I laugh. "You're welcome to all my chocolate, as long as I can have all your lemon drops."

"Done and done." She squints at the lake. "I really hope Luther doesn't destroy his boat today. My brother tries to

turn everything into a competition. Last year we lost six
boats when he decided everyone needed to reenact some
battle or another and he set fire to the enemy ships." At my
gasp, she hurriedly adds, "After the guests abandoned them,
of course."

*Merchwood parties really are different! I'm almost sorry
I missed it.* I shade my eyes and scan the water, picking out
the Kangan's boat by the way it's flying across the lake
while everyone else is lazily drifting. His small craft nearly
collides with another, grazing the other boat's side and
sending it rocking through the water.

I wince. "I hope he knows how to swim."

"He does, but ask the Fortunes to help whoever falls
victim to his antics this year."

"You'd better ask them yourself. The Fortunes and I are
not on good terms right now."

She lies on her side and props her head up on her hand,
her eyes sparkling. "Do tell."

*No need to make her feel guilty for sticking me next to
Alexander at supper. She thought she was doing a kindness.*
"Nothing serious. They just seem determined to make my
life miserable. The carriage wheel broke twice—*twice*—on
the journey here. Then I found out there was a fire near my
home in Wittrow that my dolt of a brother decided not to tell
me about because he thinks I'll faint if I get a hangnail.
Never mind that I used to wrestle him whenever we argued
and I always trounced him."

She laughs. "Someday I must meet this infamous brother
of yours."

"I'll be happy to introduce you, but he's dully formal
when he first meets someone." I shrug. "Nerves, I think. I
hope you're prepared to talk about crop rotations, and

whether the library should be alphabetized or organized by subject."

"He sounds like Lord von Bron." Aliz crinkles her nose. "There's only so much to say about the weather and how the roads were on the journey here."

"Really?" *That's not the Alexander I knew.* "He must've gotten boring in his old age."

She flicks a piece of grass at me, then steals another raspberry off my plate. "Old age, indeed. I'll be sure to mention that the next time I see him." Aliz looks over my shoulder and grins as she sits up. "His ears must be burning. I bet you the rest of your raspberries that he brings up the weather."

I playfully hold up my fork like a sword. "No bet, these are mine." As Alexander joins us, the little worm of guilt for asking Hartwin to investigate him comes crawling back, but I firmly ignore it.

In place of the standard gentleman's suit, Alexander is wearing a crisp linen shirt and dark trousers fitting for the outdoor event. His eyes flick to meet mine before he focuses on Aliz. "*Rirzan* Brecht, you look lovely this morning. As do you, Lady Carina. This is a beautiful day to have a water party."

The snort escapes before I can stop it. I try to cover it with a cough as Aliz widens her eyes in faux alarm.

"Oh, you poor dear. Is everything all right? Be careful. You don't want to spill your breakfast. Here, let me help you." She pulls my plate away and winks, her face turned so Alexander doesn't see. She pops a raspberry in her mouth with a satisfied grin.

Alexander looks between us, his brow furrowed. "Did I interrupt something?"

I glare at Aliz. "No. Aliz was just promising to tell me all about her journey to Merchwood."

"Another time, since Lord von Bron has already heard about it. But I did just find out that Lorria's sending a delegation to the High King's palace next month. I wonder if the rumors about them and the Kingdom of the Wolves are true."

I steal my plate back. "What rumors?" I hold up the last raspberry and quirk my eyebrow at her before devouring it.

She scrunches her face, acknowledging my victory. "That one of the daughters is engaged to one of the princes from that kingdom. Or both daughters are engaged to both brothers, depending on the rumor. I wish I could be there for their visit, but Luther insists he needs my help with some project or another that he hasn't bothered to tell me about."

Alexander says stiffly, "It's probably the charity drive." At our blank faces, he adds, "*Kangan* Brecht wanted to organize a charity drive for the people who lost their homes in the fires last month. He's managed to get them temporary lodgings, but it would bankrupt the kingdom to replace all their possessions and rebuild their homes. He wants to speak with the merchants about selling things at cost, or donating items in exchange for reduced rents."

Aliz sits up, her eyes bright. "That's a wonderful idea. Why didn't the oaf just tell me that himself?"

"I'm sure he was going to, but he has many matters to attend to. It most likely slipped his mind."

"Do you know where he was planning to start, or how he wants it organized?"

Alexander shakes his head. "You should speak with him."

What's he doing? I stifle a groan. I didn't think it was

possible, but this is even more painful than sitting through supper with him. It's like every trace of his personality has disappeared. No wonder Aliz isn't impressed.

Even my worst enemy doesn't deserve this torture. *There must be some way to help him.* "Your mother did something similar when the valley flooded in Wittrow. Why don't you tell Aliz about it and give her some tips? And you could help her come up with the list of supplies and which merchants to approach."

Alexander frowns at me. "I'm sure *Rirzan* Brecht has organized drives like these before." When I grimace and tilt my head pointedly toward Aliz, Alexander straightens and says gruffly, "But of course, I'm at your disposal, *Rirzan* Brecht."

Aliz kindly doesn't laugh or take offense, although I'm sure she's as appalled as I am at the lackluster offer. "That's very thoughtful of you."

This is dreadful. Alexander has turned into a block of wood. I try to keep my dismay hidden, but Alexander glances at me, then winces.

I have to do something to break the painful silence. "You're right about this being a lovely day for a water party. But why's it called a water party? If we're going out on a lake, then it should be a lake party, or a rowing party. Shouldn't a water party have more water? I think it should be held during a storm to be worthy of the name."

A hint of humor lights Alexander's eyes. "With or without umbrellas?"

I smirk. "Without, of course. What's the point of a water party if you don't get wet?"

"It would make going out on the lake more dangerous."

"Only if there's lightning."

Aliz grins. "We could start a new trend. Society's always looking for the next party craze."

Alexander blinks at her in surprise, then slides into an easy smile. "They'll rush to try anything new, and then claim they invented it. Like how everyone was wearing birds on their head last season."

When Aliz bursts into giggles, my jaw drops. "Birds? Live birds?"

He chuckles and nods. "The women had these elaborate cages as part of their hairstyle. The men had larger birds trained to sit on top of their heads by holding onto their hair. Thank the Fortunes that only lasted for one ball before they figured out keeping a bird on your head for an entire evening can have some, er, unpleasant results."

I knew they had crazy fashions, but not that crazy. Perhaps staying out of society's a good idea. Then again, Alexander and Aliz seem to think the whole thing was hilarious. There's a flash of jealousy that I'm left out of the joke, though I know it's not their fault.

Alexander asks Aliz about the horse Luther gave her and her eyes light up. She describes the mare's jumping prowess in detail, answering his questions about its lineage and training while I pick at the remains of my breakfast. Horses are fine enough, but I've always preferred walking.

"—take you out for a row?"

My attention snaps back to their conversation, and I set my fork down. Feeling impish, I slide my arm through Aliz's and lift my chin. "Sorry, she promised to go with me as soon as I finished my breakfast. And I'm done now, so we should go."

His eyes glint with challenge. "Then let me take you both out. I insist."

Aliz and I exchange a look, silently acknowledging there's no way out of his invitation without being outright rude. I'm tempted to tell him to stuff it, but Aliz's admonishing look warns me off.

She turns to Alexander, all gracious elegance, while I resist the urge to stick my tongue out at him. "Thank you, that would be lovely."

We stroll down to the boats in awkward silence. Alexander offers me his hand, which I take ungraciously and climb in, settling on the bench at the front.

As Aliz is about to join me, a young boy runs up to her and grabs her hand. "*Rirzan* Brecht, you're needed at the palace right away."

She frowns down at him. "What's going on?"

The boy tugs on her hand urgently, pulling her away. "I don't know. They just said you need to come now."

She looks helplessly over her shoulder at me. I shrug and smile, waving her on her way.

I stand up. "Since we—"

Alexander shoves the boat into the water and jumps in.

I fall back onto the seat with a curse and glare at him. "What are you doing?"

He sends us sailing across the lake with a few quick pulls on the oars, then puts them up. "We need to talk."

Pig-headed, annoying, arrogant—I lunge for the closest oar, but he has an iron grip on it. "Take me back to shore!"

"Not until we get a few things straight between us." Alexander leans forward, his eyes narrowed. "We need to find a way to move past what happened."

Anger burns hot in my chest. My fists clench and I shoot up, the boat violently rocking under me. "After everything you put me through, you want to pretend like it never happened?"

His face goes pale, then flushes. He leaps up, matching me glare for glare. "You know it was an accident."

"Ignoring me for five years is an accident? Did you have amnesia? Get shipped off to the Rus icefields? Oh, no. Evil fae must've held you in thrall and only freed you a few days ago. That would explain everything."

BOOM!

The boat lurches and I'm thrown forward into Alexander. He grabs my shoulders, but the damage is done. We tip backwards and I desperately flail my arms, trying to right us. We teeter for a precarious second, then splash into the lake.

The icy cold shock makes me gasp, and I choke on water. I push for the surface, finding the ground closer than expected. My head and shoulders pop above the water. I cough, trying to clear my burning lungs. Alexander shoots up next to me, spluttering and wiping the water from his face.

We're only a stone's throw from the shore in shoulder-deep water. There are no shouts or screams. By some trick of the Fortunes, we're shielded from the picnickers by a small copse of trees on a rocky outcropping, and the other boaters are too far away or distracted to pay attention to us.

Alexander runs his eyes over me, then whips around to the boat that crashed into us. "Luther," he bellows. "What are you doing?"

Kangan *Brecht?* I shove my hair out of my face and glare at our attacker. He doesn't bear much resemblance to Aliz, with his black hair and granite features, but his eyes have the same tilt and color as his sister's. Right now, one of the most powerful men in the kingdom is looking at us with a panicked expression.

"I'm sorry! Please don't tell Aliz. If she finds out, she'll never let me near a boat again. She still hasn't forgiven me for that juggler who accidentally set the boat on fire at the Wintertide party."

I say dryly, "I thought it was last year's battle reenactment."

He winces. "That too." Luther holds out his hands to us, pleading. "What can I do to keep this between us?"

Alexander nods at me. "It's up to Carina."

Luther turns his begging eyes to me. "Please, please, please don't tell her. I throw myself on your mercy, Lady Lux. Anything you want, just name it."

I wring out my hair. "Right now, all I want is a dry dress and a pot of tea." At his beseeching look, I decide to take pity on him. "The only harm is to my dignity. Your secret's safe with me as long as you don't tell anyone else about it." *There's already enough gossip about me and Alexander.* I shake a finger at him. "And you stay far, far, *far* away from me the next time I'm in a boat."

He puts his hand over his heart, clearly relieved. "On my honor. Thank you."

Alexander frowns. "Not quite no harm done." He points to a large crack in the side of our craft.

Luther groans "Not again." Then he brightens. "We can sink it before Aliz sees it. I'll get an ax."

Alexander rubs his chin, his eyes narrowed. "What if we tow it to the middle of the lake and set it on fire? We can say it's for Sunselt, like the old Vyking stories. If we get the other guests involved, then your sister might not be as upset."

The *Kangan*'s eyes light up. "Let's turn it into a

competition. We can shoot flaming arrows at it and whoever hits it wins a prize. I'm sure I can find something around Merchwood to give them."

I shake my head. *He'll never learn.* "And that's my cue to leave."

I slosh off into the forest, leaving them to deal with the boat. I should lock myself in my room for the rest of the party. Every time I go anywhere, disaster happens. First, I fall out of the tree, and now I've gotten dumped into the lake. With my luck, next time I'll stumble into a sinkhole or an abandoned mine shaft.

Laughter sounds ahead of me and I stumble to a stop. A man and woman around my parents' age are sitting on a blanket in a little hidden meadow, having an animated conversation too low for me to hear. The woman's bright red hair glows in the sunshine. She snickers as the man waves around a long walking stick with a silver grip, punching the air with it as though to emphasize a point.

I slowly ease away, carefully moving my feet so as not to alert them to my presence. The last thing I need is someone to see me looking like a limp dishrag and spread more rumors.

The Fortunes are laughing when I meet the same maid in the entryway. Her eyes widen and her mouth drops open.

So much for not adding to the gossip. I storm past her. "I don't want to talk about it."

It's definitely time to lock myself in my room.

7

The welcoming ball is the official start to the Sunselt party festivities. It also has the added benefit of replacing supper this evening, so I won't have to suffer through another meal with Alexander. I expected the ball to be held in the oversized dining room, but I'm directed to the other end of the house where a set of double doors is open, music and chatter spilling out into the hallway.

Aliz and her brother are stationed next to the entrance to welcome their guests. I join the receiving line, craning my neck to survey the crowd. Based on what we know about the earliest victim, Hartwin thinks the Bane's in their late thirties or older, meaning at least half the people here are suspects.

I thought I'd be excited to attend my first formal ball, but my stomach's full of butterflies. Most of the other unmarried girls in attendance are younger than me, but they have so much more experience with these things. Being sequestered in the Anglish countryside for most of my teenage years with only my ill mother and the staff for company left me free of society's expectations, but it also means I'm playing catchup to fit in.

My green silk ballgown with inset silver panels and embroidery felt impossibly elegant when I was in my room. I even took the time to arrange my long black hair into a woven crown around my head, with silver threads intertwined through the strands. But compared to the finery on display, I feel like a little girl playing dress up. Diamonds, rubies, and emeralds sparkle from fingers, ears, and throats. Almost all the women have elaborate updos that probably took hours to put in place, while the men are polished to perfection in their black silk suits. I run a hand down my skirt, trying not to let my discomfort show.

The line moves quickly, and soon Aliz greets me with a friendly smile. She introduces me to Luther, whose broad grin and wink would be a dead giveaway of our earlier boating mishap, if Aliz didn't have a blind spot when it comes to her brother.

Luther kisses the back of my hand. "Ah, Lady Lux. May I call you Carina? It's too bad we couldn't meet sooner. Aliz hasn't stopped prattling on about her wonderful new friend. It's a pleasure to finally meet you, for the first time, right now. We must have missed each other at the lake this morning, but I'm looking forward to talking with you and seeing if you live up to the legend."

My cheeks heat as I try not to laugh. *He's shameless.*

Aliz swats her brother's arm. "Stop teasing her, Luther. You'll scare her away and then I'll never forgive you." She turns to me. "Luther promises to be on his best behavior if you'll save him a dance."

The flames in my cheeks grow impossibly hotter as the butterflies in my stomach whip into a frenzy. "I look forward to it."

I move through the ballroom doors so they can greet the next guest. I glance back over my shoulder and lock eyes with Alexander farther back in the line. His face is blank except for the deep line between his brows. He dips his chin, then raises an eyebrow. I look away, ignoring the ache in my chest.

The ballroom's twice the size of the dining room, leaving plenty of space between the tables lining two walls and the dancers in the middle of the room. The other two walls are full of clever glass doors that pivot in the middle, letting in the cool breezes from the gardens. Even with the open doors, the room's warm from the lingering heat of the summer day and the crowd already gathered inside. The musicians are nestled on the second floor behind a low railing, their sweet music drifting out across the room. Candles and lanterns line the rest of the upper floor, with mirrors reflecting the light downward to fill the ballroom with a soft glow.

But most impressive are the climbing roses lining every wall and winding up the columns to make it feel like we're in the middle of a garden. Overflowing pots of greenery and mosses, covering the tabletops and scattered around the edges of the room, add to the illusion and fill the air with their sweet floral scent.

If this is a small country party, I wonder what the fancy balls in the cities are like! But they can't be better than this. Merchwood parties are famous for a reason, and I can only imagine what Aliz has planned for the rest of the festivities.

An older man approaches me and bows. "Ahh, you must be the lovely Lady Lux I've heard so much about."

I smile at him and curtsy. "Only good things, I hope." It's hard not to stare as he's completely bald, with even his eyebrows missing, making it hard to judge his age. But the deep creases around his eyes and mouth and the frail look of his skin make me guess he's somewhere north of eighty.

He laughs. "Enough to intrigue me. I'm Lord Zimmer, but everyone calls me Ziggy. And this is my daughter, Lotta." He gestures behind him and the redhead I saw this morning by the lake joins us.

I greet her, then turn back to Lord Zimmer. "Is this your first year at Merchwood, sir?"

"Come now, friends don't stand on polite formalities or talk about such mundane things!" He leans closer and whispers dramatically, "Let us speak of murder and scandals."

My eyes widen as Lotta chuckles. "Shush, Pappa. You just met the poor girl. We should talk about the weather and our favorite teas before you bring up something so shocking."

I give her a cheeky grin. "Cinnamon." I turn back to her father. "Now Ziggy, about those murders and scandals."

He lets out a hearty laugh that makes people turn their heads. "I told you she was one of us."

Lotta holds up her hands in good-natured surrender and smiles. "Don't say I didn't warn you. My father has no sense of decorum. He invites the most peculiar people to supper."

"Because the odder they are, the more fun they are."

I pretend to be offended. "What does that say about me, then?"

He winks at me. "Only that you hide your eccentricities better than most." He taps the side of his nose. "I can always spot them. Don't worry, your secret's safe with us. But I think it's only fair to warn you that if you spend too much time around us, everyone else will know you're odd too."

His daughter shakes her head. "Don't let Franz hear you say that. You know how he values his reputation."

Ziggy waves away her warning. "Franzy is a popinjay. But he's young. He'll learn."

She laughs. "Not that young."

"Bah, you're all spring chickens. Where is that scoundrel, anyway? He promised me a game of cards." Ziggy wanders off into the crowd.

Lotta gives me an embarrassed smile. "As I said, no sense of decorum. Please don't take it personally. He's just easily distracted these days."

I grin. "No offense taken, but I am dying to hear about the murders and scandals."

Humor returns to her face. "And he'll be delighted to tell you, but you might have to suffer through some odd stories first. Please excuse me, I'd better find him before accidentally insults someone less forgiving."

She hurries off and I turn my mind back to the business at hand. Lord Zimmer and Lotta proved to be a fun diversion and hopefully new friends. He's too old and scattered to be the Bane, and Lotta seems devoted to her father which wouldn't leave her time to plan elaborate poisonings. *Unless it's an act.*

My humor dims as my stomach twists. *I hope it's not one of them.* I have a little more sympathy for Hartwin. Having to constantly question everyone and everything around you is exhausting. If I had to be paranoid as long as he has, I'd be cranky too.

I dismiss my hopefully unfounded worries about Lotta and Ziggy, and search the crowd for Lord Marx. If he's the Bane's target, whoever he's around is going on the suspect list. Sadly, he doesn't appear to be here yet. I sigh, then pick out a man that fits the Bane's age range, preparing on my best feather-wit act to get him relaxed and talking.

An hour later, I'm stifling a yawn at the fourth story of someone's trip to Vunheim for their famous Ramsfeel celebration. It didn't take long to get the trick of talking to a group, rather than singling someone out for conversation. The ball's magic and iced wine selection has everyone relaxed and eager to one-up each other. It's easy to steer the conversation towards travel and shared acquaintances while I listen for any connections to our Bane list.

When the fifth Vunheim story starts, I excuse myself and head for the refreshment table along the wall. Mayhap some of the little tea cakes will give me enough strength to survive another hour of dull conversation. Or at least I can dream about them when someone starts waxing on and on about Vunheim. Vunheim, Vunheim, Vunheim. Blah, blah, blah. Is going to Vunheim some rite of passage that I don't know about?

A man with slick black hair intercepts me before I reach the tables with the coveted treats. "Lady Lux, allow me to introduce myself. Lord Wentzel, at your service. Lotta said you met her father, Lord Zimmer. Quite the character, isn't he?"

Though he's smiling charmingly at me, something about him makes me cautious. Besides, I never trust a man who gets between me and my dessert. "He's quite entertaining." It takes a moment to place Lord Wentzel, but his fancy walking stick triggers my memory. "Were you speaking with Lady Lotta by the lake this morning?"

His eyes widen slightly, but the smile doesn't falter. "Yes, she's a good friend. We live near each other in Weals. Have you been?"

I shake my head. "No, I grew up in Wittrow. And I've been in Angland the past few years."

"Ah, wonderful country! Were you in Landsheer?"

A thrill of excitement runs through me. *One of the Bane's victims was in Landsheer, and Lord Wentzel's the right age to be the Bane.* "No, but I've always wanted to go. When were you there last?"

He fingers the ruby stick pin securing his black cravat, the large stone winking in the candlelight. "Hmm, it must have been two years ago now. Yes, for Lady Kimmer's spring ball, which turned out to be a raging bore. But luckily, Lady Troyer decided to throw the most darling little salon that same week. Saved the trip from being a total disaster."

A flash of disappointment flows through me and my shoulders slump. The Bane's victim there was fifteen years ago…but Lord Wentzel must travel to Angland frequently if he's well acquainted with the nobility. And there are no known Bane victims two years ago, so that wouldn't give him an alibi. Pleased to have a good suspect at last, I smile sweetly at him. "My goodness, it sounds like you know everyone in the kingdom. I feel so silly that I've only seen Mannhyne county. What other kingdoms have you visited?"

"Near and far, and everything in between. I never like to stay in one place for too long." Lord Wentzel gestures to the middle of the room. "Could I tempt you to join me for the next dance? I'll tell you all about my favorite trip to Vunheim for Ramsfeel."

I stifle a sigh.

Alexander steps next to me. "She already promised this dance to me."

I glare at him. "No, I didn't." *Of all the arrogant, egotistical, high-handed—grrrr.*

Lord Wentzel eyes him for a moment, then bows to me with an easy smile. "Another time then."

As he walks away, I spin back to Alexander, anger burning in my chest. "What do you think you're doing? You have no right to—"

"You can thank me later. Your slippers are thin and he always treads on his partner's toes." He takes my arm and starts to lead me to the dance floor.

I dig in my heels and jerk away, ready to strangle him.

Alexander's smile doesn't waver as he holds out his arm. "Everyone's watching."

He's right, burn it. The busybodies around us are spying on us out of the corners of their eyes, and a few of the bolder ones stare straight at us while trading whispers behind their fans.

I silently groan, torn between wanting to storm away, and keeping the gossip hounds at bay. I'm here to capture the Bane. Nothing matters more than that, and that means keeping up appearances.

The Fortunes must be cackling at all the bad luck they've thrown at me. Pressing my lips into something between a grimace and a smile, I take his arm and move to the middle of the ballroom as the first strains of a waltz float through the air.

Panic shoots through me and I gulp, squeezing my eyes shut. *Why couldn't it have been a reel, or a quadrille, or something that would let me escape him for a few moments?* If talking to him has been painful, dancing so closely will be a thousand times worse. *I can't, I can't, I can't.*

I slowly pick up my skirt, then place my other hand in his, trying to hide my trembling. Alexander wraps his arm around my waist, his touch light, but it doesn't stop my heart from fluttering. Every nerve's alight where he touches me, forgotten longing mixed with fury making every brush of his fingertips feel like my skin's on fire.

Focus on the Bane. Don't think of anything else. I stare over his shoulder at the crowd, refusing to make eye contact. Now would be a good time to see if Lord Marx has joined the ball, but it's impossible to concentrate on anything except Alexander.

He clears his throat. "We need to finish our conversation from this morning. I think there's been a misunderstanding."

I grit my teeth. "There's nothing to talk about. Let's just finish this dance and go back to ignoring each other."

"Is that what you want?"

Though his voice is carefully neutral, there's an underlying sadness that makes me finally look at him. Alexander's face is drawn, and there's a tightness around his eyes I hadn't noticed before.

My heart lurches. I steel myself against the sympathy trying to soften my resolve. "It's what's best. For both of us."

He looks away, and the silence sits heavy between us as we move through the waltz. It's been years since we last took lessons together, but to my everlasting annoyance, we move effortlessly through the dance, stepping and spinning as though we practice every day. His warmth surrounds me, luring me in, tempting me to press closer to him.

It's a special kind of torture knowing that this will be the last time we dance together. I'll make sure it is because I might just break down and forgive him if I spend too much time with him. And if I do, when he leaves again, it'll completely destroy me. Because he will leave again, probably when I need him most, just like before. It's better to keep my distance. I can't live through that twice.

It's oddly unexciting when I see Lord Marx by the entrance. It looks like he waxed his overly long mustache for the ball because it's sticking straight out as he tilts his head back to drain his wineglass. I whirl around the ballroom with Alexander, silently counting down to the end of the song, doing my best to keep Lord Marx in sight.

My heart breaks into a frantic gallop and a cold sweat covers my skin. *No! Not now.* My feet trip over nothing. My pulse pounds as my heart races impossibly faster, feeling like it's trying to beat its way out of my chest. No! I clutch Alexander's coat, my knuckles white as I gasp.

"Carina? What's wrong?" He grips my elbows, his voice growing alarmed. "Are you ill?"

I pant, staring blindly at the floor. "No, I—I just need some air." I take a trembling step away. My knees give out. Cursing, I slump against him, my muscles turn to water.

Alexander mutters an oath as he wraps an arm around my waist and half carries me through the nearest door, my feet stumbling along. Thank the Fortunes we were on the edge of the dancefloor so our exit doesn't draw too much attention.

My breath comes in desperate gasps and my heart thunders in my chest. My vision goes fuzzy around the edges. *It'll pass. It'll pass. It'll pass.* I keep chanting the words in my head as my lungs squeeze against my ribs, trying to get air. *It'll pass. It'll pass.*

When Alexander starts to guide me to a bench by the door, I shake my head and gesture weakly at the dark gardens below. He glances behind him, then scoops me up in his arms, hurrying down the stairs and through the gap in the hedges.

Around the first corner's a large fountain with a wide rim. Alexander sets me down on the edge and I press my forehead to my knees, waiting for the spell to finish.

After too long, my frantic heartbeat slows, leaving me drained and hollow. I gratefully gulp in the cool night air as the vice around my chest loosens. The light scent of edelweiss and the tinkling of the fountain behind me soothe the last of my fears.

I sit up, surprised to find Alexander's coat wrapped around my shoulders and his steadying arm around my waist. His green eyes, full of concern, look almost black in the moonlight.

Alexander. Suddenly I'm thirteen again, holding my breath, wishing with everything in me he'll kiss me. Then I blink and reality comes rushing back in. My heart hardens as my stomach flips. I lean away from him, determined to put as much space between us as I can.

I shift uncomfortably on the cold stone, not quite meeting his eyes. "Thank you for your help. I'm all right. You can go back to the ball now."

"All rig—Carina, what was that? What happened?" He runs a hand through this hair, his eyes wide. "Are you still ill? I thought you'd recovered."

I wince and look away, pulling his coat tighter around me. "It's nothing for you to worry about."

He stiffens. "You are."

"I'm not sick!" He was bound to find out eventually, but it doesn't make me any less annoyed. I shrink back into his jacket, the words sour in my mouth. "Sometimes my heart will beat really fast for a few minutes. But it's not dangerous! I'm always fine after. I just have to wait for it to pass."

His fists clench. "Is it… What caused it?"

"The menders don't know. It's probably an aftereffect of…everything that happened back then." It's his turn to wince, and I rush to add, "But they're guessing. It could've happened anyway, even without all that."

Alexander looks unconvinced. "Are you really all right? You're not trying to spare my feelings?"

I jerk my head back, my jaw clenching. "No! Like I said, it's nothing to be concerned about. It hardly ever happens. I wouldn't have even told you about it if I didn't have to."

He looks away, but not before I see the flash of hurt in his eyes.

Anger flares hot and deep in my chest and I straighten. *He doesn't get to make me feel guilty.* "I'm fine," I snarl. Nobody's going to treat me like I'm going to break apart. Not again."

His face tightens and his fists clench. "But if you—"

"Don't. I've waited too long and fought too hard to be here. You're as bad as Cristoph, trying to keep me wrapped up in silk, out of sight and out of the way. My brother would rather pretend nothing happened. But it did. And I won't let them get away. Not this time. Not when I'm this close. I'm fine. Getting a little out of breath doesn't mean I have to be sent away to sit in my room all day."

"I would never think that. But you were so pale and shaky, and I…" Alexander pauses, then his voice softens. "I'm worried about you."

Now he's worried. Not five years ago when I needed him. Hot anger burns as I fix him with a hard look. "Don't be. I can take care of myself."

My chest tightens. Icy fear shoots through me that I'm about to have another attack. I shove his jacket into his arms.

My knees are still shaky, but I can't stay here for another second.

I dash off into the dark, ignoring Alexander calling out behind me. I race around the side of the house, then duck in through the first door I find and fly up the stairs to the fourth floor without stopping. When I'm nearly to my door, I almost collide with a tall, thin woman with white hair and pale blue eyes coming out of a room. She curses and jumps back to avoid me. I mutter my apologies, hurrying past her on shaking legs.

The last of my strength gives out as I stagger to my bed and collapse. I curl up around my pillow, my chest aching, and wait for the room to stop spinning. As I recognize the normal weaknesses after one of my spells instead of the onset of another one, my breathing slows and my muscles relax.

Not the best way to end my first ball. If I'm being honest with myself, the worst part was in the garden with Alexander when I forgot his betrayal. That brief moment gave me back all the hope and happiness I'd felt before my mother and I were poisoned. Then, the future was wide open, and it always included Alexander. Losing that again is almost enough to crush me.

I bury my face in my pillow and sob. I don't even know why I'm crying, except it's all too much and so unfair. Everything feels empty and hopeless. Why do I think finding the Bane will fix anything? Or that I can do it when so many other have failed?

Because I won't stop.

The determined voice breaks through my misery. My thoughts calm and I swallow around the painful lump in my throat.

Alexander's just a distraction. I need to pull myself together and focus on the real reason I'm here. Swiping the back of my hand across my eyes, I sit up. I'll make sure my mother gets justice. No matter what it takes or who tries to stop me.

The Bane won't escape this time.

8

In the light of day, everything that happened last night feels ten times worse. Not only did I lose my chance to find out who Lord Marx was talking to, which could have led me to the Bane, but I humiliated myself in front of Alexander. Knowing I'll have to see him again makes me want to hide under my blankets until it all goes away. Only my renewed resolve forces me out of bed. I linger over the sticky bun and cinnamon tea on my morning tray, hoping that the day will disappear if I wish it strongly enough.

Finally, I give into the inevitable and reluctantly dress in a pale violet gown trimmed with black ribbons. I must have forgotten to pack the matching amethyst earbobs, so I put on the black pearls, then arrange my hair into a long braid. There's something about a braid always makes me feel like I could conquer the world. Taking a deep breath, I square my shoulders and march out of my room.

The morning brunch is served on the back terrace today, the gardens and wild woods providing a serene backdrop to the meal. A quick scan of the crowd confirms Alexander's nowhere in sight, and I breathe a sigh of relief. I'll have to face him eventually, but I'm happy to put it off it as long as possible.

I dish up a scoop of eggs and add a piece of toast smeared with raspberry jam, then pick a table to join. The woman are all a few years younger than me and still in their giggly phase, but I'm hoping to hear some gossip with my breakfast.

The chatter flows around me, jumping from how fun the ball was and who danced with who, to complaining about misplaced jewelry and ribbons and slippers, then arguing about whether there were more waltzes or quadrilles. The lack of sleep's wearing on me. Pressure builds behind my eyes as I listen to their petty squabbles and high-pitched voices. I subtly rub my forehead, trying to figure out a way to steer the conversation toward Lord Marx before my brain explodes.

When someone mentions their trip to Vunheim for Ramsfeel, I leap out of my chair. They all stare at me in surprise.

My cheeks heat and I clear my throat. "Does, um, uh, anyone know where the barn is? I wanted to take a ride this afternoon."

A young man stacking dishes at the next table pipes up. "I'd be happy to escort you, milady. The path can be hard to find."

The girls at my table titter, making my cheeks burn hotter. "Thank you. That's very kind."

I bid the women goodbye and hurry down the stairs with my guide, trying to keep up with his bouncing steps. My mind flashes to Alexander carrying me down another set of stairs last night, and it's hard not to cringe. I shove the memory aside. I can deal with that later. Or better yet, try to never, ever think of it again.

"I'm Edgar Goff, by the way. And I know who you are, Lady Lux."

"My apologies. I was cloud gathering." I focus on my companion, noting that except for the dimple in his right cheek, he's average to the point of forgettable. A blandly pleasant face, floppy hair somewhere between brown and blond, and a touch shorter than me. He's too young to be the Bane—he's probably barely out of short pants—but he could still be helpful. "Have you worked at Merchwood long?"

"A few years now. *Kangan* Brecht always brings on extra staff to help with the Sunselt party." The young man frowns. "I'm sorry I wasn't able to get you a different seat for supper. *Rirzan* Brecht insisted that you be next to Lord von Bron. But I'll keep asking her about it. Mayhap she'll change her mind if I give her enough reasons."

The rumors that Alexander hates me have spread farther than I thought if the staff know about it. My chest tightens. "Oh, um, that's all right. Thank you for trying, but I wouldn't want you to get into trouble. And I would miss talking with Lady Dorthea."

"All right." His face brightens, and he takes my elbow, steering me toward the garden. "There's a little cascading fountain in the corner I know you'll like. And if we come back tonight, I'll show you how they used the old Roma trick of lining the paths in white stone so you can see it in the moonlight."

My stomach knots and I pull my arm away. "I'd rather see the barn first."

"Of course." He starts down the path again with the same bouncing step, seemingly unfazed by my rebuff. "Are you going back to Angland when the party ends?"

The knot loosens, but I continue to watch him warily out of the corner of my eye. "I'm not sure. It's been a while since I've been back to Wittrow. Or I might travel." *It depends on whether we catch the Bane.*

At the corner of the house, Herr Goff stops and points to the tree line. "That opening right there? That's the start of the jumping course. I'd be happy to take you around it."

I shake my head and force out a laugh. "No jumping for me. I was thinking a nice, leisurely trot along the lane."

"Are you sure? You're an excellent rider. Most of the jumps would be easy for you." Herr Goff shuffles closer to me, blushing furiously.

I barely stop myself from snorting. Only if an excellent rider falls off their horse on every jump. Why would he think—oh! Is he trying to flirt with me? I suppress a grin as my shoulders relax. Aw, that's so sweet. He'll get better at it with some more practice. I'd better let him down gently.

A hand clamps on his shoulder, pulling him away from me.

Alexander's jaw clenches as he stares down at Herr Goff, his other hand tight on the fishing pole slung over his shoulder. "I can assist the lady from here."

Herr Goff frowns. "But I promised to escort her to the barn."

I silently sigh. It'll be better to get my humiliation over with in private. "Thank you, Herr Goff, but I'm afraid I'll have to save my ride for another day. There's a private matter that I need to discuss with Lord von Bron."

Herr Goff turns to me, looking crestfallen. "Are you sure? I could wait for you and take you to the barn after."

Alexander scowls.

I hurriedly take Herr Goff's elbow and move him out of Alexander's reach. "No need. I'll ride another time. Thank you for your help, though. It was very kind. And I look forward to finding that fountain in the gardens."

The young man gives me a brilliant smile. "It was my pleasure." He glances over my shoulder at Alexander, saying to me, "I'll be around if you need me. Just call out."

Alexander mutters darkly as Herr Goff strolls away. The young man's barely out of earshot when he drops the fishing pole and whirls on me, his lips pressed into a thin line. "What were you doing alone with him? How do you know he was taking you to the barn and not luring you out into the woods?"

Anger flares bright in my chest and I step closer to him, glaring. "That's none of your concern. And since when do you go fishing?"

"Since Luther invited me a few years back. And you're always my concern because every time I turn around, you're chasing down trouble." He folds his arms, his eyes narrowed. "I know why you're here."

He can't know! Can he? My pulse speeds up as my stomach jumps. "Because I wanted to go for a ride and they don't keep horses inside the palace?"

"No, at Merchwood."

I widen my eyes, feigning confusion. "Because I was invited?"

Alexander leans forward, his face stony. "You're here to find the Bane."

My heart freezes. "Who?"

"Carina." He draws out my name, lacing it with exasperation. "Do you know how much danger you'd be in if the Bane was here?"

"None. They don't care about me. My family wasn't their target."

Alexander frowns. "So you're admitting that's why you're here."

Burn it. I wrap the end of my braid around my hand, thinking quickly. "There's nothing to admit. I'm here to enjoy the famous Sunselt party, just like you."

"If that were true, I'd sleep better." He pinches the bridge of his nose with a sigh. "You may have not been the Bane's target, but they'll figure out what you're up to easily enough. And they won't hesitate to kill you if they think you're a threat."

I shrug and smile innocently. "Then there's nothing to worry about since I'm not looking for the Bane."

"So you wouldn't have a problem leaving Merchwood." He levels a challenging look at me. "I'll get a carriage ready. We can leave within the hour."

Of all the high-handed, arrogant, stubborn— "But then I won't get to enjoy the party."

"You can come next year."

My eyes narrow. "Aliz and Luther will think I'm rude if I leave early."

Alexander steps closer. "They'll understand, since the alternative is getting poisoned again."

He's not going to give this up. I clench my fists as my jaw tightens. "I'm not going anywhere. You can't make me."

He raises an eyebrow. "I can't, but your brother can. Does Cristoph know where you are?"

Alexander always had a talent for finding my weak spots. "Of course," I bluff. "He was going to come too, but he had an emergency at home. Now, if you'll excuse me, I need to—"

"You know I can tell when you're lying."

He can, burn him. It's easily the most annoying thing about him. "And you know I've never listened to Cristoph before, and I'm not about to start now. I'm not leaving here until I capture the Bane." Blood pounds in my ears as heat rises through me. "I won't stop. Not when I'm this close."

"I want a truce."

"And if you think—" I blink. "What?"

"A truce. A ceasefire. A peace agreement." He tucks his hands in his pockets and rocks back on his heels with a nod. "I think we can help each other."

This is the last thing I expected when I woke up this morning. I eye him suspiciously. "Why would you want to help me?"

"I want to catch the Bane." His lips press into a grim line. "You're not the only one who has a score to settle with them."

But your life wasn't ruined. To be fair to Alexander, he didn't escape unscathed. I'm sure the guilt wore on him, though he seems to have gotten over it easily enough. "I already hired someone to find them." I smirk. "A professional. He used to work for the Spymaster, and he knows everything there is to know about the Bane. So there's nothing for you to do."

Alexander grumbles something under his breath, then grins triumphantly. "But he doesn't have an in with the nobles, which is why you're here. And I can talk to the men more easily than you. They won't be suspicious if I'm asking about their travel and business dealings. That's what you're trying to find out, right? So you need me."

Burn it. He figured that out fast. "We don't know that the Bane's a man," I challenge. I flip my braid back and lift a shoulder. "But I'm only here to see them get arrested. I'm not investigating anything."

He chuckles. "You really are a terrible liar."

"I'm an excellent liar." I fold my arms and glare at him. "I don't want your help. I can't trust you. Not after what you did."

His eyes turn into green storms. "It always comes back to that, doesn't it? The one horrible, stupid mistake that ruined our lives. How was I supposed to know the Bane poisoned those chocolates? I thought I was doing something nice for you, and I was wrong. I'm sorry." His voice is heavy with bitterness. "I used to hope you'd forgive me, but you won't, will you? You know it was an accident, but you don't care. I'll always only be the man that destroyed your family." Alexander looks away, but not before I see the pure agony on his face.

My stomach twists. *Is that what he thinks?* "I never blamed you for that."

"Yes, you did," he says hoarsely. "You hate me for killing your mother."

Tears sting my eyes and I touch my locket. "You didn't kill her. The Bane did."

His gaze snaps back to mine, a shattered look in his eyes. "Then why? Why do you hate me?"

Does he really not know? I wrap my arms around my waist, a hollow ache growing in my chest. "After I got sick, all I wanted was for my best friend to tell me everything would be all right. That we'd get through it together. But you left me." I stare at my feet, my shoulders hunched, the pain of those lonely years boiling back up to the surface. "You abandoned me when I needed you most, and you never came back." I swallow hard around the lump in my throat. "That's why I hate you."

"No!" Alexander reaches for me, his eyes wide, but I flinch back. His hands fall to his side. "No," he says quietly. "I tried to visit you, but they said you were too ill. So, I wrote you. Every day, for months, I wrote you pages and pages, begging you to forgive me. I only stopped when your brother told me how much I was hurting you."

Lead fills my stomach. "I didn't know." My mind whirls through those early days, trying to figure out what I missed. "They never told me."

Cristoph was always overprotective, but why would he do that? He knew it wasn't Alexander's fault, not really. And how many times did I cry in his arms that Alexander never came to visit, or answered my notes? Did Father put him up to it?

All those wasted years thinking my best friend had turned his back on me. Bile burns in my throat. I want to kick something, to scream. *Alexander was practically part of our family. Why would they turn their backs on him like that? Why lie to me?*

Part of me refuses to believe it, refusing to consider my family deceived me. But it makes a horrible kind of sense. I knew Alexander wouldn't abandon me and refused to believe it, which is why it finally broke me when I thought he had.

I blink back tears, my voice shaky. "Do you swear you're telling the truth? That you tried to see me and they wouldn't let you?" I hold my breath, not sure what answer I want.

He looks at me, his gaze steady, sincerity shining in his eyes. "I promise. As soon as I heard you were sick, I tried to see you. And I would never have stopped trying if I knew you wanted me there."

It's impossible not to believe him. I choke out, "Why didn't you sneak in to see me anyways? Why haven't you reached out to me in all these years?"

He smiles sadly. "Why haven't you?"

Why, indeed? Pride, fear of being rejected, and a thousand other excuses. So many mistakes that could have been avoided if we'd tried to talk to the other even once.

I rub a hand over my face, exhaustion washing over me. This is too much, too fast. It's impossible to reshape the past five years in a moment. I shove aside the confusion and mountain of emotions swirling through me until I can climb a tree and work through it alone. Right now, I have to deal with the urgent problem in front of me.

Alexander knows I'm here to find the Bane. He wants to help. But now that I know neither one of us is to blame for what happened, or mayhap we both are, I don't know if I can be around him. It was easier to keep him at arm's length when I had my righteous anger to use as a shield. It was simple. He was the villain. Now? Now he's just Alexander. The too-handsome, too-charming man who probably still knows me better than anyone else. And that makes him dangerous.

He broke me once. I can't risk it happening again.

But he's right. I have a better chance of finding the Bane with his help. That's all that matters. I'm older and wiser now. I know how to protect myself. We'll catch the Bane, and then I'll be on my way and never have to think about him or see him again. At least, that's what I tell myself. "Fine. You can help find the Bane. But we still aren't friends."

Alexander gives me the grin that always led to trouble.

"I had something else in mind. I thought I would court you."

"What?" A thrill of excitement races through me, chased by a shiver of panic. *He can't be serious.*

"It's a perfect cover. We'll be able to spend time together to plan and share information, and nobody will be the wiser to our scheme."

My mouth goes dry and I gulp. *This is not good. How much time does he think we'll be spending together?* He may not have broken our friendship like I thought, but that doesn't mean I want to start it up again. I need to protect myself from another heartbreak.

My stomach twists as my mind frantically searches for a reason to squash his plan. I blurt out, "What about Aliz?" My shoulders relax. *Yes, Aliz. Perfect!*

He frowns. "What about *Rirzan* Brecht?"

"You're supposed to be courting her." I put my hands on my hips, giving him a stern look. "If you suddenly start courting me too, she won't take you seriously. No woman will."

Alexander waves away my argument. "I was never officially courting her. Besides, I'd already decided to drop that idea. She isn't interested, and I don't want a wife that has to be talked into liking me."

My lips twitch. "Proven to be resistant to your charms, has she? That must be a first for you." I shake my head, taking pity on him. "It's because she thinks you're using her to go into business with Luther."

His head jerks back. "I would never do that! My project with Luther will happen regardless of *Rirzan* Brecht's feelings about me." He shrugs. "I just thought that we'd make a good match, and it'd a mutually beneficial alliance."

I snort. "How romantic. I'm shocked she hasn't fallen at

your feet, begging you to marry her."

He rakes a hand through his hair. "What do you want to hear? She's beautiful. Kind. Smart. Funny. And she's not afraid to speak her mind."

I shift my weight, ignoring the knots in my stomach. "Do—do you think you could love her?"

"I thought we could be happy." For the first time, he looks away. "But I would never promise to love her. I won't lie to her." He lapses into a brooding silence, then shakes his head, muttering, "It doesn't matter anymore." Alexander leans closer, his eyes intent. "So, do we have a deal? We'll pretend to be courting while we work together to catch the Bane?"

Everything in me is shouting to say no and walk away. Spending time with him is risking my heart again. But he may be my best chance and that's the only thing that matters.

I purse my lips. "We can't officially be courting. We'll just be old friends who are getting reacquainted. And if people misinterpret that as something more, then that's on them." I narrow my eyes. "And you have to promise to never, ever mention Vunheim."

His forehead wrinkles. "What's wrong with Vunheim?"

"Nothing, I just never want to hear about it again." I lift my eyebrow. "That's my best offer."

"Done and done." He grins at me. "Should I call you sweetheart, or do you prefer darling?"

I groan. "I'm going to regret this, aren't I?"

He smirks. "Definitely."

9

I spend the night tossing and turning, one moment thinking it was brilliant to let Alexander help me, the next cursing my stupidity and swearing it'll never work. But the debating's really just a way to distract myself from the earth-shattering revelations I'm still trying to wrap my head around.

Alexander didn't abandon me. We were both deceived by my brother—and he'll be getting an earful the next time I see him—but so what? It doesn't change the past.

A part of me yearns to go back to what we had, but that's a fantasy. Those children are gone, replaced by the people we've become. And now we're stuck together until we catch the Bane.

So…what do I do about it?

Nothing. It's better for both of us to keep the door to our past firmly closed. We'll capture the Bane and then go our separate ways, finding our futures elsewhere. It's the only option. I can't keep Alexander away from my hunt for the Bane now, and in any case, he wouldn't let me. But I can put aside my hurt long enough to do what I came here for, and then get a fresh start somewhere else. Somewhere that the Bane has never tainted. Mayhap by the sea, or I can spend time traveling around the continent. Once I'm rid of the Bane, there's nothing to keep me here.

I pick at the sticky bun the next morning, my stomach twisting. I'm supposed to meet Alexander in the library, but I'm stalling, and I can't even say why.

Sure, I won't be wishing him to die by a thousand jellyfish stings anymore, but we're not going to be best friends again. I'm only tolerating him for the short time until we find the Bane. And I'm sure he feels the same way about me. *Then why am I so nervous about seeing him?*

My chest tightens as I shove the plate away. *Enough dilly-dallying.* I drag myself to the wardrobe and glower at the garments, flipping through them with mounting annoyance. *No. No. Ugh, what was I thinking? No. No.* My hand pauses on an ice-blue dress and a flash of inspiration hits me with a bang.

Aliz. I smack my forehead and grin. I can't believe I forgot about her. Since Alexander was serious about courting her, I can help them. Not to try to talk her into falling in love with him. Just to convince her to give him a fair chance as a real suitor. A little encouragement should get her to be open-minded.

But Aliz probably wants her husband to love her, not just to have a 'mutually beneficial alliance.' I shake my head at Alexander's uninspiring description. The man needs a lot of help with romance.

Aliz is my friend, and her happiness matters to me. I can't encourage her into a marriage that'll make her miserable. I tug on my braid, feeling my way through the problem.

Alexander only said he can't promise to love Aliz, but that doesn't mean he won't fall in love with her. My fingernails cut painfully into my palms and I force my hands to relax. I'm not tricking anyone or misleading them. I'm just helping them start fresh. Then I'll step aside and the Fortunes can take it from there.

Feeling better, I hurriedly dress and meet Alexander in the library on the first floor. He looks eager to tackle the day with his jacket thrown over the back of his chair and his shirtsleeves rolled up to reveal muscular forearms. He flips through a stack of parchments covered in his handwriting and ink splatters, his hair messy from running his hand through it. The moment I close the door, he pelts me with questions.

"Did you hear from your investigator? Who are the other victims besides Lord Schnoebelen and potentially Lord Marx? What cities did you say they'd been in? Lonnheim, Wittrow, Norger, and was it Assan or Landsheer? Is it always poison from a plant? Has the Bane ever used venom or metal poisoning? How were the victims identified? How does your man know it was the Bane and not someone else who killed them?"

I groan and drop into a chair, throwing my arm across my eyes.

He chuckles. "You never were a morning person."

"Nobody decent likes being up this early. Are you sure you want to go through with this?"

"Trying to push me out already?" Alexander lifts my arm away from my eyes and waits until I meet his gaze. "I'm not going anywhere. Now, when do I get to meet your investigator?"

Never, if I can help it. "Hartwin's not going to be happy

that you know what we're doing. He barely let me come, and I'm his boss. We'd better wait until we have some information to put him in a good mood." I make a face. "Well, a less sour mood. I don't think he knows how to be happy."

"Then I'll make sure we find out something today, so I can meet him tomorrow." Alexander taps the stack of parchment. "At the performance this afternoon, we should make sure we're not asking the same questions. We don't want the Bane to get suspicious. Do you want to ask about the locations, or the people?"

We spend the next hour planning. It's easier to relax when we're focused on our strategy, keeping everything emotionless and detached. But as much as I'd like to pretend I've moved on from our past misunderstanding, every time he challenges one of my ideas, it takes everything in me not to snap at him. I have to force myself to take a slow breath, then calmly respond.

I'm trying not to be angry at him, but it's hard. The misplaced resentment, built up over all those years, is still lurking, ready to strike at the slightest provocation. *It'll be easier once I don't have to see him anymore and I give Cristoph a good verbal thrashing for interfering. And mayhap a dunking in the lake as payback.*

As we prepare to leave for the musicale, I decide I'd better let Alexander know about my other plan so he doesn't accidentally mess it up.

I stand and stretch, casually saying, "I've decided to help you with Aliz."

He stops rolling up the stack of parchments and eyes me warily. "Help me how?"

"By getting her to see you as a real suitor." I smile

brightly, ignoring the sharp ache in my chest.

Alexander's face goes blank. "I told you, I'm not interested in courting her. I don't want a wife who has to be convinced to like me."

I should've guessed he'd be stubborn about this. "It's nothing like that. I'm just going to get her to give you a fair chance, and she then she can decide whether she likes you or not. She's halfway there already. She only needs a little nudge." When he starts to protest, I give him a pointed look. "And you need to stop acting like a piece of wood when she's around. How is she supposed to be swept off her feet if you talk like a pompous dolt every time you have a conversation?"

He frowns. "I'm not that bad."

I snort and fold my hands behind my back, making my voice deep and monotone. "You are lovely this morning, *Rirzan* Brecht. This day is lovely. This chair is lovely. This parchment is lovely. This piece of dust is lov—"

Alexander's brow wrinkles. "I don't sound like that."

I smirk. "You absolutely do. But don't worry, we'll work on it."

His frown deepens. "We can't afford to be distracted. We need to focus on the Bane."

He could at least pretend to be a little grateful. "Stop complaining. I'm helping you win over the woman you want to marry." I reach up to touch my mother's locket, but it tumbles to the carpet. "Oh!" I scoop up my precious necklace, frowning at the clasp. "It broke."

"Here, let me look at it." Alexander carefully takes it out of my hand. I chew on my lower lip as he examines the small piece of metal. "It's just bent." He presses the piece between his two fingers, forcing it back into position. "Easy enough to fix for now, but the metal's weakened. You should get it replaced soon."

I turn around and lift my hair so Alexander can slide the necklace around my neck. I breathe a sigh of relief as its familiar weight rests above my heart while he fiddles with the clasp. It's hard not to giggle imagining the frown on his face as his fingers try to maneuver the tiny catch.

"Is this your mother's locket?" His hand brushes my neck, sending a delicious shiver down my back.

"Yes. She promised it would always protect me." I swallow the lump in my throat and laugh, trying to keep the mood light. "I guess she knew I'd keep falling out of trees. Good thing you were there to catch me."

The door opens and Aliz peers into the library. "Oh, there you are, Carina. I wanted to—"

Something over my shoulder catches her eye. She stops, a hand pressed to her mouth, her eyes wide. I glance back, but there's nothing there except Alexander, who shifts uncomfortably, his face tight.

And he thinks he acts normal around Aliz. I make a face at him to say, *"See?"* then turn back to her. "Yes?"

"What?" She blinks, then focuses on me, a silly grin spreading across her face. "I, um, wanted to see if you'd like to sit together at the musicale."

Alexander clears his throat. "I need to speak to *Kangan* Brecht."

I frown. "Now?"

Aliz gives him an odd smile. "We'll save you a seat."

He nods at us, then ducks through the doorway.

I shake my head, my brow furrowed. "Why did he run off? He's going to miss the start of the performances." *Not to mention losing time to talk to the guests like we planned.*

"Why, indeed?" Aliz's lips twitch.

She's laughing at me, but I don't know why. I bite the tip of my tongue, annoyed but unwilling to be distracted by her teasing. "By the way…" I toy with my locket. Ugh, this is awkward. "You might notice I'm spending more time with Alexa—Lord von Bron. I mean, obviously I am. You just saw us together. But we're not together, *together*."

I take a deep breath. *Great Fortunes, I'm totally bungling this. Why is this so hard?* I shift my weight. "What I mean is, you shouldn't get the wrong impression. We're just friends, and we haven't seen each other in a long time, so we're catching up. That's all. Alex—Lord von Bron's courting you, not me. And I don't want there to be any misunderstandings between us since you're both my friends."

That giddy smile appears again. "Oh, I understand perfectly."

I silently groan. *Burn it. I knew people were going to get the wrong impression.* If I keep trying to convince her, I'm just going to make it worse.

There'll be time enough to set her straight her after I've come up with a better explanation and she's gotten over this silly mood. I harumph, then gesture for her to lead the way.

To my astonishment, the ballroom has already been redecorated for the musicale. The walls of roses and pots of greenery have disappeared, replaced with wide strips of silvery cloth that stretch from the floor to the second story ceiling and sway gently in the breeze from the wall of open glass doors.

A small stage is set up at one end of the room. Sitting on it is a pianoforte, a large harp, and a few instruments I don't recognize. The long banquet tables against the walls have disappeared. Now rows of chairs face the stage, with small tables and chairs scattered behind them.

There's still half an hour until the performances will start, but there's already a good crowd in the room and loitering outside the glass doors.

I shake my head in amazement. "I don't know how you do it, Aliz. This is gorgeous. You always manage to put the perfect touch on these events."

She gives a satisfied nod as she looks around the ballroom. "It's really the staff. They do an amazing job making everything run smoothly. And it's no more than any hostess would do."

"Nonsense, Merchwood parties are famous for a reason. Who else would go to the trouble of making sure I have my favorite sticky bun and cinnamon tea every morning?"

She tilts her head to the side. "But I—"

A crash comes from the hallway, followed by the tinkling of breaking glass.

Aliz rubs her forehead as she hurries toward the noise. "Pardon me. I need to check on that."

"Should I…?" I take a step after her, but she waves me back.

"I'll find you after I sort out this mess."

Burn it. My stomach tenses. I was hoping Aliz would take the focus off me when we chatted with the other guests so I could slip in a question or two about the Bane without drawing attention. But really, I hate being at these things alone. I can spend hours by myself wandering outdoors or reading a book, but facing a crowd by myself makes me want to hide under a table.

Dorthea waves from the far side of the ballroom, then makes her way over to me, her vivid yellow dress making it easy to track her process. "Ah, Carina. Lovely to see you here, dear. Are you going to be performing?"

"Oh, no." My stomach tightens at the idea. I shake my head vehemently. "No, no, no, no."

She laughs. "So that's a no?"

"Definitely no. *Rirzan* Aliz wants her guests to have a good time, not be tortured. Are you?"

"My talents don't lend themselves to the arts. But if they want to hold a debate on whether we should trade with Rus, or if the Roma were more technologically advanced than the Gerrs, I'd be happy to participate."

"You think we shouldn't trade with Rus?" That's a new one. I thought Rus was a good ally.

"I think we should be cautious of relying too heavily on any one partner." She smiles. "But I won't bore you with an economics lecture. Is this your first time seeing Herr Meisl?"

My heart leaps into a frantic gallop and a cold sweat breaks out over my skin. *No! Not now! It's too soon.* I force a smile, struggling to keep my breathing normal. "My apologies, but I need to step outside for a moment."

Her brow furrows. "You look pale. Are you all right, dear?" She puts a hand on my arm. "I'll go with you."

"I'm fine. It's just the heat. Please, stay." I nod to her, then hurry to the glass doors. Gasping, I focus on each step, trying not to stumble as the room goes blurry. My knees tremble as my heart thunders in my chest.

Once I'm outside, I make a beeline for the nearest empty chair and sink down gratefully, pretending to admire the view while waiting for my heart to slow. *It'll pass. It'll pass.* My pulse pounds in my ears as my chest squeezes my lungs. Spots dance before my eyes, a fuzzy blackness growing on the edges.

Finally, the spell runs out and I can take a deep breath. Despite the warm summer air, I shiver, wrapping my arms around my waist, feeling hollow. I've never had two attacks so close together. It's usually at least a few months between one spell and the next. It's frustrating to never know when they're going to come over me, but there was some comfort in knowing I'd have a respite after one hits. Now even that small grace is gone. A heavy weight fills my stomach. *Will they come more often now? Am I triggering them somehow?*

It doesn't matter. I can't quit now. I have to capture the Bane, regardless of the cost. *And these attacks won't kill me. Probably.* Since the menders don't know what causes them, they can't be sure. But I'm not going to let anything stop me.

A woman says, "I must insist. You can't do that again. It's too dangerous."

I look around for the source. Lotta and Lord Wentzel emerge from the garden, her annoyed face and his mulish expression a sharp contrast to their merriment in the woods. He gives a sharp retort, too low for me to make out the words. Then he laughs and kisses her on the cheek before sauntering away, spinning his walking stick.

She shakes her head at him, her red hair glinting in the sun, before turning and spotting me at the table. "Lady Carina, have the performances started yet?"

"Not for a few more minutes." I join her and we walk toward the doors. "Are Ziggy and Lord Wentzel coming?"

"No, my father was feeling under the weather. And Franz is being incorrigible, as always." She laughs. "You'd think a man who has been to Deval as many times as he has would enjoy some culture, but he'd rather play cards all afternoon."

That's one of the Bane's locations. A thrill runs through

me. "Oh, I've never been there. Have you?"

She shakes her head. "My father can't travel as much as he used to, and I have to keep an eye on him. He'd have brandy and cigars for supper every night if it was up to him."

I chuckle as we enter the ballroom. There's no sign of Aliz, and the chairs are filling in quickly. Lotta and I find four empty seats in the middle of a row. To our left, Lord Marx is speaking with a tall, thin woman with a hooked nose. *I ran into her in the hallway after the ball. Now how can I find out who she is?*

Thank the Fortunes only Alexander knows when I'm lying. I lean over to Lotta and whisper, "This is embarrassing, but do you see that woman with the white hair at the end of our row? I met her the other night, and I've completely forgotten her name. Do you know her? She has a room on my floor, so I'm bound to keep running into her, and I'd hate to insult her by asking again."

Lotta peeks around me, then nods. "Lady Fauser. She has the room next my father. You're on the first floor too?"

I frown. "No, I'm on the fourth."

A secret liaison? Or is the Bane researching their next victim? I thought the woman was annoyed because I almost ran into her, but mayhap it was because she didn't like having a witness who could place her in that room. *Hartwin needs to hear about this.*

Lotta snickers, her eyes lighting up. "Ooh, you've stumbled on a scandal. No good house party would be complete without one. I wonder who she's seeing?"

I force out a laugh. "I haven't a clue, but I'll keep an eye out and see if I spot her again."

Our conversation is interrupted when *Kangan* Brecht steps onto the stage and introduces the first performer to polite applause. The young woman sits at the pianoforte and plays a forceful rendition of an old ballad. It's hard not to wince as she pounds the keys, her enthusiasm speeding up the tempo and bringing the normally sedate piece to a booming finale. There's a moment of stunned silence, then everyone claps as she curtsies, her face beaming.

A man takes the stage next with some kind of stringed instrument, and Lady Fauser slips out of the ballroom. I'm dying to follow her, but caution keeps me in my seat. Lady Fauser smartly sat at the end of the row, so her departure went mostly unnoticed, but I'd have to climb over half a dozen people to leave. *A trick to remember for next time.*

Lotta leans closer. "Herr Meisl is the last performer. He's a famous violinist in Deval. Franz saw him play at a private event at Lord Schnoebelen's palace, and even he had to admit it was exceptional. The uncultured oaf." Her tone is full of fondness, whatever argument they had earlier already forgiven.

Lord Schnoebelen was one of the Bane's victims. I sit up, trying not to bounce in my seat. *Lord Wentzel has two solid connections to the Bane.* My toes curl in my slippers as I force my face to stay neutral so I don't make Lotta suspicious.

Or she could be the Bane and trying to mislead me into suspecting Lord Wentzel. My instincts say it's not her, but I'm not willing to leave anything to chance when the stakes are this high.

Alexander takes the chair next to me, nodding a greeting to both of us. I raise my eyebrow. He shrugs a shoulder, then focuses on the man playing on the stage. A knot forms in my chest, but I brush off his odd behavior. It's normal for things to be a bit awkward between us. He can keep his secrets, and

I'll keep mine.

There are four more performers of varying talents, then it's the highly anticipated Herr Meisl's turn. Two men lug large boxes to the front of the platform, while a shorter man carrying a delicate violin takes center stage. Lotta nudges me and nods, an excited smile on her face.

The man puts the bow to the strings, pauses dramatically, then does a sweeping flourish, producing a piercing screech. I clap my hands over my ears and wince. Unperturbed, he brandishes the bow again, sawing on the strings, creating a shrill wailing that sets my teeth on edge.

I whisper to Alexander, "Is it supposed to sound like that?"

He shakes his head, cringing. Lotta's mouth is hanging open, and the audience's reactions range from pained to horrified. The violinist staggers forward, teetering on the edge of the stage, then lists to the side, his eyes closed. As he hits a particularly grating note, he bumps against one of the boxes. The lid pops open and dozens of terrified doves fly straight at us with sharp cries.

Everyone shrieks and covers their heads, running for cover. Chairs slide across the floor, adding obstacles to the mad stampede. Alexander wraps an arm around my shoulders and we stumble for the doors with the crowd surging around us. He pulls me close to his chest, shielding me from the onslaught.

We burst out of the doors and race for the corner of the house, the birds zooming overhead.

I tilt back my head and laugh as the doves disappear into the sky. "What is it about society and birds?" I shake my head. "Poor Aliz. I don't think she was expecting the musicale to end like this."

He runs a hand through his hair, grinning. "At least the party will be memorable."

"For more reason than one." I pause dramatically, savoring the moment. "We need to meet Hartwin. I know who the Bane is."

10

After I put the handkerchief in my window, I thought Hartwin would take at least a day or two to contact me, but within hours he sends a message asking me to meet the next morning.

I try to talk Alexander out of coming, but he refuses to be put off, insisting he has to introduce himself to our partner. This time we meet the former spy behind the barn next to a steaming pile of manure.

I wrinkle my nose, my eyes watering from the fumes. "I prefer the greenhouse."

Hartwin jerks his head at Alexander. "Who's the fop?"

Alexander stiffens, and I put a hand on his arm. "Why Hartwin, I'm shocked you don't recognize Lord von Bron. Perhaps you're not as observant as I thought."

He sniffs, then spits on the ground. "What'dya bring him into this for? I told you not to tell anyone."

"Don't be sore. You're still in charge of the investigation, but Alexander has his own score to settle with the Bane. And we have information for you." I fill him in on

what I heard, my excitement growing as I outline Lord
Wentzel's connections to the Bane's history.

He's as impressed as always, which is to say not at all.
"That's it? I thought you'd be farther along by now."

"And what have you found out?" I challenge him.

He glares at me. "Half the staff's hired on just for this
event. I'm still working on tracking down their past
employers."

I smirk. "I thought you'd be farther along by now."

As Hartwin shoots daggers at me, Alexander steps
forward. "Has the Bane made an attempt on Lord Marx?"

Hartwin ignores him until I lift an eyebrow. He
grumbles, "Not yet."

"What about an accomplice? Could the Bane be working
with someone, or at least buying the poisons from someone
else that we can use to figure out who they are?"

Now that's an idea. I'm impressed by Alexander, and
annoyed I didn't think of it myself.

The question earns Alexander something that almost
isn't a scowl. "It's possible, but unlikely. The Bane's had a
long career. Having an accomplice increases their risk of
being discovered, especially with how much they have to
move around. The Bane knows leaving any witnesses
increases the chance of being betrayed for a reward or as a
bargaining chip."

Alexander presses, "But that doesn't guarantee there
isn't an accomplice out there. Mayhap even one from when
they were just starting out and were more careless."

Hartwin snarls, "And if there had been one, I would've
found them by now."

*If Alexander's not careful, Hartwin will make him the
'Bane's' next victim.* "We'll keep gathering info on the

nobles. Let us know if you turn up anything on the staff."

Hartwin grunts and looks at me. "And I'll let you know when I have your other thing."

It takes a moment to understand him. *The blackmail on Alexander.* My stomach twists with guilt and I tug Alexander's arm. He keeps his eyes trained on Hartwin, giving him a curt nod as we leave.

I force out a laugh as we walk around the barn. "He must like you. He barely insulted us."

Alexander presses his lips into a tense line. "I don't like him."

"You don't like anybody. Actually," I tease, "you don't like any men who talk to me." When he doesn't say anything, I nudge him with my elbow. "You agree?"

"I wouldn't dare contradict a lady," he quips.

"Since when?"

"Since right now."

I laugh. "You shouldn't give me so much power. Now I know I can say the most outrageous things, and you'll have to agree."

"Not agree, just not contradict." He winks at me. "What's the other thing Hartwin's doing for you?"

My chest tightens. "Just something I wanted his help on a while ago, but it doesn't matter anymore." Technically not a lie. I'll have to remember to tell Hartwin to drop it the next time I see him alone.

Instead of turning toward the palace, Alexander surprises me by leading me to the front of the barn. "Luther lent me one of his carts so I can take your necklace into town and get the clasp fixed. Would you like to come with me? We could explore the shops and have lunch at the inn."

Oh. Butterflies fill my stomach and a warmth blossoms

in my chest. "That would be fun. Thank you."

Alexander drives the borrowed cart while I sit stiffly beside him on the bench, twisting my fingers together. There's no reason to be nervous. The hurt from his abandonment still hovers in the background, but it's slowly fading away. And before our estrangement, I spent plenty of hours alone with Alexander. We never lacked for things to talk about, and our quiet periods were always comfortable. *So why do I feel so flustered?*

The horse trots along the road and over the bridge as the silence stretches. I run my finger over the delicate flower embroidery on my sleeve, trying to find a way to break the awkwardness between us. "I haven't had a chance to talk to Aliz."

He tilts his head to the side, giving me a quizzical look. "You sat by her at breakfast."

"No, I mean I haven't talked to her about how you're actually courting her. But I'll make sure I drop some hints after we get back to the palace."

Alexander tenses. "There's no need." When I open my mouth to protest, he adds, "*Rirzan* Brecht will be suspicious if you suddenly start singing my praises out of nowhere."

I wave a hand through the air. "It'll be fine. We've already talked about you, so it'll just be more of the same as far as she's concerned."

"Really?" His green eyes light up as he grins. "What did you say? How handsome I am? Charming? Brilliant?"

"That you think there's a ghoul in your attic, and your foot got stuck in the jam jar."

"I was seven!" Alexander eyes me warily. "You didn't really tell her that, did you?"

I smirk and flip my braid over my shoulder. "Not yet."

"Then I'm sure she'd love to hear how you tried to dye your hair blond, and when it turned green, you panicked and cut it all off so your mother wouldn't find out." He chuckles. "I still remember her face when she saw you. She almost fainted."

"Don't you dare!"

"I won't if you won't."

"Done and done." I grin. "Besides, I can find plenty of other ways to embarrass you."

He chuckles. "So can I."

True. I giggle. "It's too bad that dye didn't work. I would've been a stunning blond. Mayhap I'll visit one of the beauty shops in Lonnheim and give it another try."

Alexander scrutinizes me for a moment, then solemnly shakes his head. "You can't improve on perfection."

I playfully swat his arm. "You're such a tease."

"Hmm," is his only response as he flicks the reins.

He's jesting… Isn't he? I tuck a strand of hair behind my ear, the butterflies in my stomach swirling. No, he's just being nice. Alexander always had a way of charming me.

I shift on the seat, eager to change the subject. "Do you remember when we decided to run away to Lenmark and be pirates?"

"You wanted to be a pirate. I was going to find buried treasure."

My shoulders relax. "Then why did you make me call you the pirate king?"

"Just helping you get ready for pirate life. Besides, you made me call you the pirate queen."

"And Cristoph refused to come because he gets seasick in the bath. He was so mad when he thought we were going to leave without him."

"He should've known you'd never do that to him."
Alexander leans back on the seat. "Speaking of your brother, where does he think you are?"

I smirk. "Resting in the Anglish countryside."

Alexander throws back his head and laughs. We trade memories from our childhood, and soon my cheeks ache from smiling. My need to find the Bane and the fears that have haunted me since the poisoning float away while we're talking.

Alexander fills me in on some of his recent travels and the people I know from town. I don't have much news to add from my side, but I describe the country house where my mother and I lived, and all the areas I explored once I was well enough to venture outdoors again.

When he asks about the people I know there, I distract him with questions about Wittrow. I don't want to spoil the lighthearted conversation by confessing I didn't make friends or socialize much. I always thought our stay in Angland was temporary, and I was still hurting from his betrayal. Besides, I had Mother and the house staff, and Father and Cristoph would visit. It was enough.

It's a surprise when we reach the town, though it's been a couple of hours since we left Merchwood. I expected a large city since it's close to the summer palace, but it's only slightly larger than the village near our estates in Wittrow. A mix of bright stores and tidy homes line the main thoroughfare, with clusters of buildings set down side roads and around the town center. People hurry on their errands or linger in doorways chatting with friends.

Our first stop is the blacksmith at the edge of town. There's a small shop attached to the smithy for customers to place their orders and browse the selection of common items he keeps in stock. The young girl running the counter assures us that her father does fancy gold work and it'll only be a week to create a new clasp for my locket. It's painful to leave my mother's necklace behind, but it would be devastating to lose it if the clasp broke again.

With our errand taken care of, we decide to explore before getting lunch. The town might be small, but the variety of stores is as good as I'd find in any city. Alexander trails bemusedly behind me as I run from one to another, exclaiming over the trinkets and treats. I spend far too long drooling over the bookstore, promising myself I'll come back and buy out half the shop after we capture the Bane.

During lunch at the quaint little inn, Alexander has me in giggles with his impressions of Lord Marx and Hartwin between bites of crispy golden potato pancakes and a tender sauerbraten smothered in gravy that melts in my mouth.

After our meal, we set out at a slower pace, ducking into the different stores that capture our fancy. He insists on buying me an enormous bag of lemon drops while blatantly ignoring my suggestions to get a present for Aliz. *The man is too stubborn. Can't he accept that he's frustratingly oblivious about women and I'm just trying to help him?* I sigh. *I have my work cut out for me.*

As we leave the candy shop, Alexander frowns. "What's he doing here?"

"Who?" I crane my neck, trying to pick out the man he's looking at.

"Chef Kloss. Luther introduced me to him after he was hired last month. I wanted to talk to someone about soap's boiling point, and Luther thought—"

"He's new?" My pulse speeds up. *Could the chef be the Bane?* A chef would know about poisonous foods, mayhap even how to extract poisons from plants. I run off in the direction he was looking, then skid to a stop, narrowly avoiding being bowled over by Alexander. "Which one is he?"

He chuckles and points out a short, thickset blond man across the road. When Chef Kloss glances over his shoulder, I duck behind a nearby rain barrel, dragging Alexander down next to me.

He whispers loudly, "What are we doing?"

"I want to see where he's going. He could be the Bane."

The humor disappears from his face. "That's unlikely."

I peer around the edge of the barrel to keep an eye on the chef and hurriedly going through my reasoning.

Alexander shakes his head. "Nobles don't change chefs that often. Even if the murders are years apart, what are the odds Chef Kloss could find a new job near the victims when he needed to? And he couldn't just disappear for days without questions being asked."

He's just mad because I figured it out first. "He doesn't always have to work as a chef. Mayhap sometimes he posed as a baker, or a carriage driver, or a fishmonger. And he could have sent some poisons, instead of going personally, like the ones sent your parents." My lips pinch together. "Besides, Hartwin could be wrong about which murders belong to the Bane."

Alexander stands, his jaw clenched. "It's not him."

I glare up at him. "Then it won't hurt to see what he's doing." Before he can respond, I dash after Chef Kloss. Alexander falls into step beside me, glowering.

My shoulders tense. "You can wait for me by the cart. I won't be long."

"I'm not going to leave you alone with a murderer."

"And I thought you said it was impossible for him to be the Bane." I get a flash of grim satisfaction at the annoyance in his eyes.

"Just because he's not the Bane doesn't mean he's not dangerous."

There he goes again, being overprotective. Like I haven't taken care of myself these past five years without his help, thank you very much.

"Besides, you might get stuck in a well."

I gasp. "You know that wasn't my fault. The rope broke. It could've happened to anyone."

He smirks. "You're the one who climbed down there to capture sprites."

"Because you dared me to!"

"That's not how I remember it."

We pause our bickering when Chef Kloss turns down a shady side alley between two stores. As we creep forward, I'm amused by how quickly Alexander joined in my snooping despite all his protests. My pulse speeds up, and every nerve's tingling as I peek into the lane, holding my breath. Chef Kloss is standing at the end of the alley near the trash pile, looking nervously behind him.

We dart back, hiding behind the corner. After a few moments, we inch forward to the corner again, me crouching low to the ground with Alexander leaning over me.

The chef's talking in a hushed voice to someone hidden in the doorway. Chef Kloss hands over a heavy pouch, receiving a dark green box the size of my hand in return. I clutch Alexander's arm, trying not to squeal. When Chef Cluck turns toward us, we stumble back and race away from the alley, skidding around the nearest building to get out of sight.

I give Alexander a gloating smile, feeling like I'm going to burst from excitement. "Now who's wrong?"

He frowns at me, but I can tell he's curious. "It could be something else."

"Or it could be evidence he's the Bane." I clap my hands together, bouncing on my toes. *Another clue!* "I can't wait to tell Hartwin."

He shakes his head. "We can't go around accusing random people of murder."

"We aren't." *Not exactly.* "Hartwin will investigate him and try to find out where he's been the past year. Meanwhile, we can spy on him and find out what's in that box."

"We'll need to be careful."

"Yes, yes, yes. No letting him catch on that we suspect him. Keep acting normal. I'm not a feather-wit."

"No, but you do get into a lot of trouble."

"Usually with your help." When he shakes his head again, I know I've won. I grab his hand and pull him toward the cart. "Let's hurry and get back to Merchwood before he does. We can intercept him when he arrives and find a way to see what's in that box."

Alexander and I argue most of the way to the palace. He wants to let Hartwin handle it since he's the professional, while I insist that we watch the chef so he doesn't claim his next victim and destroy the box. In the end, he reluctantly agrees with my plan—once I make it clear I'll do it with or without him.

There's no sign of Chef Kloss on the road. I dance

impatiently in my seat as we drive over the bridge, protesting loudly when Alexander takes the turnoff to the barn instead of driving to the palace entrance. As soon as the cart stops, I jump out and make a beeline to the kitchen, ignoring Alexander's shouting, determined to find a good hiding spot before Chef Kloss arrives.

When I slide to a stop by the kitchen entrance, my jaw drops. He's already in there, bellowing at the other staff while he chops onions and carrots. The mysterious green box is perched on a high shelf above him, tucked between two clay jars. Chef Kloss spots me hovering around the doorway and barks at a pot girl, jerking his head in my direction.

She scurries over to me, wringing her hands in her apron. "Can I get you something, milady?" She nods at Alexander as he trots up to us, his lips pressed in a grim line. "Sir?"

I give her a bright smile. "No, I—" Alexander clears his throat loudly and I barely keep from growling. "*We* were hoping to observe Chef Kloss's cooking. His dinners have been amazing, and I simply must know how he does it." Alexander snorts, but I ignore him and keep my hopeful gaze pinned on the girl.

Her eyes widen and she chews furiously on her bottom lip. "I'm so sorry, milady, but Chef doesn't allow any visitors in his kitchen." She darts a look over her shoulder, then lowers her voice. "He's very strict."

I keep the smile fixed on my face. "Surely he can make an exception this one time. I must insist."

The hand wringing and lip chewing double in intensity. "I—I don't know."

The poor girl looks like she's about to keel over. Disappointment fills my chest and my smile dims as I nod.

"Another time, perhaps."

As Alexander and I walk away from the kitchen, I whisper, "He probably doesn't want anyone in there to see what's in the box, anyway. We can check back later when the kitchen's empty and see what he's hiding."

"Or we can find Hartwin and he can deal with it, since it's probably nothing."

"Then why would Chef Kloss be so secretive about buying it? There's something going on, I know it." I start, then realize my hand unconsciously reached for my missing locket. *I hope the blacksmith can hurry the repairs.*

"We should still tell Hartwin," he insists.

I raise an eyebrow and smirk. "I thought you didn't like him."

He narrows his eyes. "I don't, but that doesn't mean he isn't the best person to find out what's going on."

Stubborn, annoying beast. "Fine." I stop in the hallway and put my hands on my hips, glaring at him. "I'll go signal Hartwin, if you promise to stay here and make sure the chef doesn't leave with the box."

"Done and done," he says dryly as he leans against the wall, his arms crossed. "If he steps out of the kitchen, I promise that I'll wrestle him to the ground and keep him in a headlock until you get back."

"Make sure that you do." I flounce off without a backward glance.

My annoyance fades as I climb the stairs. This could be it. I've finally found Bane. The box probably has the poison he plans to use on Lord Marx. If Hartwin knows what it is, we can figure out how he's going to give it to Lord Marx and catch him in the act. But we have to be careful and make sure he doesn't know we're watching him. I frown. I hope

Alexander wasn't serious about that headlock.

A door opens in the hallway to the right. My heart jumps into my throat and I dash out of sight, pressing my back against the wall. I hold my breath. *Who is it? Did they see me?* Then laugh at myself. *See me doing what, exactly? Walking up the stairs? Very suspicious.* Chuckling, I push off the wall, glancing at the hallway to see Lady Fauser opening a door halfway down. Still laughing, I nod a greeting. She starts, then nods back before going inside.

As I continue the climb up to the fourth floor, something about the encounter nags at me. It's not until I reach my door that it hits me. I spin around, eyes narrowed. *Lotta said her room on the first floor, so what's she doing on the third floor? And why was she on the fourth floor during the ball?*

I mull it over, then shake my head. *I'd better tell Hartwin about this, too.* My hand closes on empty air and I hiss through my teeth, realizing I reached for my missing locket again.

I dash over to the window and stuff the handkerchief in the corner, then pause. A small package with a note's sitting on my vanity. The room was locked when I got here, so one of the staff with a key must have delivered if after breakfast. Feeling paranoid now that we're close to catching the Bane, I use one of the hand towels to pick up the note and break the seal.

> *This will help with your spells*
> ~Dorthea

The knot in my chest loosens as I open the box and the spicy scent of cinnamon fills the air. Inside's a little silver strainer sitting on a supply of looseleaf tea. A warmth grows inside me and I press my fingers to my smiling lips. It's a bit embarrassing that she saw how unwell I was at the musicale, but I'm touched by her thoughtfulness. I'd love to brew up a cup right now to see how it compares to my favorite, but Alexander will come looking for me if I dawdle much longer.

I race back down the stairs, hoping to catch sight of Lady Fauser. The third-floor hallway's empty, but I mark the room she went into, making a note to ask Aliz about its occupant later. I'm tempted to knock on the door and confront Lady Fauser, but Alexander would definitely sew me in a sack and ship me off to Cristoph if he thought I was trying to confront the Bane without him.

I intentionally take the long way around the first floor so I can go by the kitchen, slowing my steps as I pass the archway, confirming the box is still on the shelf. Chef Kloss is busy fussing over a pot bubbling over the fire while the rest of the kitchen staff cuts, chops, and peels large piles of vegetables at a long counter.

Alexander gives me a pointed look as I join him at the end of the hallway. "Didn't trust me to keep an eye on him?"

"No, I just like watching the kitchen staff work," I lie.

His exasperated sigh says he knows I'm fibbing, so I hurriedly change the subject and tell him about Lady Fauser. "What if she's the Bane instead of the chef? Is that Lord Marx's room? I should've asked Hartwin where it is. What do you think she's doing in there?"

He shrugs. "A rendezvous with a paramour?"

"In the middle of the afternoon?" I blush, ignoring his chuckle. "Never mind. We should split up so we can watch them both."

"No." His response is so forceful that I jump. In a softer

tone, he adds, "If one of them is the Bane, it would be dangerous to be caught alone. We need to stick together."

It's annoying when he's right. "Then let's watch the chef. We need to make sure that box doesn't disappear."

His cocky grin makes my stomach flutter. "I was hoping you'd say that."

11

I look skeptically at the storage closet, then at Alexander. "When you said you found a good hiding spot, I imagined a nice empty sitting room, or a couch in the root cellar next to a plate of lemon cakes."

"Well, I was going to invite Chef Kloss to join us for tea, but I thought staying out of sight was more important." He gestures inside. "Plenty of room for both of us, and it gives us a good view down the hallway without being seen. People would talk if we spent hours standing in hallway."

"They'll definitely gossip if they find us in a dark closet together," I point out.

"Then we'd better make sure they don't see us." His playful grin brings on a flood of warm summer memories, making my heart flutter. His brow furrows. "Burn it, wait a moment." Alexander takes off his coat and spreads it on the ground, then grandly gestures for me to sit. "I should've gotten a blanket, but this will have to do."

I try to protest, but he insists. A little ball of warmth glows in my chest as I settle on the jacket, smoothing out my skirt as I avoid his eyes. Over the years, he's given me his jacket a thousand times, but now it feels different in a way I don't want to think about.

What am I doing? I mentally shake my head. I've been thinking about the past too much today and losing focus. Look at all the time we wasted in town when I could've been finding out why Lady Fauser is sneaking around the palace, or even identifying another suspect. *This party is turning me into a feather-wit.* I square my shoulders, determined to keep all my attention on capturing the Bane.

As far as hiding places go, the storage closet isn't terrible. There's room for us to sit across from each other, and the gap between the door and its frame is large enough to easily peep through. I squint down the hallway, keeping a sharp eye out for any movement.

My enthusiasm for playing lookout soon fades. There are only a few people who come and go from the kitchen; otherwise, the area is quiet. I shift my weight, trying to get comfortable. My fingers drum against my thigh and I sigh. Alexander leans back, his eyes closed.

I glare at him. "Why aren't you watching?"

"It doesn't take both of us. I'll take over when you're tired."

Fine. I tug on my sleeve, smoothing a wrinkle out of the fabric. A man walks out of the kitchen carrying a tray of stacked plates. *No box.* My hand closes on empty air and I curse, desperately wishing I had my locket back. I twist the end of my braid around my fist, then blow out a breath. "You said you talked to Chef Kloss about soap. Why?"

"I'm working on a new way to make it." He grimaces and adjusts his shoulders, then relaxes against the wall.

"How are you going to do that?"

He opens an eye. "I wouldn't want to bore you."

"No, I want to know. It might help us figure out if he's the Bane. Why soap? What are you doing?" To my surprise, I'm really curious. When he still hesitates, I say, "Please?"

Alexander sits up, his eyes bright. "Right now, we mix the oil, water, and lye together and pour it into the molds. Then it takes about seven weeks for it to cure and be ready to cut into smaller blocks to sell. But if we heat it while mixing it, it'll only take one week for the soap to cure."

My eyebrows shoot up. "That's amazing. How did you figure that out?"

He shrugs self-consciously. "A lot of experimenting. I got the idea from that summer we tried to make candied apples."

I grin. "And ended up with a blackened brick of goo that ruined Leila's stock pot. Not our most successful scheme."

He chuckles. "But not our worst."

"At least some good came out of it. Now you have a brilliant new idea. What are you going to do with it?"

"That's what I'm hoping to talk to Luther about. He has a small soap factory in Gretzberg with enough space for the furnaces and boilers to try out the process on a larger scale. We've been talking about going into business together for a while. This seemed like the perfect fit." He scratches his cheek and makes a face. "If I ever get a chance to tell him about it. Every time I start to bring it up, we get interrupted."

I lean forward, excitement thrumming through me. "You will. And he'll be just as impressed as I am."

"I hope so. But if he isn't, then there are other people I'll ask."

I peek through the crack in the doorway, watching a few more servers leave the kitchen with small trays. "Cristoph?"

He's always writing about some investment or another.

Alexander's jaw tightens and he looks away. "No."

A sour taste fills my mouth. *Of course not.* Alexander's rightly furious about Cristoph's meddling and will probably do everything in his power to avoid him. It's different for me. Cristoph might be a self-righteous idiot sometimes, but that doesn't mean I'll stop loving him.

Alexander clears his throat. "In any case, I'll speak with Luther first."

I smile brightly, pushing aside the moment of discomfort. "Try to ask him before he does another battle reenactment and burns down the palace."

His shoulders relax and he laughs. "No need. Even if I don't catch him before the party's over, I'm visiting him in Bomen soon. And we wouldn't be able to get the furnaces and boilers in place before next summer, so waiting another month won't change anything." He grins. "Except make me very impatient."

My smile turns forced as my chest tightens. "It sounds like you spend most of the year visiting Luther." *No wonder he decided Aliz would be a smart match. They already spend most of their time together.*

"This year I have. But now I'll probably be spending more time in Wittrow." His eyes meet mine, then dart away as he rubs the back of his neck.

Because if he and Aliz get married, he'll want to live near his family. I bet they'll love her. My stomach twists. "I'm sure your parents will be glad to hear that. They must miss you."

He leans back against the wall and frowns. "They're in Pilla for a few more months, but I'll see them before Wintertide. They'd love to see you when you come back to

Wittrow." He grudgingly adds, "And I'm sure Cristoph would be happy to have you home."

If I go there. As happy as I would be for Alexander and Aliz, it would be awkward to live next to them. *Perhaps after a few years, when I've gotten used to the idea.* I rub the sharp ache in my chest as I turn my attention back to the hallway.

As servers stream out of the kitchen with more dishes, I realize how late it is. "You'd better hurry. They're about to serve supper."

His brow furrows. "So?"

I tilt my head to the side and give him a questioning look. "This is the perfect chance for us to get more information about Lord Marx. You need to find out everything you can about him now that we know he's the Bane's target."

Alexander nods slowly. "All right. I guess we can come back here after supper and see if the chef's still here."

"No need." I smile sweetly. "I'm going to stay and watch him."

His eyebrows shoot up. "No, you're not. You can't stay here alone."

I match his glare and cross my arms. "Yes, I can. Chef Kloss is still our best suspect, and I'm not going to let him out of my sight for a moment. What if he hides the box while we're gone? We'll never find out what's inside it." I smirk. "Besides, Lord Marx thinks I'm impertinent, but you're like the son he never had. And you said that it'll be less suspicious if you're the one asking the men about their travel and business deals instead of me." It's nice to have the logical argument on my side for once.

Alexander scowls. "I'm not dressed for supper."

Why does he always have to be so stubborn? "It'll take you five minutes to get ready, whereas it would take me at least an hour. You're out of excuses. Now go."

He argues for a few more minutes, trying to convince me to either let him stay or come with him, but I stand firm. After he grumblingly slips out of the storage closet, I take a deep breath and close my eyes, pressing my forehead against the cool stone.

I didn't realize spending time with Alexander would be this confusing. My emotions keep swinging between happiness and hurt, relaxation and resentment. I hate feeling so confused. I haven't felt this off-balance since I thought he'd abandoned me. It would be so much simpler if I could turn my heart off until we catch the Bane and I never have to see Alexander again.

It would be easy to pretend the past doesn't matter. But it does. We both made mistakes, but he should have tried harder. It might be unfair, but it's true. *I was too tired, too weak to go to him. Alexander should've come to see me, no matter what Cristoph said. He could've fixed all this five years ago, but he didn't.*

I wrap my arms around my waist and shift my weight, trying to get comfortable. *I may have moved on, but that doesn't mean I'm going to let my guard down now.*

I don't hate him, but I can't trust him. I won't. Being friendly doesn't mean we're friends. As long as I keep my wits about me and make sure I keep him at arm's length, everything will be fine.

Satisfied with my plan, I stretch my sore spine with a groan. Spending hours hunched over, peering through a crack in the door, isn't great for my posture. I put my hand down to stand—then jerk it away.

Alexander's coat. He forgot to take it with him.

I scramble up, chewing on my bottom lip, staring at the rumpled garment. The minutes tick off. *Stop being silly. It's just a jacket.* I gingerly nudge it to the side with the toe of my slipper, then settle on the cold stone floor with a wince and return to surveilling the hallway.

Soon the heavy stream of people coming in and out of the kitchen creates quite the crush, and the number of carts and covered trays makes it impossible to see if anyone has the box. But if Chef Kloss is the Bane, he wouldn't entrust a deadly poison to someone else, and he hasn't left the kitchen. I have to believe it's still in there with him.

The crowd in the hallway ebbs and swells between the courses. I didn't realize how long the supper service would feel when I'm trapped in a cold storage closet with a constant parade of amazing foods flowing past me. The captivating smells of savory beef and roasted vegetables fill the air, making my mouth water. My stomach grumbles and I promise it I'll raid the kitchen for something delicious the moment it's empty.

Hopefully Alexander's getting more clues about the Bane. Lord Marx should be extra chatty since I'm not there, although Dorthea will probably keep his ego in check. Alexander doesn't seem to mind his belittling comments. He's always been so easygoing and willing to give people the benefit of the doubt, unlike me.

My fingers are mindlessly brushing back and forth across his jacket's soft sleeve. I force my hand to move away and put my clenched fists in my lap. The longer I'm around Alexander, the more I turn into a feather-wit.

My jaw tense, I put my eye against the crack in the door and watch the hallway.

As soon as I catch the Bane, I'm leaving. And I'm never, ever, ever coming to another Sunselt party.

The stone floor quickly draws my body heat away, leaving me chilled. My comfort isn't helped by being forced to sit still in the small space.

After an hour or so of shivering, I give in and put on Alexander's coat with a muttered oath. *It's better than freezing to death.* I pull it tight around me, pretending I'm not breathing in the scent that's purely Alexander.

The dessert course is served, and then there's a steady pattern of staff members taking drinks and tea to the guests while most of the kitchen staff are packed into the kitchen. Based on the splashes and voices, I'd guess they're washing the mountains of dishes that were piled on the returning carts.

I stifle a yawn. I may be used to spending hours alone, but I'm not usually trapped in a storage closet. Eventually the staff starts drifting out in ones and twos, the noisy kitchen quieting as the hours crawl by.

Chef Kloss steps into the hallway and my pulse speeds up. I press against the door, trying to catch every detail. He has his shirtsleeves rolled up, revealing healed cuts and a long burn scar on his right forearm. His blond hair is slick with sweat, and he mops his red face with a large handkerchief. *The green box is too large to be in his pockets, so it must still be in the kitchen.* Chef Kloss glances over his shoulder and nods, then walks down the hallway and turns out of sight.

I hold my breath, forcing myself to count to five hundred to make sure he's gone, my heartbeat thundering in my ears. As soon as the time is up, I leap out of the closet and race to the kitchen, skidding into the empty room. My eyes fly to the shelf that held the box.

It's gone.

My heart plummets. Cursing under my breath, I drag a stool over and climb up for a closer look. The cannisters hold loose tea, dried beans, and other mundane kitchen staples. The box isn't hidden inside any of them or tucked behind anything up there.

I narrow my eyes and look around the room. *It must be here somewhere.* I grab an apple and absently devour it as I get on my hands and knees to dig through the nearest cabinet.

"Carina?"

I jump, banging my head with a curse. Eyes watering, I rub the sore spot as I crawl out of the cabinet to glare at Alexander. "You scared me."

He folds his arms, green eyes flashing. "Imagine how I felt when you weren't in the storage closet."

Someone's cranky when they stay up past their bedtime. "I'm obviously fine, except for a new headache." I wince as I touch my head.

A line appears between his brows. "Why didn't you wait for me?"

"I saw a chance, and I took it. Besides, you've been gone for hours. I didn't know if you were coming back." I gesture at the shelves. "Help me look for the box."

Alexander begrudgingly carries the stool to the far corner of the kitchen, starting an orderly search of the shelves while I duck my head and shoulders into the lower cabinets, shoving pots and pans aside.

He raises his voice to be heard over my racket. "I followed Lord Marx after supper. He played cards all night. Nothing seemed suspicious, but I have a list of everyone he spoke with for Hartwin. Did anything happen while I was gone?"

"Nothing except the box disappearing. When Chef Kloss left, he didn't have it, so it must be in here somewhere." I stick my head into the next cabinet, then sneeze loudly. "Why do they need so many pots? These probably haven't been used in years."

"If the dust isn't disturbed, it's probably not in there," he points out reasonably.

I ignore him, continuing my search. "He wouldn't have trusted anyone else with it. But why hide it? Why not take it with him?"

"Or he took it with him and you missed it."

I grit my teeth. I can't strangle him. But I can give him a good kick in the shin if he keeps being annoying.

He dusts off his hands and frowns as he looks around. "It's not in here."

"Then leave," I snap. "I'll find it myself."

Alexander stiffens, then turns and digs through one of the sacks on the floor. We work in silence, bumping into each other with muttered apologies as we make our way around the kitchen. My stomach growls loudly and heat rushes to my cheeks.

His shoulders relax and he hands me a ripe pear with a smile. "Why don't you sit for a moment? I'll keep looking while you eat."

I give a token, "I shouldn't..."

"Yes, you—"

"All right." I plop down on a stool and he chuckles.

My first bite of the juicy pear has me groaning. Alexander keeps his promise to continue searching while I gobble the sweet fruit, sticky juice running down my chin. I laugh when he hands me a napkin, his eyes sparkling with humor. As I finish the pear, he passes me a thick slice of bread smothered in honey and raspberry jam. Alexander finishes my supper service with a large apple strudel, the flaky crust melting in my mouth, the buttery flavor mingling with the spiced apples and raisins.

Refreshed, I use the sink to wash up, then dive back into our search with gusto. Alexander entertains me with impressions of Lord Marx and the other guests playing cards as we dig into barrels and sacks, seeing no sign of the mysterious box.

Just when I'm about to admit defeat, a faint outline under one of the barrels catches my eye. "Come look at this."

Alexander crouches next to it, his brow furrowed as he runs a finger over the lines. "It looks like the tile is loose."

He muscles the heavy barrel to the side, then lifts the stone away, revealing a small metal safe with a dial on the face.

I clap my hands and whoop. "We found it!"

He frowns and nods slowly, then tests the handle. "Locked."

My shoulders sag. *Burn it.* I don't know why I expected the Fortunes to finally give me some luck. "Mayhap we can take it with us."

Alexander hesitates, running a hand through his hair. Then he shrugs and takes off his dinner jacket, handing it to me. "Give me a little room."

I inch back, craning my neck around him. Alexander rolls up his sleeves, braces his feet against the floor with both hands on the handle, and heaves. His muscles strain and he grunts, his face turning red with effort.

He relaxes with a curse. "It's too heavy. It doesn't look that big, so it must be weighted."

I sigh. Alexander is several times stronger than me and the safe didn't even wiggle when he tried to lift it. There's no chance we could get it out, even if we worked together. *That's why the chef was so confident about leaving the box behind. Nobody can carry the safe off. They'd have to break into it.*

Alexander interrupts my musings. "Chef Kloss probably hired a couple of men to move it in. I'd bet Luther doesn't even know it's here."

I raise my eyebrows. "That seems like a risky move. What if Luther fired him?" I shake my head and answer my own question. "He'd just sneak in and get it out the same way." It's not like there are guards patrolling the hallways every night. "Can we open it?"

He shrugs, then pulls on his dinner jacket. "Hartwin probably knows how to."

A spark of anger flares in my chest, and I put my hands on my hips. "That's it? You're giving up?"

His eyes narrow and gestures to the safe. "I don't have any tools to pry it open, and we don't know how many numbers are in the combination. But if you want to waste your time, go ahead."

Glaring at him, I sit on the floor, then turn my attention to the safe's dial. It starts at 0 and goes up to 60, the numbers marked off in increments of 5. My heart sinks as I realize how impossible this task is, but I clench my jaw and spin the dial. Alexander sighs and settles on a stool a few feet away.

I ignore him, trying a simple 1-2-3-4 combination to start.

The Fortunes owe me. Now it's time for them to pay up.

Gentle arms scoop me up.

I mumble, "What time is it?"

"Late." He chuckles quietly, the sound vibrating in his chest. "Or early, depending on how you look at it."

"All right." I snuggle closer, breathing in the scent of home. "G'night."

He laughs again. "Sweet dreams."

12

I bolt up in bed, drenched in sweat, heart racing. Clutching the blanket to my chest, I frantically look around. It takes a few minutes to place the strange room and remember I'm at Merchwood. I sigh, flopping back on my pillow and throwing an arm across my eyes.

The nightmare is fading, but pieces of shadow still cling to me. Darkness. Alexander shouting my name, panicked, as he searches for me, his voice growing more and more faint. A faceless Bane grabbing me from behind, then flames blazing across my face and clothes. I shudder from the imagined pain of the fire scorching my skin.

Dawn is barely peeking over the horizon, but there's no point in trying to go back to sleep. I crawl out of bed and grimace at my reflection in the mirror. Face powder can only do so much to hide the dark circles under my eyes, but a cup of strong tea eases the throbbing pulse in my head.

When I'm on my second cup, someone slips a note from Hartwin under the door, telling me to meet him after breakfast. I dress and hurry down to the library to wait for

Alexander, my steps light, surprised at how much bigger Merchwood feels with empty hallways. I pass a painting of a small mountain village and grin.

After we prove Chef Kloss is the Bane, we should go to Vunheim for their Ramsfeel celebration so I can see what all the fuss is about. And then it'll be my turn to bore everyone with stories about my trip.

Outside the library, I freeze. When did I decide Alexander and I are friends again?

I knew this was a risk when I started working with him, but all my reasons for keeping him at arm's length are suddenly hard to remember. And I might have been a little hasty deciding we couldn't be friends. Who else but Alexander would help me spy on a man around town? Or spend hours sitting in a storage closet and ransacking a kitchen when they think it's a complete waste of time? And I'm not worried about him tattling to Cristoph, so perhaps I do trust him—to an extent. Enough that I won't mind seeing him after we stop the Bane. Enough that I'm including him in my future.

Butterflies fill my stomach and I twist my hand around my braid as I stare sightlessly at the library door. Nobody knows me better than Alexander. We've both learned from our mistakes and we're both sorry about the roles we played in what happened back then, so there's no reason we can't be friends now. Besides, he wants to court Aliz, so there's no risk of getting my heart broken again.

The thought isn't as comforting as it used to be. In fact, it's downright uncomfortable, but I can't pinpoint why.

"Carina?" Alexander says from behind me.

I spin around, practically bumping into him. Alexander's eyes are still soft from sleep, and the rumpled shirt and trousers look like the same ones he was wearing last night. My fingers itch to comb through his tousled hair and trail down his unshaven jawline.

I suck in a breath and hastily put my hands behind my back, my cheeks heating. *I must be more exhausted than I thought.* I blurt out, "What are you doing here?"

His lips twitch. "I was invited. But if you mean in the hallway, I couldn't sleep. I thought I'd spend a few hours reading before breakfast." He scratches his chin and stifles a yawn. "If I don't fall asleep in the chair. Why are you up so early? I thought you'd be asleep until supper." The concern in his eyes sends a warm shiver through me.

"Oh, um, I was coming to find you. Hartwin wants to meet. After breakfast." I toy with my sleeve as my cheeks burn hotter. "I thought you'd want to know, but then I realized how early it is and that you probably wouldn't be awake yet."

He chuckles. "I guess the Fortunes decided to help you." Alexander ducks his head and rubs the back of his neck. "Since we're up, do you want to walk down to the lake?" When I hesitate, he winces. "You're tired. We can go some other time."

"No, I'd like to." I don't know who's more surprised by my breathless response. I clear my throat, my stomach fluttering. "We have plenty of time, and I need something to take my mind off of everything."

He gestures for me to lead the way. My pulse speeds up and I sternly tell myself there's nothing wrong with spending time with an old friend. Our footsteps echo off the stone as we walk through the palace, feeling like we have Merchwood to ourselves. The start of the day hasn't yet extinguished the night's chill, and I'm grateful I brought my shawl. When we step outside, I take a deep breath of the crisp morning air. It feels good to stretch my legs and banish the last bits of my nightmare.

The stroll to the lake is even prettier in the early morning light, with flowers opening to the sun's rays and thin fog blanketing the hills. The fresh scent of dewy grass fills the air while early birds call to each other. There's a lightness in my chest and an easy looseness to my step. Alexander seems equally at peace, an inscrutable smile on his lips. When we reach the water, he tilts his head to the dozen row boats sitting on the shore.

"Shall we have a do over?"

I pretend to think it over, tapping my chin with my finger. "It depends. Where's Luther?" I playfully shudder.

He chuckles. "I think we're safe, but I'll keep a sharp lookout just in case."

The boat slides easily across the silent water, the mist swirling around us. Alexander puts up the oars, letting us drift. We chat easily about the party, and he tells me more about his experiments to perfect the new soap process. Before long, I'm giggling at his descriptions of his poor parents patiently suffering through weeks of horrible smells coming from the spare room until they politely banished him to one of the garden sheds.

Alexander shrugs ruefully. "Even that wasn't far enough, so they decided it was time to take a long, long vacation to the coast. They came home when I outgrew the shed and moved my experiments to a warehouse outside town. A coincidence, I'm sure." He winks.

I laugh. "At least you weren't playing with that new exploding powder. You could've brought the entire house down."

He leans forward, his eyes lighting up. "What new powder?"

"Something from Lenmark. Someone was talking about it at the ball." I fix him with a stern look. "Do not tell Luther about it."

He makes a crossing motion over his heart, his gaze distant. I hide my grin, knowing I've lost him for the next few minutes as he contemplates all the things he could destroy. *No wonder he and Luther get along so well.* I tilt back my head and enjoy the sun's warmth on my face, letting the gentle rocking motion of the boat lull me into a peaceful doze.

Alexander puts his hand on my arm, his finger against his lips, then tilts his head toward two large white storks in the shallows. The birds are standing close together, nuzzling and grooming each other. One throws its head back and clacks its beak before returning its attention to its partner.

Normally I'd be captivated by the sight, but all I can think about is the warmth of his hand, my skin tingling under his touch. My arm breaks out in goosebumps as my breath catches. Alexander turns back to me with a grin, his cheeks flushed. His eyes catch mine and he freezes, mesmerized. My heart flutters and I lean forward as though pulled by an invisible force, needing to be closer to him. Confusion and hope and a thread of fear swirl around my mind, overwhelming me.

I wrench my gaze away, breaking the moment.

Alexander leans back, resting his elbows on the seat behind him. I don't know if I'm relieved or disappointed by the additional space between us. The lines between friendship and something else are blurring and I don't like it.

A little voice inside me whispers that I'm lying to

myself. I ignore it.

He clears his throat. "Have you thought of enrolling at the university in Lonnheim next year?"

My brow furrows. "No. Why would I?"

"You used to talk about it all the time. University was the first step in your plan to become the most famous president of the Royal Naturalist Society in history."

That feels like five lifetimes ago. I pick at the lace on the edge of my shawl, avoiding his eyes. "I gave that idea up a while ago."

"Then what are you planning to do?" he presses. "After you catch the Bane, what's next?"

I shift on my seat and shrug. "I haven't thought about it."

His eyes narrow, then he takes a deep breath and relaxes. "Perhaps you should. There's a big world out there, and nothing holding you back. You could take up painting, or sewing, or become a fire juggler."

A snort escapes me. I clap my hands over my mouth, but Alexander's sudden bark of laughter sends me into a giggling fit.

Between snickers, I say, "If I became a fire juggler, I bet Luther would hire me."

"Only if you promised to burn all the boats at his next Sunselt party."

"It'd probably be safer to train lions, or go cliff diving."

He gives me an incredulous look. "Do you really think Luther would turn down the chance to have lions at his party? I'm shocked he hasn't thought of it already."

I laugh. "Cliff diving it is, then." I bite my lip, then ask, "Did you go to the university?" There's so much I don't know about our time apart.

He shakes his head with a mischievous grin. "But I was thinking about going next year. They have an engineering class I'm interested in."

Oh. Butterflies swirl in my stomach, and I have a hard time meeting his eyes. "That sounds perfect for you." I smooth out a wrinkle on my skirt, my brow furrowing.

Alexander's life has been so different from mine since I went to Angland. I feel like time stopped when the Bane came into my life and I've never gotten past it. But he has. He's made friends, and traveled, and has new interests and hobbies. I could have had all that too if I had let go of my need to catch the Bane. But I've never been able to.

My hand touches my chest and I silently curse, swearing I'm going to get my locket back from the blacksmith tomorrow, broken clasp or not.

I shield my eyes and glance at the sun overhead, then smother a sigh. "We should probably head back. Hartwin's expecting us soon."

He gives me a wry smile and picks up the oars. "We can't keep our spy waiting."

The walk back is just as silent as our walk to the lake, but now there's a nervous energy buzzing through me. We pause at the palace long enough to grab toast and jam, then hurry to the dairy near the edge of the property. Hartwin's already waiting for us near the back door. The eyepatch is missing today, but it's the fury burning in his good eye that makes me gulp.

He glares at us. "I hope you two had fun playing spy last night. You stopped my man from getting into the safe and finding out what that chef is hiding."

A fist squeezes my heart and my stomach plummets. "You already know?"

"'Course I do. I've had my eye on him for a while. I know all about that box and the safe. What I don't know is why you two barged into my investigation and botched it up."

I lift my chin, forcing my gaze to remain steady. "Your man should've approached us, and then we could've opened the safe together."

He snorts. "They don't know you, just like you don't know them. Unlike you, I want to catch the Bane, so I don't go spilling tales to everyone who looks at me." His voice drips with scorn.

My cheeks flush as I flinch and stare at the ground.

Alexander puts his hand on my shoulder. "We were only keeping watch because we hadn't heard from you, and we didn't want Chef Kloss to poison anyone. If you'd answered Carina's signal sooner, we wouldn't have interfered."

"And if you hadn't been involved at all, this might already be over. Stop wasting my time and leave the investigating to me." Hartwin stomps off, throwing over his shoulder, "Don't contact me again unless you have some real news."

"He's right." My voice is thick and I swallow hard around the lump in my throat. "And you're right. We should've let Hartwin handle this." *I always say catching the Bane is the most important thing, and now I've ruined our only chance.*

Alexander shakes his head. "We had no way of knowing Hartwin was already on to him. We did the best we could with the information we had."

The knots twisting in my stomach loosen. "Still, I wish we could've gotten into that safe last night. But I guess Hartwin will deal with that soon enough."

He raises an eyebrow. "You're not giving up, are you?"

I blink. "No?"

He grins, mischief lighting his eyes. "Good. Because we're going to find out what's in that box, with or without Hartwin's help."

My lips slowly curve in a smile, a lightness filling my chest. "It's not like he can fire us."

"Exactly." He rubs his hands together. "It's time for another stakeout."

Knowing Hartwin has a man monitoring Chef Kloss takes the pressure off us to watch him during the day. We agree the chef is unlikely to retrieve the box when the kitchen is busy and full of people coming and going. If he is the Bane, he'll want to be as discreet as possible. Having the safe secretly installed shows a level of forethought and planning, so he won't be hasty now. Night is when we'll act.

If he follows the same routine as yesterday, Chef Kloss is unlikely to do anything until after the kitchen is clear and quiet. And as much as it pains me to admit, it's unlikely we'll be able to break into the safe, so we'll leave that to Hartwin's man. Instead, we'll try to catch Chef Kloss using the poison and figure out how he's going to give it to Lord Marx.

Alexander has caught my excitement. We skip today's entertainment—the acting troupe includes a fire eater, and I refuse to go anywhere near Luther when fire is involved— and spend the day distracting each other while we explore the gardens, then take a late afternoon ride through the forest.

He insists on waiting for me to check my room for intruders before leaving me, saying he'll see me at supper. I take my time to thoroughly wash up from the dusty ride, then slowly flip through the dresses in the wardrobe, fretting about what to wear.

I finally narrow it down to two gowns, debating between them for what feels like hours before I put on the lavender dress with silver embroidery. Then I immediately change into the scarlet silk gown with the off-shoulder sleeves and sweetheart neckline My curled hair is held up with a simple gold clip, and I pull a few strands loose to frame my face. Gold and diamond earrings complete my outfit, and I dab a tiny bit of perfume behind my ears before I leave.

I hum an old ballad as I make my way to the dining room. Alexander is already there, his lips curving as I approach.

"You look lovely this evening, Lady Carina."

My insides glow, but I fight the smile trying to break out. "Thank you, Lord von Bron. Today was lovely. And this chair is lovely. And this napkin is lovely. Wouldn't you agree?"

His grin widens as he tries not to laugh. "Indeed. Everything is very lovely."

I settle into my seat, my insides thrumming. It's hard to focus as I try to make plans for spying on Chef Kloss tonight while being strangely preoccupied with Alexander's nearness. My foot taps out an impatient rhythm. Poor Dorthea has to keep repeating her questions, and I can only manage distracted one- or two-word replies. If my life depended on it, I couldn't recall a single dish served during the supper.

Alexander, on the other hand, is chatting easily with Lord Marx and the other diners. He reaches down and gently squeezes my hand under the table while keeping up the spirited debate with the man next to him. The knots in my stomach loosen even as my pulse speeds up. When the next course is served, I reluctantly pull my hand away, puzzled at why it's so hard to let go.

An eternity has passed before dessert is finally served. I bolt down the plum cake topped with crumbly streusel without tasting it, eager to get the evening gathering started so we can get it over with.

The diners drift into the nearby rooms as supper ends. I'm antsy to get back to the kitchen, but Alexander and I agreed it's best if we keep up appearances with the other guests this evening by being seen socializing. I avoid the parlor and wander into one of the gaming rooms instead.

The huge crystal chandeliers and thick red carpeting provide a luxurious backdrop for the card tables spread around the room and the chessboards along the walls. Through the open archway come the sounds of billiard balls clacking and clouds of hazy cigar smoke. Lotta waves to me from one of the tables, and I join her, Ziggy, and Lord Wentzel.

Ziggy's added a pith helmet to his dinner attire, which seems perfect for him. He tilts it back with a grin. "Our wayward friend has returned to the trenches. What tales have you brought us?"

"Murders and scandals, and perhaps a bit of mystery." I wink at him as I claim the open chair.

"Our favorite currency these days. You must visit us next time you're in town so we can read the crime sheets together." He turns to his daughter. "We should invite Herr

Dorn, too. He's always good for the latest murder updates. We'll make it a party." Ziggy coughs into a handkerchief, and Lotta's eyebrows pinch together.

"Papa, why don't we retire early tonight? You should get some rest."

He waves away her concern. "Nonsense. A glass of brandy and I'll be back in fighting shape. Besides, I haven't told Lady Lux about battling swamp trolls during the war."

He launches into a story about his command being sent to investigate the disappearance of an entire barracks, leading to their ambush in the swamp. Ziggy is an excellent storyteller, making me gasp and laugh throughout the tale. Lotta and Lord Wentzel must have heard the story a thousand times judging by the ways they help prompt Ziggy when he forgets a detail, but they're enjoying it as much as I am.

As Ziggy wraps up the final battle with the bandits disguised as swamp trolls, Lord Wentzel gives a dramatic shudder. "All that blood. Horrible. I'll stick with to theater, where the only ones trying to murder me are the critics."

Lotta laughs. "Don't pretend you're helpless. We all know there's a sword hidden in that walking stick."

Lord Wentzel widens his eyes innocently. "Only so I can ensure your safety, darling Lotta. And to keep my hordes of fans from carrying me off and ravishing me."

I ask him, "Are you an actor?"

Lotta groans good-naturedly as his chest puffs out. She leans over to me and loudly whispers, "Now you've done it. Franz's favorite topic is himself."

"That's because I'm the most fascinating person in the room." He turns to me, smiling charmingly. "Present company excepted, of course."

Lotta gives a very unladylike snort. "Don't believe him, Carina. In his mind, nobody is more amazing than he is."

Ziggy chuckles. "Not even Franz can live up to his reputation."

Lord Wentzel playfully frowns and puts a hand over his heart. "You wound me."

She shakes her head. "Impossible. Your ego is indestructible." Lotta reaches over and pats his hand with a grin. "But you're almost as enchanting as you think you are, pet."

Ziggy coughs again, his lips taking on a blue tinge.

Her smile tightens. "Time to say goodnight, Papa." When he protests, she says firmly, "No arguments. I'll come read to you until you fall asleep."

Ziggy grumbles, but stands, swaying a little on his feet. Lord Wentzel offers his arm to the older man, and Lotta gives him a grateful look. I hastily say my goodbyes, promising Ziggy I'll see him again tomorrow and that I'll visit the next time I'm in town.

Despite the concern for Ziggy, I'm feeling refreshed and relaxed after their visit. I meander through the rooms, catching snippets of conversation flowing around me but not trying to join any of the groups. It's enough to be seen by the other guests tonight to keep the gossipmongers at bay.

In one parlor, a tall woman has Alexander trapped in a corner. It takes a moment to put a name to the face. *Gisele.* The one Aliz said was interested in him my first night here. Alexander's back is pressed against the wall, his posture stiff, clearly wanting to escape but unwilling to be rude. Gisele is oblivious to his discomfort as she tosses her blond hair and smiles brightly, keeping up a steady stream of one-sided chatter.

I catch Alexander's eye and send him a sympathetic smile, then tilt my head, silently asking if he wants me to rescue him. His rueful grin and faint shrug lets me know he appreciates the offer, but he's fine for now. Gisele looks over her shoulder, frowning fiercely when she spots me. She puts her hand on his arm and steps between us, moving closer to him as he tries not to squirm.

I chuckle silently. Poor Alexander, forced to endure her misguided pursuit in the name of chivalry. He always was too much of a gentleman for his own good. I'm tempted to stay and watch the show, but I shudder to think of the next torturous tactic Gisele will use if I'm around.

In the game room next door, Aliz brightens when she spots me, and a knot forms in my chest. She's lovely as always in a yellow satin gown that makes her hair glow like gold in the candlelight. She makes her way across the room, people turning their heads to watch her.

She surprises me with a hug. "Carina, I missed you this afternoon. It feels like it's been ages since we've talked."

The knot loosens and I grin at her. "I see you managed to keep Luther from burning down the palace."

She groans. "Not for lack of trying. The dolt even snuck away after the show and tried to get the fire eater to give him lessons. Thank the Fortunes the bucket brigade was on high alert all day, so the damage was limited to a singed curtain and a ruined rug."

I laugh. "That man loves to set things on fire. Which is why I stayed far, far away."

"If only I could do the same. But he's pretty tolerable in most aspects." Her eyes light with mirth. "Speaking of which, where's your handsome, almost-as-wealthy-as-my-brother, not-too-obnoxious friend? You two have been spending a lot of time together.”

I shift uneasily, rubbing the ache in my chest. “I told you we’re just catching up on news. And we haven’t been spending that much time together.” My stomach churns as I bite the inside of my cheek.

I should tell Aliz how much Alexander admires her, or say he asks about her, or gush over how he’s always complimenting her kindness, but the words stick in my throat. *Besides, she already seems friendly toward him. She doesn’t need any more encouragement to see him as a suitor.* I swallow hard, suddenly queasy.

She moves closer, a line appearing between her eyebrows. “Is everything all right?” Aliz touches my arm, lowering her voice. “Did something happen with Lord von Bron?”

My chest tightens. “Fortunes, no.” I force out a chuckle. “Whatever could happen with him? I just didn’t sleep well. And I probably spent too much time in the heat today. Nothing for you to worry about. I’m sure I’ll be back to normal tomorrow.”

She hesitates, then nods slowly. “All right. But if something’s bothering you, I hope you know you can talk to me. About anything.”

And I could. Aliz would come with me to the library, no questions asked, and let me pour my heart out. I could tell her how all I’ve wanted to do for the past five years was catch the Bane. How it’s taken over my entire life. How muddled I’ve been feeling about Alexander. My confusion over whether I want him to be my friend, or something more, or nothing at all. How I want her and Alexander to have a fresh start and be happy together, but the idea twists me up inside until I feel like I can’t breathe. How the world used to make sense and now nothing does. Aliz would listen patiently, give me a hug, and promise to do whatever she could to help me.

And then she'd firmly turn away Alexander and any attempts to court her. Because she's my friend, and she doesn't want to cause me any pain. Like I should be doing for her, instead of the cowardly weasel I've been.

My lips stretch into what I hope is a reassuring smile. "I know. I'm fine. Really. But you should go rescue him. Last I saw, Gisele had him trapped in the parlor over there."

The line between her brows deepens. "Why didn't you help him?"

I shrug. "He didn't want me to."

Her eyebrows shoot up. "I doubt that."

"Well, he didn't. But I'm sure he'd welcome your help." I smile brightly, swallowing around the hard lump in my throat.

Aliz narrows her eyes, studying me. She looks at the parlor for a long moment, then shakes her head and turns determinedly back to me. "Carina, about me and Lord von Bron. I—"

My pulse speeds as my mouth goes dry. "You don't have to say anything." *I really, really don't want to hear it. Not now.*

"Yes, I do." She takes my hands, her face earnest. "I'm not interested in Lord von Bron as anything except a friend. If he proposed to me today, tomorrow, or a year from now, I'd say no. But he wouldn't propose to me. He doesn't love me." She squeezes my hands. "I think we both know who his heart belongs to."

My cheeks heat and I look away, my pulse thundering in my ears. I can't pretend anymore that I want her and

Alexander to be together, or that my feelings aren't involved. She's graciously made it clear that she's already stepped aside, and she'll support whatever decision I make about Alexander.

But I don't know what to do.

When I was young, falling in love was simple. Now, it's complicated. Risky. Scary. Part of me wants to run to him, while the other part wants to run as far away as I can. And even if I love Alexander, it doesn't mean being with him is the right choice. His rejection already crushed me once, even if it was unintentional. There's nothing to say he couldn't do it again. We weren't able to navigate the obstacles back then, but could we manage it now? *I don't know…*

Her face softens. Aliz, being the amazing friend she is, doesn't press me or pester me with questions. Instead, she gives me another hug, then leave me to my thoughts, reminding me she's here if I need to talk.

It's easier to pretend our conversation never happened when she's out of sight. I idly wander over to one of the empty tables and shuffle through the cards, trying to keep my hands and mind occupied so I don't have to think. There's still some time to kill before I meet Alexander, and then we'll be spending hours together. Alone.

It's going to be a long night.

The conversation with Aliz keeps creeping back into my mind, no matter how much I try to ignore it. My nerves are stretched thin, and it's hard not to snap at the people who talk to me. The hours drag by until the room starts emptying and I can finally excuse myself, pretending to yawn as I go.

I hurry to my room and change from the more restrictive dinner gown into a simple blush day dress. Not knowing how the night will go, I opt for my boots instead of slippers (*there might be a foot chase!*) and a wool shawl to keep from freezing. I sigh with relief as I take out my hair clip and let the curls tumble loose, lightly massaging my scalp to relieve the tension. I start to braid my hair—then stop and instead tie it back with a ribbon, my cheeks pink as I studiously avoid my reflection.

I pace around my room, counting down the minutes until I'm to meet Alexander. From the hallway come the occasional faint footsteps, lowered voices, and doors opening and closing. Eventually the floor falls quiet.

It's still a half hour until our agreed time, but I can't wait any longer. Tucking two apples in my pocket, I slip out of my room and down the stairs. I keep a wary eye out for stragglers as I hurry to the storeroom, taking care to use a longer route that avoids the kitchen, snickering at the memory of getting lost in these same hallways after my first supper. I reach the store room as Alexander comes trotting down the hallway and we exchange sheepish grins.

He whispers, "Is Chef Kloss there?"

"I didn't check yet."

He blinks, then he runs a hand through his hair, smiling. "Shall we see together?"

Footsteps come from around the corner. I grab Alexander's hand and drag him into the storage closet, yanking the door shut moments before Lady Fauser comes into view, talking animatedly with a young woman I don't recognize.

"—met Chef Kloss in Macco, oh, must be ten years ago now. The man has a temper, but nobody can deny his talent."

My eyebrows fly up. *One of the Bane's victims was in Macco.* I can't place Lady Fauser's accent, with an odd emphasis on the t and slight lisp on the s. She and the young woman disappear into the kitchen, their voices fading.

Alexander and I look at each other, the silent question about whether we should follow them hovering between us.

I shrug a shoulder. "Let's wait. If Lady Fauser knows the chef, we don't want her saying anything about us being in the kitchen."

He nods slowly. "And we don't want to start any rumors about people finding us together in the middle of the night."

My stomach jumps. "Of course. Right. Yes." It's funny how the thought doesn't bother me as much as it used to.

We settle on the floor and lean against the back wall. His

arm brushes against mine, sending a delicious shiver over my skin. *My nerves are so jumpy. It must be because we're so close to catching the Bane.* The conversation with Aliz tugs at the back of my mind, but I refuse to think about it.

Alexander checks the hallway. "They're still in there."

Get going all ready. I yawn, then hand him an apple before tackling mine with gusto. The tart crispiness is exactly what I need to distract myself. Too soon, the fruit is gone and an awkward silence falls over us.

If only Aliz hadn't said anything, we could be talking and joking like before. It's a comforting lie. Nothing's changed for Alexander, but he's picked up on my uneasiness. The poor man must be so confused by my sudden moodiness.

No matter what, he's still my friend. I nudge him, determined to act normal. "Do you think they're breaking into the white punch, or eating all the tea cakes?"

Alexander laughs, his shoulders relaxing. "They're probably trying to find the chef's stash of preserved cherries. That's what I'd be doing."

"I'd go for icing sugar. That tastes good on everything."

"Even bratwurst?"

"Especially on bratwurst. Sweet and savory. Perfect." I try to keep a straight face, but a giggle cracks through.

We keep upping each other on what we'd filch from the kitchen, then Alexander tells me more about experimenting with the soap process, detailing his specular disasters and their hilarious results. It's proof that his parents spoil him, that they let him get away with it for so long. I'm enjoying the stories, but the lack of sleep is catching up with me. I rub my aching eyes, trying to get rid of the gritty feeling.

Alexander's brow furrows. "Chef Kloss probably won't

show up for a few more hours. Why don't you rest? I can keep watch."

I'm about to protest when an enormous yawn overtakes me and he chuckles.

"If you insist." My eyes slide closed. "Just for a few minutes."

"Mrrmph." I snuggle deeper into my pillow, wrapping my arms around its warmth. "Rhmph."

Alexander's breath hitches and the heartbeat under my cheek speeds up. I shoot up, knocking the top of my head against his chin. I must've fallen asleep on him and mistaken him for my bed.

My face flushes. "Sorry."

"It's fine." He rubs his jaw with a laugh. "I forgot how dangerous is it is to wake you up."

The fire in my cheeks burns hotter. "I'm definitely not a morning person." Keeping my gaze averted, I stretch, then retie my mess of hair with the ribbon. "What time is it?"

"Around three in the morning. Lady Fauser and her friend left the kitchen an hour ago, and it's been quiet ever since."

And he stayed up, letting me sleep. A warmth grows in my chest. "Thank you for keeping watch. I'll get better at these stakeouts."

"You had your turn last night, so I figured this one was mine."

I glance down the hallway, squinting at the shadows. "They probably won't start breakfast for a while." The reminder of my favorite sticky bun makes my stomach grumble. "Do you have anything else to eat?" I make my best pitiful face.

He shrugs. "Sorry. It's hard to hide soup in my dinner jacket."

I sigh. "That's all right. I should've brought more."

"Hmm, now wait a minute. What's this?" Alexander grins and takes something wrapped in a napkin out of his pocket.

I squeal, unwrapping it to find a slightly squashed piece of plum cake. "This is why you're my favorite."

He blushes and my heart flutters. I busy myself with the cake, insisting over his protests that he take some.

"Asking someone to forgo their dessert is too much. Nobody should have to make that sacrifice." Between bites of the amazing cake, I ask him, "Do you think Chef Kloss will show up tonight?"

Alexander lifts a shoulder. "If he doesn't, then we'll come back tomorrow. And the day after. And as long as it takes."

The thought of spending weeks alone with Alexander in a storage closet sends butterflies whirling in my stomach. I smirk. "Hartwin'll give us an earful when he finds out, but he can't stop us."

He laughs. "Not that you'd ever let him."

A clatter comes from the hallway, making us jump. We peer through the crack around the door and I hold my breath, trying not to get excited in case it's a false alarm.

Chef Kloss slinks down the hallway, stopping every few feet to look behind him. I squeeze Alexander's hand, my mouth dry, as the chef ducks into the kitchen. *This is it.* Belatedly, I realize I'm crushing his hand and relax my grip…but I don't let go.

I nod toward the door and raise my eyebrows. He shakes his head, flashing his fingers to indicate we should wait ten minutes. He's not wrong, but it's so hard to sit here, my pulse thrumming with anticipation, keeping my eye pressed to the gap between the door in case the chef suddenly leaves.

I make it eight minutes before I jump up, eager to go. Alexander insists on taking the lead as we tiptoe to the archway. A loud oath sounds from the kitchen. Alexander and I glance at each other, then creep forward to the open arch.

Chef Kloss is alone, furiously swearing and chopping at the far counter. When I spot the mysterious green box by him, my pulse speeds up and I bounce on my toes.

Tonight's the night. He's going to poison Lord Marx and we're going to stop him!

My brow wrinkles as I try to make out the chef's muttering. "Is that Irelish?"

Alexander shakes his head. "Maccon, I think."

My insides thrum. Macco again. I hold my breath, leaning closer, my knuckles white as I press against the stone wall.

Butter, sugar, flour, milk… "He's making the sticky buns for breakfast. It'll be easy enough to swap out Lord Marx's poisoned one when it's delivered to his room. Then we can arrest Chef Kloss and expose him as the Bane."

Alexander shifts his weight, darting a look at me before turning his attention back to the kitchen. "It's too early. They'd be stale by breakfast. And he has peaches over there. It's something else."

Before I can reply, my stomach growls. I freeze, ice flooding my veins. The chef pours several jugs of milk into a small pot, then hangs it on a hook high over the fire. I breathe a sigh of relief. I chew on my lip, waiting as he stirs the milk, occasionally testing the temperature. After a few minutes, he nods to himself and moves the pot off the fire.

Chef Kloss glances over his shoulder suspiciously. We duck back, then carefully peek back into the kitchen. He's sniffing the box's contents, a beatific smile spreading across his face. I grip Alexander's arm as I lean forward, my heart pounding. *What? What is it?*

Humming, Check Kloss carefully scoops out a small spoonful of something that looks like bits of red yarn. Putting a hand below the spoon, he carries it over to the cooling pot and drops the red yarn bits into the milk.

Alexander and I exchange puzzled looks, then watch as the chef layers sliced peaches in three dozen cake tins before mixing up a gigantic bowl of batter. My toes are numb and I'm ready to fall asleep on my feet when he finally returns to the milk. Chef Kloss stirs the pot, then carefully pours the milk—now a pretty yellow-orange color—through a strainer and into the batter. He folds in the chopped peaches from the counter, then ladles the batter into the prepared tins.

My shoulders sag, and a heaviness fills my chest. I hate to admit defeat, but unless Chef Kloss is going to poison the entire party, it's unlikely whatever ingredient is in the box will confirm he's the Bane.

My heart sinks. What do we do now?

Alexander and I walk silently down the hallway, deep in our own thoughts. When he turns toward the stairway, I surprise us both by taking his hand and tugging him toward the library. Once the door is safely closed, I slump against it and sigh dejectedly.

"I really thought he was the Bane."

Alexander's eyebrows crease together. "He still could be. We can keep watching and see if he does anything."

I shake my head. "You were right. He's a chef, so he can't be the Bane. It wouldn't make sense." My chest aches. I touch the spot where my locket normally hangs, missing my mother terribly. "But I really, really wanted it to be him."

His face softens and he holds out his arms. My breath catches as tears sting my eyes. I wrap around him, pressing my forehead against his chest as he slowly rubs a hand up and down my back. Alexander's warmth surrounds me, helping fill the hollowness inside me. I swallow hard, refusing to cry.

It's harder than it should be to pull away. I finally step back, forcing a bright smile. "I guess we'll have to find another suspect before Hartwin does."

Alexander hesitates, then says, "Why don't we wait a few days? There's still plenty of time before the party ends."

I swipe a hand across my eyes, taking a deep breath. "It's already half over. And if we don't find the Bane now, we may never catch them." My hands curl into fists and I straighten. "I can't let that happen."

Alexander nods, his jaw tensing. "Then we keep looking. But now, we need some sleep."

It's impossible to argue, exhaustion already pulling me toward my bed. We silently walk to my room, the palace empty and full of shadows. After I unlock my door, Alexander lingers a moment, his eyes intense.

I give him a wan smile. "I'm all right. Go to sleep."

He pauses, then lightly touches my cheek. "I'm on the third floor. Third door on the right. If you need me, just knock."

I nod, knowing I won't—because I want to too much.

His eyes hold mine for an eternity. Then he slowly walks away, glancing over his shoulder before he disappears down the stairs.

After locking the door, I flop on the bed and throw my arm over my eyes. *What am I doing?* I have enough trouble with losing our best lead on the Bane and knowing Hartwin's going to find a way to blame me for it. I don't need to add worries about Alexander to the mix.

Even if it was nice to have his arms around me again…

Very nice.

14

While Sunselt is officially about celebrating summer's midpoint, it's really an excuse to hold an outdoor party. The garden decorations are surprisingly subdued, letting the beauty of the flowers and greenery take center stage. Small tables are spread around the lawn, including some shaded by fancy silk tents.

At the end of the lawn is the entrance to the hedge maze, while off to the side people are playing ten pins and hoops, and others competing in a beanbag toss. Jugglers and minstrels in bright costumes mill around the grass, entertaining guests, while the staff circulates with trays of tempting tidbits and refreshing punch.

It looks like most of the guests are here and having a grand time. I stifle a yawn as I look around for someone I know. Dorthea catches my eye and waves me over to join her circle. To my pleasant surprise, Lord Marx is there, making it the perfect opportunity to finally speak with him again.

While the group argues about one of the obscure rules of

snooker, I smile at Dorthea. "I forgot to thank you for giving me that wonderful tea. Cinnamon is my favorite."

She chuckles. "I'm glad you like it. I suffered from a similar malady when I was younger, and it was a tremendous help. After a month of drinking it daily, I was cured. I hope it'll do the same for you. The town didn't have a large supply, so I sent a message to my local shop and they'll send you enough to last the summer."

My smile wavers. I'm touched by her kindness, but I don't want to mislead her. "That's very thoughtful of you, but I'm not sure it'll help me. The menders say nothing can." *And I've seen too many of them over the years to ever want to see another one again.*

Dorthea pats my hand. "Indulge an old woman and try it. It can't hurt, and you did say cinnamon was your favorite."

A warmth glows in my chest and I squeeze her hand. "Of course. Thank you again."

She nods to the side. "I see our dinner companion isn't wasting any time staking his claim."

I crane my neck, spotting Aliz and Alexander sitting together on a bench at the edge of the garden, their heads close together. The conversation looks serious, but then Aliz laughs and Alexander grins. My chest tightens. Even though I know Aliz has no interest in Alexander, that doesn't mean he's not interested in her. *Mayhap I was mistaken about his feelings...* I quickly turn away, my stomach twisting. "They're good friends."

"Hmm. More like Lord von Bron and her brother's wealth makes a good match. The von Brons have always been opportunists. I heard he's been showering her with presents, including some fancy soaps made special for her, to get Kangan Brecht to invest in them." She shakes her head.

"A fool's folly. He'll lose the family fortune trying to make it work."

A spark of anger flashes in my chest. "I'm sure Lord von Bron knows what's doing. He wouldn't approach *Kangan* Brecht otherwise."

Dorthea raises an eyebrow. "Have you heard his plan?"

"No, just the idea," I reluctantly admit.

"I didn't realize you were spending time with Lord von Bron these days." She eyes me curiously.

I shift my weight, my spine stiff. "It's hard to avoid each other. And he's one of the few people I know here."

Her face softens. "Of course. If there's anyone I can introduce you to, please let me know. I may not travel much in society's circles these days, but all of us old folks know each other. And if there's someone I don't know, I know someone who does."

I laugh lightly. "You're not that old."

"I've lived several lifetimes, dearie. That's why I stay in the countryside now. I had my fill of people long ago." Her eyes twinkle.

I grin at her, then turn my attention to the rest of the group, trying to get a feeling for everyone. There are eight of us, including three men and two women I don't know, all within the Bane's age range. *I need to get them talking about Lord Marx. If one of them is the Bane, they might slip.*

Spotting an opening in the conversation, I jump in. "Lord Marx, what are your plans after the house party?"

He gives me a disapproving look, his long mustache twitching. "I'll be traveling to Rus."

My pulse speeds up. *The Bane will have a hard time poisoning him after the party unless they want to chase him across the continent.* I widen my eyes innocently, playing into his impression of a silly girl. "Oh, but it's dangerous to travel so far. Aren't you afraid of running into trouble on the road?"

He puffs out his wide chest and strokes a finger down his mustache. "It is treacherous, but I've taken the trip many times. I know how to avoid the hazards."

One man asks, "Do you have business in Rus?"

I don't recognize him, so I make a note to ask Dorthea about him later. Anyone who shows an interest in Lord Marx is of interest to me.

Lord Marx rocks back on his heels, taking out a handkerchief and mopping his flushed forehead. "No, I'm visiting family."

Dorthea whispers to me, "Family who helps smuggle gold and spice out of the country." She gives me a knowing look and taps the side of her nose.

I force a smile as my stomach knots. *How does she know that? And she made that other comment about trading with Rus earlier.* The conversation continues around me, moving on to other travel plans and upcoming parties, but my mind is stuck on Dorthea.

She knows a lot about Lord Marx. Did she pick that up from the suppers I've missed, or is it something more? And she clearly dislikes Alexander's family. But she's a known recluse…who just happened to come to the party Lord Marx's attending. What about the tea she sent me? Is that some innocent herb lore, or has she studied plant uses, including poisonous plants?

A buzz goes up from the crowd and a woman pipes up, "This must be Chef Kloss's special dessert."

A stream of servers carrying trays spread out among the crowd, passing out slices of golden cake set on silver plates.

It's a beautiful little dessert with a fluffy orange cake base and peach chunks baked in. On top of the cake are layers of sliced peaches, topped with a generous dollop of light orange cream. A sweet, flowery scent mixes with the peach aroma.

I take a bite and sigh happily as peaches and cream flood my taste buds, the floral flavor adding a pleasant depth to the dish.

The woman holds up a bite on her tiny silver fork, studying the cake. "This is amazing! There's peach, but what's that spice?"

The group looks at each other, shrugging, until Dorthea speaks up.

"Saffron. I'm amazed Chef Kloss could get enough to cater the party. It's scandalously expensive, and difficult to find in this kingdom since we have a trading ban on Fasser."

That's probably what he was buying in the marketplace alley. But how does Dorthea know what it is if it's so scarce? Everyone murmurs appreciatively while I stuff another bite of cake in my mouth, the sweet flavor now sour. More innocent knowledge, or is she the Bane?

I look at her out of the corner of my eye, trying to keep an open mind. The same gray eyes and black hair streaked with silver I noticed at the first supper. Shorter than me, which isn't unusual for a woman, with a thick waist and swollen joints on her fingers. Her bright purple dress is a little old-fashioned, but not so much that someone would remark on it. A tasteful gold necklace and the bracelet with the luck bead are her only jewelry.

What did I expect, a big vial of poison hanging around her neck? There's nothing suspicious about her appearance, but it doesn't make me any less troubled.

Dorthea shifts her feet, then winces. She excuses herself

and walks over to a bench, subtly rubbing her hip, her steps slow. If I had to guess, I'd say she has joint pains, but it could be an act. *I'll ask Hartwin about her.*

My enthusiasm for investigating the guests, and Lord Marx, have disappeared. When I spot Aliz alone on the bench, I leave the group to join her.

As I make my way across the gardens, a young man holds out a tray filled with small chocolate tarts. "Would you like one, Lady Lux?"

I fight the urge knock the tray away. *He doesn't mean any harm.* It takes a moment to place the pleasant but unremarkable face with a dimple in one cheek. "Herr Goff, it's nice to see you again. No, thank you." I move to step past him, but he shifts to block me.

"Did you find that cascading fountain in the garden? I can show you now if you'd like." He gestures to the garden entrance.

I take a deep breath, trying not to snap at him. *He's just young and overeager.* "Not yet, but I don't want to interrupt your duties. I'll ask *Rirzan* Aliz where it is. Have a good day." I dart around him, hurrying over to join Aliz.

She gives me a tired smile. "Enjoying the party?"

I settle on the bench next to her. "Of course, but are you?"

"I'll be glad when it's over." She rubs her forehead and chuckles heavily. "Luther needs a wife so she can take up the hosting duties and I can finally be a guest."

I grin. "He's terrified of you. I'm sure you can get him married before next summer with a little effort."

"I plan to do everything in my power to make sure he does. There's a few ladies I'm going to introduce him to before the party ends, and another four in Bomen next month. If he doesn't match with any of them, there's always Wintertide." At my raised eyebrows, she laughs. "No need to worry. I value our friendship far too much to saddle you with him."

"Thank you?" It stings a bit that she doesn't consider me good enough to marry her brother.

She must sense my hurt. "Carina, honestly, I'd love to have you as a sister, but you two would be terrible together. Luther's far too reckless and impulsive. You'd throttle him in a week."

"Good point." I'd rather have a husband who doesn't end up dunking me or lighting my boat on fire. I fidget with my sleeve. "You and Alexander looked pretty serious. What were you talking about?"

Aliz shrugs. "Nothing in particular. About the party and how he's hoping to meet with Luther to discuss some business next week."

"That's all?" I press. They certainly looked serious when I saw them.

"I might've mentioned Chef Kloss promised another special dessert for the closing ball, but don't ask me what it is." She shakes her head. "He's a genius in the kitchen, but he's incredibly paranoid about anyone figuring out his recipes. He won't even tell me the secret ingredient in today's cake."

"Saffron," I answer absentmindedly. *Hmm.* Nothing to be suspicious about, but I can't help but feeling uneasy. "Do you like the soaps Alexander gave you?"

She brightens and the knots in my stomach tighten. "They're so darling! Little white seashells infused with pink salt and a lovely honey scent. I've never seen anything like them before. I know he has a different idea for his soap making business, but everyone would love these. He should show them to Luther, don't you think?"

I wouldn't know since I've never seen them. My heart heavy, I force a smile and nod. "But you know how stubborn he can be."

A hint of humor lights her eyes. "Almost as stubborn as you."

"I can't help it if everyone else is usually wrong and I'm right." I ignore the ache in my chest, and decide to put Alexander out of my mind. "How well do you know Lady Goethe?"

Aliz takes two glasses of white punch off a passing tray and hands one to me. "Not well. She hardly ever leaves her estate in Eaglan. This is the first time she's come to our Sunselt party, although we invite her every year. Why do you ask?"

So, Dorthea was telling the truth about staying out of society. Some knots loosen, though I warn myself to stay alert for other clues. "She's been very kind to me. She even sent me some cinnamon tea, although I didn't have the heart to tell her I already get it with my breakfast tray. Thank you again for that."

Aliz purses her lips. "I meant to ask you about that. I'm flattered you think my hosting skills are so remarkable, but I didn't know you like sticky buns and cinnamon tea."

My insides turn to ice as her words sink in. "You didn't arrange it?"

She shakes her head. "I checked with the kitchen staff. Someone ordered it on the first day, but they couldn't remember who since there were a lot of requests and they were busy preparing for all the guests. They think it was a man, but they weren't even sure about that."

A cold sweat breaks out over my skin. *The Bane! Have I been poisoned again?* Bile rushes up my throat and I swallow hard, wrapping my arms around my middle.

Aliz grabs my arm, her eyes wide. "Carina, are you all right?"

"I'm fine. I'm fine." I force myself to take a few deep breaths, fighting off the panic threatening to overwhelm me. It's been weeks. I don't have symptoms. And I feel normal—except for the bone-shaking terror. I've had a few more of my heart spells, but those could just be a coincidence and it's been a while since the last one. If I was poisoned, I'd be dead or seriously sick by now. I haven't been hallucinating, or feeling lethargic, or the thousand other terrible things that happened when I was poisoned with velvseiess.

Most of my fears retreat and my muscles relax. But who made the request to the kitchen staff?

Alexander. He's the only one here who knows those are my favorites, and it would be just like him to have them sent to my room without taking any credit. *Although I'll have to tease him mercilessly for making me think I was poisoned again.*

A warm glow fills my chest. I smile at Aliz, feeling happier than I have in months. "I'm all right. Really."

She frowns. "Are you—"

A young girl runs up and frantically whispers in Aliz's ear while I wait, curious at what's happening now. Aliz's face grows grave as the girl finishes relaying her message.

She asks the girl to find Luther, then turns back to me. "I'm sorry, but I have to go. Lord Zimmer is ill."

Poor Ziggy, I hope he'll be all right. "Is there anything I can do to help?"

She hesitates. "Can you find Lady Lotta? She needs to come to his room right away. Oh, and let her know the mender is on his way from town."

"Certainly." As she hurries away, I search for Lotta, my mind whirling.

Is Ziggy really ill, or is it something else? Is he the Bane's real target? Hartwin was sure it was Lord Marx, but what if he's wrong? What do I know about Ziggy?

I find Lotta watching the juggler and deliver Aliz's message. She seems grim but unsurprised as she nods a thanks to me, then hastens to the palace. Errand finished, I search out Alexander, which doesn't take long since he's looking for me. Mindful of the large crowd nearby, I pull him next to the fountain where we can't be easily overhead.

"Where have you been? You won't believe what happened!"

He raises an eyebrow. "I had a busy morning. What's going on?"

My jaw clenches. *Not too busy to talk with Aliz.* I quickly fill him in. "What if Ziggy's the Bane's next victim, not Lord Marx?"

"Or it could be a coincidence," Alexander argues. "He's old and not in the best of health."

"Or it's not, and we've been focusing on the wrong victim the entire time. If Ziggy's already been poisoned, we'll have to act quickly to catch the Bane before they vanish." I grit my teeth. *All that time wasted.* "Lotta hardly ever leaves his side, and I think she lives with him, so she's probably not the Bane. But Lord Wentzel is always around them, so he would have lots of opportunities to slip Ziggy the poison. Have you seen him around Ziggy's room?"

Alexander reluctantly nods. "On the first floor? He's

been in that hallway once or twice. But Lord Wentzel spends too much time with them. The Bane's a poisoner for hire. He wouldn't risk having a personal connection to one of his victims."

"Mayhap he does this time," I counter. "We can only guess at his motives. If Ziggy's been poisoned, we need to find out what it is so the menders can help him. Which means we need to search Lord Wentzel's room."

"What? No!" Alexander rakes his hand through his hair. "Let Hartwin do it."

"We can't wait for him." My hand touches my chest and I hiss through my teeth.

Seeing the gesture, Alexander's expression brightens. "Oh, I have something for you." He reaches into his pocket and pulls my mother's locket.

I gasp in delight, a weight I didn't know I was carrying lifting from my heart. "Thank you!" I spin around and lift my hair so he can put the necklace on me. "I thought it wouldn't be ready for a few more days?"

He fidgets with the clasp, saying distractedly, "I knew you missed it, so I rode to town to check this morning and he was able to fix it sooner."

And probably paid an extra fee to get it so quickly. A warmth glows in my chest and I smile down at the locket. He's a better friend than I deserve.

I grin at him, emboldened now that my locket is back in its rightful place. "If we hurry, we can search Lord Wentzel's room and come back to the party before anyone misses us."

15

Alexander grumbles, "I still think we should wait for Hartwin."

"Hartwin, Hartwin, Hartwin. You can't expect him to do everything. We're here to help him and this is helping." I peer around the corner, making sure the hallway's clear. "Are you sure Lord Wentzel's room is on this floor?"

"It's the fourth door down on the right. It's right next to mine."

As we hurry past Alexander's room, I almost ask to ask to see it, but quickly squash the urge. *Stay focused.* I test the doorknob. Locked.

"Burn it. How are we going to get in?"

Alexander heaves a dramatic sigh and motions for me to step aside. I move out of the way and he grips the handle, then throws his body against the door with a loud bang. My pulse jumps at the noise and I gasp, then glance around. *Thank the Fortunes nobody heard that!*

He stands in the open doorway with a smug smile. "It just takes a little muscle to pop these locks."

"And you'd know that from your years of picking locks?" I ask dryly, refusing to show how impressed I am.

"How do you think I got us those shovels from the gardening shed when we went hunting for pirate treasure, or into that room in the attic where my father stored the broken bits of armor?" He leans closer, raising an eyebrow, his eyes full of mischief. "I have many hidden talents."

My heart skips a beat. "I hope those skills include searching for clues, because we need to find something to prove Lord Wentzel is the Bane." I slip past him into the room.

The wardrobe and bed are similar to mine, but there's a chair instead of a window nook, and a low dresser and tall mirror in place of the vanity. Either Lord Wentzel is very neat, or one of the staff has cleaned up recently. There are no clothes draped over the furniture, no toiletry items or trinkets laid out. Even his toothbrush and toothpowder are tucked away somewhere. If I didn't know better, I'd think the room was unoccupied.

Now that I'm faced with searching through Lord Wentzel's things, I'm reluctant to start. *Hmm, I should've thought this through.* "You take the dresser and I'll start with the chair."

He crosses his arms. "Since this is your idea, why don't you take the dresser and I'll take the chair?"

My head jerks back ad I put my hands on my hips. "I can't look through a man's dresser! Who knows what he keeps in there."

He makes a face. "I don't want to search it for the same reason."

Fair. I grin. "We'll leave that for Hartwin. After all, he's getting paid."

I check the chair, searching the cushions for any hint of an opening, and tipping the frame over to inspect the bottom of the seat. After I finish, I move to the washbasin. While I search the furniture, Alexander looks through the wardrobe, carefully checking the pockets and lining of the clothes for hidden notes and items.

The doorknob rattles. Alexander and I stare at each other with wide eyes, then we dive under the bed.

There are three small trunks stored there, forcing us to press our sides together to stay out of sight. My nose tickles from the thin layer of dust covering the floor, and I bury my face in my sleeve, fighting the sneeze trying to break free. The door opens and someone walks into the room. I hold my breath. From my position, all I can see is a woman's dusty slipper and the bottom of her brown satin dress, the quality of the material suggesting a noble instead of a staff member.

The footsteps come closer. I squirm back, moving closer to Alexander. His breath catches. I look at him, instantly captured by the swirl of emotions shimmering in his green eyes. I want to look away, but I can't, held by the intense longing in his gaze. Something inside me answers, and a warmth pools low in my stomach as heat rushes to my cheeks.

Alexander gently tucks a strand of hair behind my ear, his fingertips lingering on my skin. I lean into his touch, my eyes sliding shut—then start back when a dresser drawer opens. Then another drawer opens. And another. Puzzled, I inch forward, daring a peek at the woman.

Lady Fauser? What's she doing here? The white-haired woman rummages through the drawer, then pulls out a silver stick pin topped with a large ruby. She gives a satisfied smile as she tucks it into her pocket, then slides the drawer closed.

I duck back out of sight as she moves to the door. Once she's in the hallway with the door closed behind her, she hums a jaunty tune, the music fading with her footsteps.

I crawl out from under the bed. "Did you see that? This proves Lord Wentzel is the Bane."

Alexander slowly stands, dusting his clothes off. "How? We didn't find any poison in here, or anything else to confirm that it's him."

How can he not see it? "Lady Fauser is a thief. That's why I kept seeing her in all the different hallways at odd hours. So, she can't be the Bane."

"Not necessarily. She could be a thief and a poisoner."

"Nonsense. Being the Bane must pay more than petty robbery. And the Bane would never risk exposing himself by committing other crimes. He's too smart for that." I bounce on my toes, brimming with excitement. "If it's not her, then it must be Lord Wentzel. He's the only one left."

He raises an eyebrow. "Just because you don't suspect anyone else, that doesn't mean it's him. It could be someone else at this party, or nobody."

"But everything fits." I count off the points on my fingers. "First, we know the Bane is here."

He interjects, "We don't know that for sure."

I ignore him. "Ziggy is the Bane's target because he's the only guest who's fallen ill. The Bane must have used a slower-acting poison this time."

"Or it's a coincidence. Lord Zimmer is old and laid up with a normal illness. Meanwhile, the Bane's still after Lord Marx, or someone else, or not here at all."

Heat flushes through me. *Stubborn, annoying, insufferable—* "Lotta's always around her father. She would notice if someone was acting odd around him, or if someone had been in his room. Therefore, it had to be someone close to him, like Lord Wentzel.”

“She’s not looking for a poisoner around every corner. She might not have noticed anything, or brushed it off as a one-time oddity.” He folds his arms and rocks back on his heels. “Or she could be the poisoner. Mayhap she’s in a hurry for her inheritance.”

I put my hands on my hips and glare at him. “She would never do that.”

Alexander matches my scowl. “You don’t know that. It could be her just as easily as it could be Lord Wentzel, or one of the other guests, or a staff member, or someone who’s not even here. My point is that this is all wild speculation. We can’t go around accusing people because they supposedly have some imagined connection to the Bane. We need to be thoughtful about this.”

And by ‘be thoughtful,’ he means ‘do nothing until the Bane kills someone else.’ I clench my fists. There’s no point in arguing. Alexander’s going to keep throwing doubt around and refusing to admit he could be wrong. “Let’s go. I need to find Hartwin.” He’ll see I’m right.

16

After two days, Hartwin hasn't responded to my signal and I'm worried. I know he's sore from the chef fiasco, but I would've expected him to get over his tantrum and answer me by now. He might be tracking down some clues of his own—or something might have happened to him.

I try to distract myself from Hartwin's silence by following Lady Fauser, but she's thoroughly boring. The lady thief must be satisfied with whatever baubles she's already stolen, because she spends her free time playing cards and drinking brandy. Lotta will be sorely disappointed to learn that Lady Fauser doesn't even have any illicit rendezvous or paramours, just a habit of hiding aces up her sleeves.

Ziggy's menders were unsurprisingly dismissive of our suggestion that he might've been poisoned. After all, we don't have any idea what type of poison it could be, or anything to suggest he was actually poisoned aside from vague speculation. Alexander heroically doesn't gloat, which I find endlessly irritating.

When the third day rolls around without a word from Hartwin, I decide I have to find him myself. When Alexander catches me sneaking out of the palace, I try to convince him that I'm just taking a walk around the grounds, but he always knows when I'm lying, burn it.

I stomp along the path, clenching my jaw. "You didn't have to come. I'm perfectly capable of looking for Hartwin by myself."

Alexander tucks his hands in his pocket as he tilts his face to the sun. "And I'm perfectly sure you'll get into trouble without me."

I grumble, "You're the one who causes all the trouble."

He ignores me. "Besides, if the Bane's around, we need to stay together. It's safer."

That argument is getting old, but it doesn't make it any less true. There's nobody in the potting shed, and no sign of Hartwin at the dairy or outside the barn. Alexander's checking the tack room when a young man sidles up to me.

He smiles. "Lady Lux, I see you found the barn."

It takes a moment to recognize him. I suppress a sigh. "Ah, Herr Goff. It's nice to see you again."

"You may want to hold off if you're going for a ride. I don't like the look of that sky."

I glance at the gray clouds forming on the horizon and silently curse. *Alexander and I better stick close to the palace if we don't want to be caught out in a storm.* "Perhaps you're right. I'll go check on Lord Zimmer and see if there's anything I can do to help him."

The smile drops off his face. "I'm not sure there's much to do there. More than the Fortunes seem to be against him."

A knot forms in my stomach. "What's going on? Did he get worse? Have you heard something?" At the reluctant look on his face, I put my hand on his arm. "Please. If you know something, you need to tell me. Lady Zimmer's a friend, and I'm worried for her and Lord Zimmer."

He hesitates, then nods and lowers his voice. "I overhead an argument between Lord Wentzel and Lady Zimmer the morning he fell ill. Lady Zimmer was upset her father wouldn't let them marry, but Lord Wentzel assured her that he wouldn't interfere." He shrugs, a deep line forming between his eyebrows. "I don't think he meant anything by it."

But if Lord Wentzel is the Bane... "Thank you for telling me. I'm sure you're right." I glance over my shoulder, confirming the tack room door's still closed. *I need to get rid of him before Alexander comes out.* The last thing I need is for another showdown between male egos. I ask Herr Goff to walk me back to the palace, then pretend I left my gloves in the barn, sending him ahead without me.

Alexander pokes his head out the barn door, his expression relaxing when he spots me hurrying toward him. "Where did you run off to?"

"Never mind. Wait until you hear this." I fill him in on my news. "We have to find Hartwin as soon as possible. Where do you think he could be?"

Alexander grimaces. "Merchwood has more than thirty outbuildings in addition to the main palace."

I groan. "Why do they need so many?"

"Aliz said one of their relatives got it into their heads to expand the grounds and kept building all over the property." He shrugs. "I'm sure some are closed up, but I don't know which ones."

Hmm, it's Aliz now, is it? What happened to Rirzan *Brecht?* I brush aside the irrational annoyance and sigh. "Not to mention the woods, and gardens, and all the other places he could be hiding."

"Do you want to go back to the palace and wait for him to send a message?"

I square my shoulders. "No. This can't wait."

Four hours later, I'm deeply regretting my decision.

"How many burning orangeries does one palace need?"

He swipes the back of his arm across his forehead. "At least five, apparently. But on the bright side, we got fed this time."

We follow the winding path away from the orangery and through the trees, eating sweet wedges from the nicked oranges as we go. I lick the sticky juice from my fingers as I glance around. "If we don't find Hartwin in the next two hours, we should probably go back to the palace. They'll be serving supper soon, and he might have stopped pouting long enough to contact us."

He nods as he tosses the orange peel into the bushes. "Do you know where we are?"

I gesture northwest. "The palace is about three miles that way." I got into the habit of keeping a mental map while rambling around the Anglish countryside. A night spent shivering in the dark woods quickly taught me to always know where home is.

The forest has been gradually fading away from the path, leaving open rolling hills on one side. Wildflowers dot the landscape with bright yellows, blues, and whites. We stroll along in the same comfortable silence we always had together when we were children lazing around meadows or climbing trees.

A raindrop hits my nose, startling me. Then another. I look up at the angry gray clouds overhead. "Uh-oh."

Alexander grabs my hand. "Run!"

We race towards the trees as the skies open up, dumping a lake on our heads. In seconds we're drenched to the skin. The rain roars around us as the wind picks up, and it's hard to see more than a few feet in front of me. If I didn't know better, I'd swear we're in the middle of a monsoon. I thought there'd be some relief once we were under the tree canopy, but the storm continues to rage down on us, determined to keep us in its watery clutches.

Alexander yells, "Over there."

He points, but I can't see anything through the thick curtain of water. He leads me through the trees until the forest opens at a small clearing with a little white pavilion. We dash under its roof as the rain impossibly doubles in strength.

I laugh as I drag the damp strands of hair away from my face. "Why am I always getting drenched around you?"

"Me?" He pretends to be offended as he shakes out his coat. "You're the one always getting me soaked. At least it's a summer rain and not the middle of winter."

"Thank the Fortunes for small favors." I watch the storm howl around us, grateful to have our cozy shelter. I plop down in the middle of the floor with a groan and massage my calf. "I'm going to strangle Hartwin when we find him."

Alexander settles next to me, his shoulder brushing mine. "If we find him. Do you think he left?"

I ponder it for a moment, then shake my head. "He wants to catch the Bane as much as we do. If he did leave, it was to chase them, and he'll update me after. And then I'll kill him. But if he actually catches the Bane, I might be merciful and make it a quick death."

"Hmm." Alexander's face is carefully neutral. "What

will you do if we don't catch the Bane?"

"We already have. We know it's Lord Wentzel. Now we just need to find enough evidence to prove it to everyone else." I lean back on my hands with a happy sigh. "It's just a matter of time."

The rain patters on the roof overhead, tapping out a relaxing rhythm. I close my eyes and take a deep breath of the damp summer air. This is the first time at the party where I can truly relax. Now that I know who the Bane is, they can never escape me, and soon they'll be brought to justice. Alexander's my friend again. We're alone, in the middle of nowhere, out of danger's reach. At this moment, everything is perfect.

Alexander says, "Are you coming home after the party ends?"

"Not yet. Angland's so rainy this time of year. I'll probably travel for a few months first."

He frowns. "I meant Wittrow."

"Oh." I hadn't realized I don't think of Wittrow as home anymore. *Or do I?* Before, it wasn't an option because I knew Alexander was there and I could never face him again. But now there's nothing keeping me away.

Images of blue lakes and green meadows drift through my mind, the charming yellow house I haven't seen in years prominent in my memories. I twist the end of my braid around my hand, squeezing it dry. "I—I don't know. When are you going back?"

Alexander looks away. "I haven't decided."

"You could stay at Merchwood for a while. I'm sure Luther and Aliz would be happy to host you. And you could finally pin Luther down about your soap idea." *And I wouldn't mind spending more time with Aliz.* I ignore the nagging voice telling me I'm just avoiding making a decision about Wittrow.

He shrugs. "No need. Luther and I have already made an agreement. We'll work out the last details before I leave."

"You did?" I squeal and give him a hug. "Congratulations! When? Why didn't you tell me?"

His blush is adorable. "We've talked about it the past few mornings before you've gotten up. We're going to start with a few test batches, then scale up after a few months if it's working."

He really did it. "Is that for the regular soap, or the fancy ones?"

His brow wrinkles. "The regular. The other ones can only be done in small batches, and the process is more complicated. How did you hear about those?"

He wasn't going to tell me about them. My stomach twists, but I keep the smile on my face. "Aliz. She really loved your gift." I jump to my feet. "Look, the rain's stopped. We have a little time before we need to go back to the palace. Let's keep looking for Hartwin."

I hurry away from him, rubbing the hollow ache in my chest.

"Carina, wait."

He touches my arm. I stumble to a stop, but I don't turn around.

Alexander moves in front of me, waiting until I meet his gaze. "I gave those to her when I arrived at Merchwood as a hostess gift. It was before I knew you were here."

When he's this close, looking at me so intently, it's hard to breathe. The past and the present mingle together, hurt mixing with longing and something I don't want to look at too closely. "And it was very sweet of you. Now, can we find Hartwin?" Technically not a lie. I'm getting better at this.

He eyes me for a moment, then nods. "Where do you want to look next?"

"Anywhere as long as it isn't an orangery." I wince dramatically.

Alexander chuckles, the low sound hitting me deep and I shiver.

His brow creases. "Are you cold?" He rubs his hands up and down my arms.

I close my eyes and lean into his touch for a moment, savoring it, then pull away with a bright smile. "I'm fine. And once we're walking again, I'll be asking the Fortunes to dump another rain storm on us so I can cool off. Let's go this way." I set off in a random direction.

I chat lightly about the Sunselt party, exclaiming about what a wonderful job Aliz has done and laughing at Luther's attempts to set everything on fire. Alexander doesn't join in much, occupied with something he doesn't share. The next two buildings we come across are locked and covered in dust, but the third one has the door propped open. Loud swearing pours through the opening.

The knot in my chest disappears. "Hartwin, are you done sulking?"

The former spy steps out of the shadows and glares at us. "Are you trying to get the Bane to make a run for it by tromping all over the estate looking for me? I've half a mind to lock you both in the cellar until I catch 'em."

I grin. "But then you wouldn't hear all the wonderful things I have to tell you."

He crosses his arms in a silent challenge. I fill him in on what happened to Lord Zimmer and everything I can remember about Lord Wentzel, my excitement growing when I relay the information from the young staff member.

When I finish, Hartwin strokes his chin. "Ay, that could be something."

Alexander says, "What about the rest of it?"

I look at him in surprise and he shrugs.

"Lady Fauser's a thief. We saw her rob Lord Wentzel, and other guests have noticed missing items."

He just doesn't want to admit it's Lord Wentzel. But I guess we should tell Hartwin everything and let him decide what to do. I reluctantly add, "And Lady Goethe has a lot of plant knowledge. She sent me a special healing tea, and recognized saffron in the cake when nobody else could." Alexander eyes me while I hurry to add, "But I'm sure it's just a coincidence. *Rirzan* Brecht said Lady Goethe is a known recluse and hardly ever leaves her estate in Eaglan."

Hartwin narrows his eyes. "Anything else you've been holding back? Saw someone slip something into the stew? A man in a mask setting up bear traps in the hallways?"

I sniff. "Lord Wentzel is the Bane. Everyone else is just a distraction. So, what do we do next?"

"Nothing. You go back to your party and play dumb. I'll take it from here."

I'm about to protest when Alexander squeezes my elbow. "We'll signal you if we learn anything else."

Hartwin grumbles and stalks back into the building. When he's out of range, I glare at Alexander.

"Why did you do that?"

"Arguing wasn't going to solve anything. We can keep investigating just as we have been, whether Hartwin likes it or not."

Burning logical arguments. "Fine. But I'm not sharing

any more information with him until he's nicer about it."

Alexander raises an eyebrow. "Do you think that's a good idea?"

"Yes," I say mulishly.

He shakes his head, knowing I'm lying. It wouldn't make sense to keep information from Hartwin, even if he's an annoying grouser who's too full of himself for someone who still hasn't caught the Bane.

I'm in a foul mood as we trudge back to the palace. "Hartwin keeps treating us like we're a nuisance."

Alexander chuckles. "He's probably jealous you're doing a better job finding the Bane than he is. After all, he's supposed to be the professional and he's probably wrong about Lord Marx being the Bane's target."

I perk up. "Do you really think so?"

"Or he thinks we're pests."

"That's because he's an old, grouchy curmudgeon. If he showed even a hint of good manners, I'd faint from shock. You'd think a spy would be charming so he could sweet talk information out of people."

He laughs. "That's probably why he's a former spy and not a current one."

We trade outlandish theories about why Hartwin was fired as a spy as we walk back to the palace. I leave Alexander on the third floor, agreeing to meet in the library after we've both changed and washed up. When I get to my room, I kick off the boots with a sigh of relief and reach back to untie my dress before pausing. A white box with a red bow sits on the end of my bed. Though I've had other deliveries to my room, something about it makes me uneasy.

The staff wouldn't leave something on the bed, would they? No note. Did I lock the door when I left this morning?

I swore I did, but that doesn't mean there isn't a duplicate key around, or that someone couldn't break in easily, as both Alexander and Lady Fauser have proven.

Curious, I use a hand towel to open the box—and drop it. A cold sweat breaks out over my skin as I stare at the chocolates spilling across the bright bedspread. *The Bane. He knows I'm here to hunt him.* My breath comes in panicked gasps. I backpedal away from the bed until my back hits the wall. *He was in here.*

I rush over to the washbasin and retch, tears streaming down my cheeks, my throat burning. Choking on sobs, I blindly scrub my hands until they're red and raw. I slide down to the floor, shaking, and wrap my arms around my knees. I'm not sure how long I sit there before a few rational thoughts find their way through the fog. *Alexander wouldn't give me chocolates. Nor Aliz—she knows I hate it. It must be the Bane. There's nobody else who would do something like this. But why? To taunt me?*

I clench my fists. I'd love to be able to say I'm not afraid of him, but that would be a lie. I'm terrified. The sad truth is if the Bane wants me dead, there's a thousand ways to do it, and I'd never know until it's too late. Anything in here could be poisoned.

There's nothing I can do about it. I need to keep going. I stand up and brush off my dress, my jaw set. My false bravado crumbles the moment my shaking hand reaches for the wardrobe door, freezing in midair before I touch it, bile rushing up my aching throat.

I swallow hard. *I'll be brave tomorrow.* For now, I dig through my hamper and unearth a pale green dress that's reasonably clean, hoping the Bane didn't bother to poison my laundry. I hurriedly change, then rush out of my room, only pausing to lock the door behind me. *Not that it'll do any good.*

On my way to the library, I come across Aliz leaning against the front door, her eyes closed and her face tight. She must be under considerable strain with Ziggy falling ill on top of hosting this party and dealing with all the other catastrophes.

I push my fears aside and give her a hug. "Aliz, I haven't seen you since the Sunselt party. How are you?"

She rubs her forehead with a weary groan. "Everything seems to be going sideways today. Chef Kloss is threatening to quit, Lady Keil accused a staff member of stealing her emerald ring, and Luther has disappeared."

Poor dear. I take her hands and squeeze them. "How can I help?"

"I can't—"

"I insist," I say firmly. "And I won't take no for an answer."

She smiles, a spark coming back into her eyes. "Since you're so determined, could you please pass along my apologies to Lord Wentzel and check if he needs anything? I'll make sure I see him off, but right now I have to go calm down Chef Kloss if we want supper tonight."

My heart freezes at the Bane's name and I have to remind myself to breathe. "Oh, he's leaving early?" I try keep my voice even as my pulse speeds up. *Fleeing the scene of the crime?*

She looks distractedly toward the kitchen. "He has some urgent business in town."

My stomach twists. "Go deal with Chef Kloss. I'll see to Lord Wentzel." I hope she didn't notice the squeak when I said his name.

Aliz squeezes my hand, then hurries off. I climb the stairs to the third floor, dread wrestling with determination. This is it. Proof that he's the Bane. Why else would he run? He must be making arrangements for him and Lotta to run away together since Ziggy didn't die like he planned. I clench my jaw. I'll make sure Lord Wentzel doesn't get a second chance to kill him.

When I reach Lord Wentzel's door, I wipe my slick palms on my skirt, my heart hammering in my chest. Act normal. He won't hurt me, not now. The Bane doesn't know that I've figured out his true identity. He'll think he's safe and smarter than me, so I can use that to my advantage.

I brace myself and paste a pleasant smile onto my face. *Mayhap I can get him to slip and mention the chocolates he left in my room.* I knock loudly, then wait for a response. There's only silence inside. I knock again.

Alexander steps out of the room next door. "He left."

"Already?" I put my hands on my hips, hiding my relief. "And you didn't tell me?"

"I just found out myself and was about to come find you." He narrows his eyes at me. "But I see you were going to confront him alone."

Guilty. I jut out my chin. "Aliz asked me to check on him since she's busy." I peer down the hallway. "Do you think we can catch him in the courtyard?"

"No, the man cleaning his room said he left almost an hour ago."

His mouth snaps shut as a young girl in a uniform hurries up to us. She hands me a sealed note with a bobbing curtsy. Before she can scurry away, I ask her to change my room as soon as possible, carefully avoiding Alexander's curious gaze.

I distract him by holding up the note, pointing to the scrawled H in the corner. "It's from Hartwin." My eyes scan through the ink-splattered document, my jaw dropping. "He followed Lord Wentzel back to town. He just left us here!"

Alexander nods. "Good. If Lord Wentzel's the Bane, he could be dangerous."

"But—but—but he can't just leave us behind. I want to be there when the Bane's captured." I crumple the note in my fist. *After everything that's happened, I deserve it.*

"Hartwin won't capture him yet. Right now, all we have is suspicion. He'll be watching Lord Wentzel, trying to gather actual evidence." Alexander shrugs. "There's nothing we can do to help with that, and Hartwin knows how to handle it better than us. He'll figure out if Lord Wentzel is actually the Bane."

My chest tightens. "How can you not be convinced? Look at everything he's done. And we know he and Lotta are in a relationship, but her father's against them being together. That's why Lord Wentzel poisoned Ziggy."

He narrows his eyes. "We don't know that. We're guessing."

"Herr Goff told me. And I saw them a couple of times, even arguing! That's enough for me."

"But not for me." He crosses his arms, his jaw set. "There's still Lady Fauser and Lady Goethe. Not to mention all the other guests here. Or mayhap the Bane isn't here at all, and Hartwin's been wrong from the beginning."

Ice fills my stomach as I stare at him, a horrible realization slowly dawning on me. "You never thought that the Bane was at Merchwood. You've just been humoring me." *He doesn't want to find the Bane. Why didn't I see it sooner?*

A guarded look comes over his face. "I never said that."

"You didn't have to. You've been laughing at me this whole time." Tears sting my eyes and I swallow around the growing lump in my throat.

Alexander's green eyes widen. "Carina, no! I would never do that."

"Then why were you helping me?" I cry.

"I—I—" he falters, then looks away, grimacing. "If the Bane was here, I didn't want you to get hurt. Not again."

Just like Cristoph. Always thinking I'm helpless. "I've taken care of myself for the last five years. I didn't need your help then, and I don't need it now." I spin away, but pause when he touches my shoulder, glowering at the floor.

"Carina, please don't be angry. It's true. I don't think the Bane's here." He sighs heavily. "I made my peace years ago with the fact that we'll never find the Bane. Our families did everything they could, and they failed."

I clench my jaw. "That's why this party was so important. This could be our only chance at getting justice."

He levels a look at me. "Justice—or vengeance?"

I glare at him, heat flashing through me. "You didn't lose your family. I did."

"Didn't I?" he says sadly. "I lost you. And Cristoph, and your parents."

"It's not the same." I clutch my mother's locket, hating the tremble in my voice.

"No, it's not. But I'm not going to risk losing you again." He puts his hands on my shoulders, his face close as he stares intently into my eyes. "I don't care if we catch the Bane. I only care about keeping you safe."

I look away, stiffening. "But that's not what I want." My chest is hollow. He'll never understand. The Bane took everything from me. I can't rest until I know they'll never hurt me again.

Alexander's grip tightens. "I'll help you hunt the Bane, but I won't put you in danger. I can't. If I have to choose between you and catching them, I'll choose you every time."

I step back and his hands reluctantly fall away. "Then you'll choose the wrong thing." He knows I'm not lying.

This time he doesn't stop me when I walk away.

17

After Hartwin's departure, it's impossible to enjoy the party. I'm constantly on edge, waiting for news of Lord Wentzel's capture. I never told Alexander about the chocolates in my room. He's already too overprotective and I don't need to add to his paranoia. As satisfying as it would be to prove I was right about the Bane being at Merchwood, it's not worth the risk of being dragged off to Wittrow 'for my safety.' As though anywhere is safe from the Bane.

I thought I'd be thrilled at being this close to catching the Bane, but there's a shadow over my happiness that I can't shake. Without being there, it doesn't feel real. Hartwin's note used some very colorful language to order us to stay at the party. He doesn't want to alert Lord Wentzel that we're on to him, so I'm stuck at Merchwood for now. Thank the Fortunes that there's less than a week left.

The few times we talk, Alexander and I studiously avoid any mention of the Bane. It's a boulder sitting between us. Alexander and Aliz spend most afternoons huddled in the library, with Luther occasionally making an appearance. I try joining them a few times, but the conversation always stalls. Mostly I avoid the palace as much as I can. I spend my days wandering in the woods and evenings holed up in my room with a supper tray so I won't be forced to see him.

Today, I get a later start than normal after a night of tossing and turning. The sun pours through my windows as I dig through the wardrobe until I unearth a dark green walking dress. *Time to go lose myself in the forest and climb some trees.*

I take the long way through the palace and go out one of the back doors so I can avoid the library. No need to tempt the Fortunes and have my path cross Alexander's if I can avoid it.

Lotta's sitting on a bench by the garden, the first I've seen of her outside since Ziggy fell ill. It's tempting to slip by her without saying anything, but her drawn face makes my heart ache for what she's going through. I approach her cautiously, ready to leave if she looks like she doesn't want company.

Lotta looks up at my footsteps and gives me a wan smile. "Were you sent to find me?"

"I was going for a walk, but I thought I'd join you first." I shrug and smile tentatively. "But if you'd rather be alone, I can be on my way."

She scoots over and pats the space next to her. "A friend would be nice right now, thank you." As I settle next to her on the bench, she sighs. "I feel like I've been up for days, but I can't sleep."

I remember similar nights staying up late to watch my mother, then tossing and turning all night, even though I was exhausted. "How's Ziggy?"

"Good, all things considered." She chuckles. "My

father's too stubborn to give up his cigars and brandy, even while stuck in bed. He's been complaining nonstop because there's nobody to sneak them to him now that Franz left."

My stomach tightens and I furrow my brow. "I thought Ziggy and Lord Wentzel weren't getting along lately?"

Humor lights her face. "Oh, the opposite. Those two are always thick as thieves. Franz even visits with us most nights to play cards or read. I should've banned him since he's always finding ways to slip my father those blasted cigars no matter how much I scold him. But we adore him and it makes Ziggy happy to have him around. The stubborn fool." She grins.

I toy with my locket, a heavy feeling in my chest. *This doesn't make any sense.* "Are—are you and Lord Wentzel courting?"

She bursts into laughter. "Great Fortunes, no! Is that what people think?"

Heat rushes to my cheeks and I lift a shoulder. "Well, you do spend a lot of time together."

Lotta pats my hand. "We're just good friends. My husband's a captain, so he's at sea most of the year. It makes us both feel better if I live with my father while he's away. Someone has to make sure Ziggy stays out of trouble, especially when Franz's around."

"Why isn't he? Around, now, I mean. Since Ziggy's sick." I shift my weight on the stone seat, my mind whirling.

"He'll be back tomorrow. Franz volunteered to get the townhouse ready for our early return and hire some extra help for Ziggy while he recovers. He's such a dear. So thoughtful." She wrinkles her nose and chuckles. "Except for the cigars and brandy. Speaking of which, I'd better go check on my father. He's probably already bribed one of the staff to sneak him a cigar while I'm gone."

I murmur a goodbye as she leaves, my thoughts tumbling over each other in a flurry. Everything we thought about Lord Wentzel is wrong! There's no reason he would be upset with Ziggy. And Lotta spends every moment with both of them, so she would know if anything was going on. And she's clearly fond of both of them. No, Lord Wentzel can't be the Bane.

Why would Herr Goff mislead me about them? Or was he just passing along information someone else told him? Was someone trying to throw us off the trail of the real Bane? I rub my forehead. Or mayhap it was all ordinary gossip, and it doesn't mean anything at all.

Ugh, I'm glad I'm not a spy. All this speculation and guessing could drive a person crazy.

But there's one thing I know for sure: the Bane's still out there. *Should I tell Alexander?* My jaw clenches. *He's probably off somewhere with Aliz.* As much as I'd love to keep avoiding him, he deserves to know about the Bane, if only so he knows to keep an eye out. I force myself to trudge back into the palace and turn toward the library, then pause.

I don't have to tell him directly. I could leave a note in his room. Then he can't accuse me of hiding it from him, and it won't be my fault if I find the Bane before he reads it.

Pleased with my plan, I make my way back to my room, my steps light. I pen a long letter to Hartwin to have posted in town, giving him a thorough recount of my conversation with Lotta. Then I dash off a significantly shorter note to Alexander saying we were wrong about Lord Wentzel. It's tempting to ask someone on the staff to deliver the message for me, but I can't risk the Bane finding out.

When I get to Alexander's room, the door's cracked

open. *Burn it. What did I do to make the Fortunes dislike me so much?* I take a deep breath, then lightly knock as I push it open. "Alexander, I—"

A hooded figure looks up, a knitted black mask covering the bottom part of their face. They're standing by the bed, an open bottle of white powder in their gloved hand, the bedcovers thrown back. It takes a moment for the scene to make sense. My heart freezes and ice floods my veins. *The Bane. Poison. Alexander.*

Everything happens at once. I scream as I run out the door. The hooded figure lunges at me, catching the back of my skirt, knocking me to the ground. My chin slams against the floor. Tears sting my eyes. A knee pins my legs to the ground as large hands squeeze my throat.

I gasp and claw at the fingers choking me, but they don't budge. My heart thunders in my chest. The Bane's too heavy to knock to the side. As my lungs shriek for air, I reach blindly back, raking my nails across their face.

He bellows, his grip loosening. I frantically redouble my efforts, scratching and mauling at what I hope are his eyes. The hands shove me down and the weight disappears as he rears back with a roar, his gloved hands covering his damaged features.

I scramble away, gasping for air. Then run.

Pounding footsteps follow. My legs are clumsy. I try to scream, but nothing comes out. My throat is on fire. He's close. My focus narrows to my next step. Any stumble or the smallest hesitation means death.

Find people. I can't waste time knocking on doors. *Will he catch me before I can reach the bottom floor? Will anyone be there?* My breath rasps as I fight the urge to look over my shoulder. A desperate plan forms in my mind.

I leap down the stairs, buying myself a few precious seconds. At the landing, I fly to the closest door and grab the handle, shouldering it open like Alexander showed me. I slam the door closed and throw the lock as the Bane skids across the landing.

Jamming the chair under the door handle buys me the time I need to climb out the window. It's a long drop, but I've fallen out of enough trees to know how to land without hurting myself.

My teeth rattle as I hit the ground. There're only moments before the Bane breaks down the door and follows me.

I pick up a large rock and hurl it at the nearest window, shattering it. Then the next. And the next.

Shouts erupt inside the palace.

I run toward the front door, knowing people will come to investigate the noise.

A quick glance over my shoulder shows the hooded figure ducking back inside the second-floor room. *Safe.* As people come streaming out of the palace, I dive behind a hedge, collapsing on the grass. My lungs bellow, trying to draw in enough air.

The Bane will be easy to identify now, but I don't want anyone else to know there's a murderer lurking on the grounds. If the guests found out, they'd panic and leave in droves, letting the Bane escape into anonymity again.

I close my eyes and focus on breathing.

The scene from the bedroom slams into me. My heart stops and my stomach fills with lead. *No!*

I struggle to my feet and stagger towards the side door, one thought on my mind.

I have to warn Alexander.

18

When I throw open the library door, Alexander's alone inside. He looks up from his chair. "Did you…" His voice dies as he leaps up, his face white. "Carina, what—"

He's alive. I fling myself into his arms, sobbing, all the fear and pain pouring out of me. I'm shaking so hard I can barely stand. Alexander picks me up and carries me to the chair. When he tries to put me in the seat, I refuse to let go of him, so he sits down with me cradled against his chest, his arms tight around me.

I cling to him, burying my face against his shirt. As my tears flow, the panic drains away, leaving me feel numb and hollow. My throat burns and the bruises covering my body throb. Slowly my weeping dies down to soggy hiccups and I rest my head on his shoulder.

Alexander keeps his arm around me, comforting me as he tenderly brushes my hair back from my face. He uses the pitcher on the side table to dampen his handkerchief to bathe my sore eyes, then coaxes me to sip some water, the cool liquid soothing the fire in my throat.

His expression darkens when he glances at my neck, but his tone stays soothing as he murmurs, "You're safe, Carina. I won't let anyone hurt you. Can you tell me what happened?"

I sniffle, my hand clenching his soggy shirt. "The Bane. He's here." My voice is a hoarse whisper.

His brow furrows. "Lord Wentzel's in town. Hartwin followed him."

I shake my head. "We were wrong." I haltingly tell him everything between sips of water, starting with my conversation with Lotta. As I relive the events, my pulse speeds up and I talk faster and faster, horror morphing into anger. Alexander stays silent throughout my story, emotions flickering across his face too quickly for me to catch. When I get to the Bane's attack, his fist clenches, crushing the fabric of my ruined skirt, his knuckles white.

After I finish, he pulls me against his chest and buries his face in my hair, letting out a shuddering breath. His heartbeat is steady beneath my ear, the rhythm soothing the last of my fears away. My hand creeps up to cover my mother's locket. In the dim, quiet library, surrounded by the normalcy of leather-bound books and sunlight, the Bane's attack feels like it happened a lifetime ago. The strength runs out of my muscles and I sag against him, fighting off a wave of exhaustion.

Too soon, he leans back, his face a storm of rage and fear. "You have to leave. Now. My carriage can be ready in ten minutes."

A spark of outrage ignites in my chest and my back stiffens. "I'm not running away."

"It's not safe here anymore. The Bane will be furious that you attacked him and got away." Alexander's arm tightens around my waist. "He'll want revenge."

I suppress a shudder, then pull back my shoulders. "So do I. I'm not going to let him chase me away. Not when we can finally find out who he is." At the stubborn set of his jaw, I hurry to add, "He's probably already left Merchwood. He won't want to explain his injuries, especially since they'll identify him. This is the best place for me to be."

"If he knows where you are, he can find a way to kill you. We need to get you far away and hidden." His expression turns to granite. "Then I'll hunt him down."

My pulse speeds up. "I decide whether I stay or go, not you." I jump up from the chair and glare at him. "You can't try and send me away when we're about to catch the Bane. We only got this far because of me. Because I never gave up, even when everyone else did."

Alexander stands, locking eyes with me. "And I told you, I won't put you in danger. And right now, this is the most danger you've ever been in. Before, you weren't the Bane's target. Now you are."

"And I can take care of myself. I escaped him, didn't I?"

"He almost killed you!" His voice cracks. Alexander takes a ragged breath and runs a hand across his face.

My fists clench. "But he didn't. And he won't get another chance."

"You don't know that." Despair fills his eyes as his shoulders slump. "He's almost killed you twice. I can't lose you. Not again."

Alexander's pain makes me almost relent, but I steel myself against it. "I'm not yours to lose."

Alexander winces—then his face hardens. "But I'm still going to protect you."

I blurt out, "You gave Aliz fancy soaps, but you never

gave me any."

His brow furrows. "What does that have to do with anything?"

"It—it just does!"

He glares at me. "Fine. I'll give you thousands of seashell soaps. You'll get buckets of fancy soaps every day for the rest of your life. Which is going to be a long, long time because you're not staying here. I don't care if I have to carry you home kicking and screaming, but you're leaving."

He'll do it; I can see it in his eyes. This is his breaking point. Alexander doesn't care that I'll never forgive him. He'll do it without an ounce of regret because he's more afraid of me dying than of losing me.

He loves me. I knew that he did, but I didn't realize what that really meant until this moment. Alexander will always put my safety and happiness before his own. He's not trying to send me away from Merchwood out of some misguided chivalry, or because he thinks he knows best. He's terrified for me. He thinks my need to capture the Bane is overriding my sense of self-preservation and I can't see it.

I can't be angry since I'd do the exact same thing in his place. Because I love him.

I've been tying myself in knots, doing anything I can to deny it in a pathetic attempt to protect my heart. Admitting that I love him terrifies me. It means I have something to lose. Something I thought I'd lost before, and that almost destroyed me.

When I was young, I thought I was in love with him, but that's like comparing a candle to the sun. Knowing him now, understanding the man he's become, my feelings for him have changed into something so much deeper than a childhood fancy.

I've only ever loved Alexander, so I have nothing to compare it to, but there's no other name for this feeling. Even that doesn't do it justice. He's kind and brilliant and a thousand other things, and my life is richer because he's a part of it. I never stopped loving him. Even when I thought he abandoned me all those years ago, I never stopped. I just buried it deep down, sure that he'd betrayed me and we'd never see each other again. But when I found out the truth, my feelings started slipping back into my heart without my noticing.

But if something were to happen, can I trust him to fight for me? For us? Or would he give up and leave when things get hard?

The answer is simple. "Kiss me."

He blinks. "What?"

I giggle at his dumbfounded expression and step closer, sliding my arms around his neck. "I. Want you. To kiss me."

He gently cradles my waist, his eyes darkening with a deep longing. "Are you sure?"

"Ye—"

His lips capture mine, sending fire racing through me. I melt against his chest and he tightens his grip, pulling me closer. I've dreamed of this moment a thousand times, but my imagination pales in comparison to the reality. The long years of yearning and desire crash down on us, carrying us away. Everything is hunger and heat and need. Pleasure washes through me, making me feel wild and reckless because I know he'll guard my heart for me. My body hums and I press against him, his every touch making me desperate for more.

He pulls away too soon—but it'll always be too soon. *Alexander.* A sense of wonder fills me, knowing he's mine as much as I'm his.

Alexander touches his forehead to mine and chuckles. "You have no idea how long I've wanted to do that."

"Probably almost as long as I've wanted you to." I look up at him through my lashes and grin. "You were frustratingly oblivious to all my shameless flirting when we were young."

He nuzzles my ear and my breath catches. "There were no hints. Believe me, if I had seen the slightest spark of interest in anything but friendship, I would've acted on it."

"That's because you were as blind then as you are now." I kiss the tip of his nose, then press a hand to his chest, my gaze turning serious. "I'm not leaving Merchwood. But I agree the Bane will want to find me. So. Let's use that to our advantage."

He stiffens. "I told you, I—"

"Won't put me in danger. I know." I draw in a breath and let it out slowly, trying to put into words what I instinctively know. "I'm already in danger. Running away won't change that, but that's what he'll expect me to do. Which means staying hidden here really is the safest place for me right now. The Bane will leave Merchwood as soon as possible to avoid anyone seeing his scratched-up face, so we'll be able to figure out who the real Bane is in the next few days. After that, we can leave together and find Hartwin."

Alexander eyes me, but he knows I'm not lying. He nods slowly. "As long as you stay out of sight and you aren't alone at any point before we go. You can stay with me in my room."

I raise my eyebrows. *And have everyone gossiping about me for years to come if they find out?* "I'll stay with Aliz."

When he still looks unhappy, I sigh and add, "We'll ask Luther to have someone watch the room so nobody can sneak in. But only until we figure out who the real Bane is." I grip his shirt and tug him closer. "And you need to stay with Luther and do the same. You're the Bane's target. They may try to—" My voice chokes and I can't get the words out. "Before they leave. You need to be careful until we know he's gone."

"Done and done." He gives me a grim smile. "Let the hunt begin."

With the threat of the Bane looming over us, we're reluctant to part ways, but Alexander can see I'm flagging and likely to fall asleep on my feet at any moment. He's tempted to carry me around the palace as he looks for Luther and Aliz, but finally realizes it would be a terrible idea—mostly because I threaten to shave his head while he's sleeping if he tries. Alexander grabs the library's fireplace poker as an improvised weapon and we move carefully through the palace, keeping a wary eye out for anyone trying to ambush us.

After he checks my room for any hidden intruders and swears to the Fortunes a hundred times that he'll be careful, we exchange a lingering kiss, a thrill racing through me that has my toes curling in my slippers. He insists on waiting until I've locked the door and wedged a chair against it before he leaves. After his footsteps fade away, I fall back on the bed with a happy sigh, a warm glow in my chest.

Alexander loves me. Knowing it makes me feel like I've been wrapped up in a fluffy cloud—or that might be the exhaustion. Either way, everything has taken on a dreamlike quality. The future I thought was lost has come rushing back into possibility, and it looks even better than I ever imagined. In an odd twist from the Fortunes, I have more faith in us than when I was younger. Before, it was an effortless, gossamer infatuation. Was it love then? I think so, but it's hard to say since I didn't understand everything that love means. I probably still don't, and I'll spend a lifetime finding out. But like a tree that's weathered a storm, we were tested and damaged, and now we've grown back stronger. It gives me a confidence that I didn't know I was lacking all those years ago.

If only we had caught the Bane… I frown. Everything would be different if the Bane hadn't destroyed our lives five years ago. And now he'll be coming after both of us. If we can't figure out who he is before the party ends, he'll disappear into the crowd like he always does, ready to strike the moment we let our guard down. *And take everything away again. I can't let that happen.*

A knock on the door interrupts my thoughts. I spring up from the bed, my heart fluttering. "Back already?"

I'm expecting Alexander, but my hand freezes on the chair when a different voice answers. "Lady Lux, I'm sorry to bother you. Is Aliz with you?"

"Luther?" The knot in my stomach loosens.

"Yes. I'm looking for my sister. Do you know where she is?"

I wrestle away the chair, remembering at the last moment to throw on a large shawl to hide my bruised neck before I open the door. "Sorry, no. But Alexander went looking for her a few minutes ago. For both of you, actually. There's, um, a situation we need to tell you about."

Luther nods distractedly, his brow furrowed. "Right, right. Let me find Aliz first, and we'll all meet in my study in an hour."

"I can help you look for her." The Bane won't attack me if I'm with Luther.

"No, please don't concern yourself. I'm sure she's fine. Aliz probably just needed a moment to herself after all the havoc from the past few weeks. Most likely she's holed up somewhere with a book." The line between his eyebrows deepens as he gives me a half-hearted smile. "If you see her, please let her know I'm looking for her."

He hurries off before I can reply. I relock the door and replace the chair, then sink down on the edge of my bed. My prior peace eludes me as I chew on my bottom lip, wondering where Aliz is.

She definitely deserves a break, but it's hard to believe she would make Luther worry, or disappear without telling someone. Where could she have gone? I haven't seen her the past few days, but I assumed she was with Alexander when I was avoiding him. She seemed in good spirits the last time I talked to her. Busy, but she's always busy. Did something upset her recently?

It's impossible to know, and Alexander isn't here to ask. I pace my small room, pausing when I catch sight of myself in the mirror. The expected bruises are already formed on my chin and neck, but the smudges of dirt on my face and the hair half-out of my braid are a surprise. *Ghastly.* I laugh. *Love really is blind if Alexander could look at me so tenderly when I'm such a disaster.*

I untie my braid and pick up my hairbrush—then set it back down with a frown, my stomach twisting. Luther must be more worried than he let on if he didn't notice. When was the last time anyone saw Aliz?

No matter how concerned Alexander is about the Bane attacking me again, I can't sit here and do nothing until I know Aliz is all right. Besides, I need to tell Alexander about our meeting with Luther. I clean up quickly and change into a fresh dress, wrapping a shawl high around my shoulders to hide the bruises. My room is sadly lacking in weapons, so I twirl my long braid up into a bun held in place with a pair of wickedly sharp hairpins.

I'll make the kitchen my second stop so I can swipe a knife. But first, I need to see if Alexander's still in his room. Knowing him, he'll want to make sure the contaminated bedding is properly disposed of so nobody accidentally gets poisoned. With any luck, he'll still be there.

When I spot his door open, I breathe a sigh of relief and hurry in.

"Alexander, I—"

Someone grabs me from behind. A hand holding a handkerchief clamps over my face.

The world goes black.

20

Murmurs. Footsteps. Something hard digging into my stomach. As consciousness creeps back in, I slowly realize I'm slung over someone's shoulder. I try to move, but my arms and legs aren't working. My eyes refuse to open. A faint voice in the back of my mind tells me I should be panicking, but the thought drifts away into the fog, leaving me floating in a sea of gray.

The swaying motion and the sour-sweet smell clinging to my skin makes my stomach churn, and bile rises up my throat. Thankfully the person carrying me stops before I'm sick and lays me on the ground. Someone takes hold of my wrists and I feebly try to fight back, but I'm not even sure I twitch. A low growl sounds off to the side and the person by me chuckles.

Something heavy is dropped on the floor, followed by shuffling and the sound of furniture being shoved around. I'm vaguely aware that I'm lying on chilly stone, but that sickly sweet stench overpowers any other scents that might hint at where I am. My body still isn't responding, while my mind struggles through the fog surrounding it. How did I end up here?

I was in the library with Alexander. No—I was in my room. Alone? Luther came. Something about Aliz? Then he left? Or I left? It's all a muddled blur.

Hands lift my shoulders and prop me sitting up against a wall. I fight to open my eyes, but they refuse to budge. There's another growl.

"She'll come around in a minute. Then we'll all have a nice chat."

The words sound far away, though the man must be inches from me. That voice… I almost recognize it, but then it's gone.

He hums as he moves around the room for a few minutes, then pauses. "Looks like our sleeping beauty could use some help waking up."

He slaps my cheek with a cracking force.

My eyes fly open as I groan, the fog disappearing from my mind. Herr Goff is squatting in front of me, his face covered in a patchwork of angry red scrapes left by my nails.

My mind struggles to make the pieces fit. I thought the Bane attacked me, but Herr Goff can't be the Bane. Some of the murders happened before he was even born. What's going on? Why was he trying to poison Alexander if he's not the Bane?

Herr Goff playfully wags a finger at me. "You've caused us a lot of trouble, Lady Lux. I'll forgive you for accidentally scratching me and running away, since you didn't know it was me under the mask." He rocks back on his heels and says cheerfully, "And I'm sorry if I hurt you earlier. I had to stop you from yelling before you gave away the game, and I got a little carried away. But now we're square and we can be friends again."

I gulp and press back against the wall, a chill crawling up my spine. *Is he insane?*

Herr Goff stands and moves to the side, revealing Alexander gagged and tied to a chair in the middle of the room. My heart leaps into my throat as my eyes frantically run over him. There's a large purple lump on his forehead, and the ropes seem painfully tight, but otherwise he looks unharmed. My relief is short lived as I take in our surroundings.

We're in a small stone room with no windows, the scant light coming from two shuttered lanterns. A heavy wooden door blocks the only exit. I can't tell if we're still in the palace or if we were moved to one of the many outbuildings. In either case, the thick dust covering everything and the musty air means it's unlikely someone will accidentally stumble across us.

Alexander locks eyes with me, his eyebrows drawing together. I nod, letting him know I'm not hurt. My hair pins have disappeared, and my hands are bound in front of me with a leather cord, but my legs are free.

I'd be insulted that Herr Goff didn't think me enough of a threat to properly tie me up, but I'm too busy figuring out how to use it to my advantage. He's close enough to my weight and height that I don't think I can overpower him, even if I get my hands free. *Surprise will give me an edge, but only a small one. I'll have to be quick.*

Herr Goff turns his back to us and rummages through a large bag tucked under the lone table in the room. "Give me a moment and then we can get started."

While he's distracted, I try to stand, my muscles trembling with the effort. I only manage to get a few inches off the ground before I collapse, panting. My stomach drops as tears sting my eyes.

What are we going to do? I can't fight him if I can't move. Terror squeezes my heart and I swallow a whimper. *No.* I shove the fear aside, refusing to admit defeat. My nails cut into my palms as I clench my fists. *I'm not going be killed by a silly, bland twit. I'm already getting stronger, so I just need to stall until my legs are working again. Then I'll show this lump that he attacked the wrong lady.*

Our abductor straightens with a large sealed jar in his hand. "I'm so glad we could get together and figure out what to do next." He turns to Alexander, his brow furrowed. "Well, it really should be your decision. But since Lady Lux is here, it would be rude not to include her." He sits on the floor a few feet from me and grimaces as he rubs the back of his neck. "I've really bungled it this time."

My pulse speeds up. He'll be easier to overpower if he's on the ground. I subtly stretch my legs, testing my muscles, then silently curse. A little better, but still weak. I need more time. Keep him talking. "What do you need our help with?"

"Oh, right. You don't know yet. See, I was supposed to leave you" —Herr Goff nods at Alexander, who growls around his gag— "a note with instructions where to go, and then we'd ambush you after you left Merchwood." He frowns. "Which is completely foolish and leaving far too many things to chance, but she always has to make things so complicated. She should've just kidnapped you and been done with it. That would've been so much better, don't you think?"

He doesn't wait for Alexander's reaction, too caught up in his rant as he waves the jar through the air. "But everything has to be done her way and she never listens to me. Which isn't fair! It's not like she's never made a mistake. After all, *your* mother didn't eat the bonbons way back when. If she had, we could've avoided this whole mess. So obviously her plans aren't perfect either. But she still insists she knows better than me, and that we have to do it her way and go through this whole elaborate scheme instead of keeping things simple." Herr Goff makes a face.

My spine stiffens as my insides thrum. There's only one person he could be talking about. "Who is she? Who is the Bane?" I hold my breath, my hands clutched around my mother's locket.

"I can't spoil her surprise." He chuckles. "She was annoyed that her title wasn't something grander, but I think 'Bane' is fitting. She definitely makes me miserable most days." Herr Goff winces. "Don't tell her I said that."

My muscles tense and there's a roaring in my ears. *You half-witted, ignorant, foolish, AARGGHH—* I have an overwhelming urge to shake him until he tells me the Bane's name. Knowing Alexander could die if I fail is the only thing that holds me back. *He's young. Eager. Play into his ego.* Biting my tongue, I widen my eyes and force myself to ask, "Are you her partner?"

He puffs out his chest. "I'm the new Bane." He deflates a bit. "Well, I'm supposed to be. But after she finds out how I botched this, she might change her mind. Which is why I need your help." He blows out a breath and opens the jar. He lifts it to his lips, then pauses and holds it out to me. "Do you want some? It's apple cider."

I shake my head, my nerves vibrating, ready to throttle him. The boy has the attention span of a gnat. He glances at Alexander and shrugs, then gulps down the cider before replacing the lid and setting the jar aside.

"That's better. Where was I? Oh." He shakes his head. "We all agree that the Bane refusing to kidnap Lord von Bron is silly, right? And since she was planning to kill him anyway, I decided I'd save a bunch of time and hassle and do it myself. But then Lady Lux interfered."

He gives me an admonishing look. I duck my head, hiding the rage burning in me. He expects me to feel bad that I stopped him from killing Alexander? Now I know he's insane.

My heart bursts into a thundering pace and a cold sweat coats my skin. *No! Not now!* My breath comes in short gasps as I fight for air. I clutch my locket as the edges of the room fade into a fuzzy blur. *It'll pass. It'll pass.* My heart tries to burst out of my chest as it races impossibly faster. My chest is trapped in an invisible vice, slowly suffocating me. *It'll pass. It'll pass.*

Herr Goff says, "And now I have to figure out what to do because—" He frowns at me. "You haven't been drinking your tea."

I can't answer him, my lungs squeezing against my ribs as I pant for air. Alexander strains against his ropes as I slide down the wall, collapsing on my side. I curl up in a ball on the floor, pressing my forehead to my knees, waiting for the spell to pass.

Our abductor tuts, turning to search through the sack behind him. With a grin that shows his dimple, he extracts a large flask, then sits next to me. Revulsion washes over my skin. I feebly try to crawl away, but he easily pulls me up against his side, wrapping an arm around my shoulders to support me.

He holds the flask up to my mouth. "Drink this."

I turn my face away, my lips locked together. My chest

heaves, my lungs desperate for air, but I'd rather suffocate than give in.

He gives a disappointed sigh. "Why are you being so difficult when I'm trying to help you?" When I don't move, he grumbles, "Fine. If you're going to be like that, I can too." He nods to Alexander. "Drink, or I'll start cutting off his fingers."

I look helplessly at Alexander. He furiously shakes his head, his words strangled by the gag, his eyes pleading. I open my mouth and let Herr Goff pour the liquid in. *Cinnamon.* Icy terror and my struggling body make it hard to swallow, but I force it down. After a few seconds, my pulse slows and my labored breathing eases into a comfortable rhythm.

Herr Goff pats me on the head and smiles. "Isn't that better? Now be sure to drink your tea every day, like a good little girl."

Alexander's gaze runs over me as though to make sure I'm really recovered from the attack. I give him a trembling smile and he sags against his bonds.

Our captor pulls a folding knife out of his pocket and flips it open, the sharp blade glinting in the scant light. He strokes my hair and my muscles scream to run, but I'm too terrified to move. Alexander's eyes turn to green granite as he glares at Herr Goff with pure hatred, the ropes cutting cruelly into his flesh as he struggles against them.

"Back to my predicament. So now that you both knew that I was going to kill Lord von Bron, I couldn't just leave him a note, like she wanted. And Lady Lux was involved too, which was going to make her even angrier. So, how do I get out of this mess?" He frowns. "I can't manage both of you for the trip, so one of you has to go." His focus shifts to

Alexander. "Do I kill both of you? Kill you and take Lady Lux to the Bane? Or kill Lady Lux, and then take you to the Bane—which is closer to her original plan."

Keep stalling until the right moment. "Why can't you leave one of us here and come back later for them?" I hate the way my voice shakes.

He sigh deeply. "I thought of that, but it's too risky. The Bane has said over and over and over not to leave any witnesses. Someone might find you while I'm gone. And if you told them about this—" He uses the knife to gesture to the scratches on his face. "They'll know who I am and I'll never get to be the new Bane." Herr Goff shakes his head. "You only have yourself to blame for this." He brightens. "But I'm glad you came to his room before you had a chance to tell anyone else about me. Capturing you right after him saved me a lot of time and trouble."

My hands squeeze together as I fight the urge to throttle him. "I already told *Kangan* Brecht about scratching you," I bluff, my chest tight. "He's searching for you right now."

Herr Goff chuckles. "Good try, but the *Kangan*'s busy looking for his sister and doesn't know anything about me. Now, I need to leave soon, and no matter what option I pick, it's going to take some time to arrange. So, what do you think I should do?" He looks at Alexander for an answer, his expression turning chagrined. "Oh, pardon me. I forgot."

Herr Goff stands and carelessly slices off Alexander's gag, the knife leaving a thin red line down his cheek. While he's distracted, I tackle the leather cord binding my hands, tearing at the tight knots with my teeth.

Alexander spits out a soggy rag, then clenches his jaw, his cheekbones white. "If you touch Carina, I'll kill you."

Our abductor chuckles. "I knew you loved Lady Lux.

The Bane was sure you were in love with *Rirzan* Brecht and
nothing could convince her otherwise. But I knew better."
He gestures to Alexander. "What do you think? What would
you do in my place?"

Alexander leans back in the chair. "I think you should
kill me."

My heart freezes. "No!"

Herr Goff waves at me to shush. "She'll be angry."

Alexander keeps his eyes on our captor. "She'll be
impressed. You'll have succeeded where she failed."

Herr Goff rubs a hand over his mouth as he thinks it
over.

I won't let him sacrifice himself for me. I abandon my
attempts to free my hands and roll up to my knees, my
stomach twisting into knots. "You said she wanted
Alexander alive. She must have a reason for that. If you kill
him now, you'll just make her mad."

Herr Goff looks at Alexander. "Lady Lux makes an
excellent point."

Alexander glares at me. "She's confused. She has
nothing to do with any of this. I'm the one the Bane wants
dead. If the Bane has other plans for Carina, she'll be even
angrier with you if you hurt Carina now. Better to wait and
let her decide."

Herr Goff taps his chin with the blade. "Hmm, I hadn't
thought of it that way." He nods crisply. "I agree. It makes
the most sense to kill you and take Lady Lux to the Bane."

An empty pit opens in my chest as sour fear fills my
stomach. "What about needing Alexander alive?"

He waves a hand through the air nonchalantly. "I was
going to kill him before, so doing it now doesn't change
anything. And she doesn't much care for getting her hands

dirty with these things. She'll probably thank me for taking care of it."

He raises the knife and Alexander braces for the blow

I shout, "Wait!" I struggle to my feet, using the wall for leverage. "You have to poison him. It's tradition."

He grimaces. "Oh, of course." Herr Goff strides over to the bag under the table. "I brought the perfect thing."

I launch myself clumsily at our captor, crashing into him. He grunts as we stagger sideways. I scream incoherently as I claw at him with my bound hands, trying to wrestle the knife away. It falls to the floor with a clatter. My heartbeat thunders in my ears. My nails rake across his face and he bellows. Herr Goff hurls me against the wall. My head cracks against the stone, bright stars filling my vision.

He glares at me as I drop to the floor in a daze. "Stop playing around."

Herr Goff digs through the bag, then turns back to Alexander. Sometime during our struggle, Alexander's chair fell over. He curses and bucks against the ropes as Herr Goff hauls the chair upright. I struggle to stand, using the wall for support. Black spots float in front of me. Dizziness washes over me and my legs buckle, dumping me on the floor. Ice runs through my veins as I look helplessly on, desperately trying to find a way to help Alexander before it's too late.

The madman holds up a small vial of clear liquid. "A fitting selection, given your past. Any last words for your dear Lady Lux?"

Alexander's gaze finds mine. He mouths, *I love you*, his eyes soft. I nod, knowing instinctively he doesn't want me to respond in case it triggers Herr Goff, but I hope he can see the love and strength I'm sending him. I promise the Fortunes that if we get out of here alive, I'll tell him I love him every day.

He clamps his lips shut. Herr Goff sighs and pinches Alexander's nose until he gasps. The vial's contents are dumped in unceremoniously, then Herr Goff holds a hand over Alexander's mouth and nose until he swallows.

Our captor carefully replaces the stopper, then puts the vial into his pocket and dusts off his hands. "Excellent. That takes care of—"

Alexander stabs him in the heart, bits of hacked off rope dangling from the wrist holding the knife. Herr Goff looks down in disbelief, then silently crumples to the floor.

Alexander retches to the side, trying to expel the poison. For a second, all I can do is stare in shock. Then I clumsily crawl over and grab the knife, frantically slicing through our bonds.

After I cut the last rope, I try to pull him to his feet. "Hurry, we have to get you to the mender."

He shakes his head as he slumps in the chair. "I can't walk." His body shudders.

Already? A painful lump grows in my throat as my stomach drops. "Then I'll bring them here."

Alexander weakly catches my hand. "It'll take too long. Stay with me."

I steel myself against the wave of despair threatening to overwhelm me. "You're not going to die. You can't. He must have a cure." I wrench away and stumble over to bag by the table, dumping out the contents. Vials and bottles scatter across the stone, but nothing's labeled. I helplessly pick through them, screaming at Herr Goff, "Which one is it? Tell me!"

Alexander slides off the chair to the floor, his skin going gray.

"No, no, no, no, no, no." My heart feels like its being ripped out of my chest as I scramble back to him, my body trembling as I grab his hand in both of mine. "You can't die. We just found each other again. I love you. I've always loved you. Please don't die." I can barely see through my tears.

He gasps, "Promise me. Don't hunt. The Bane. Stay safe."

"You'll keep me safe, but you have to stay with me. Hang on." If Alexander dies, there's nothing on this earth that'll stop me from getting revenge.

I squeeze his hand, using the other to search through the scattered vials, determined to find something, anything, to help him. The flask spins across the floor. *The cinnamon tea! It helps me, but will it save Alexander? Was it the same poison?* It doesn't matter. I know it's safe, but I can't say the same thing about anything else in the bag. There's no other option.

I grab it and race back to him. Alexander's chest is barely moving, his lips blue.

"Drink this. Hurry."

He doesn't respond, even when I shake his shoulder and shout in his ear. Heart thudding, I pour the tea into his mouth, then clamp my hand over his face. "Sorry, sorry, sorry."

Alexander's throat contracts and he swallows the tea. It has to work. It has to. I hold my breath, waiting, hoping. *Please please please please please please.* His eyes fly open and he bolts up with a gasp.

I wrap my arms around him, sobbing with relief. He shudders and puts an arm around my waist

Alexander looks around in a daze. "Did I die?"

"You're going to be all right. You're fine now. You're all right." I'm babbling, but I can't stop. "You're alive. You're going to be all right."

Alexander blinks, then focuses on me, his eyes wide. "You love me."

I give a watery chuckle. "That's what you're worried about?"

"If I'm going to live, yes."

I wipe my tears away, a warmth in my chest. "Yes, you're going to live. Yes, I love you. I've loved you my entire life."

"I'm glad I'm not the only one." He brushes his lips lightly across my temple, then his brow furrows. "Are you all right?"

"Just tired, and I have a headache." I touch the spot where my head hit the wall and wince. "I'll be fine after a nap. Do you feel sick or hot?" I press the back of my hand against his forehead. *No fever or hallucinations.*

"I feel like I've run twenty miles carrying a pack of rocks in the middle of summer, but otherwise I'm fine." He flinches at the sight of Herr Goff's body. "Is he dead?"

"Yes." *And good riddance.* I can't feel pity for the man who almost killed Alexander, no matter how delusional he was.

"It was him or us." His tone is oddly flat. Before I can respond, Alexander says, "Let's go. I don't want to stay here another second."

Alexander and I support each out as we stagger out of the
room and into an unfamiliar hallway, shutting the door
firmly behind us. I shudder at the last glimpse of Herr Goff's
body and the nightmare we're leaving inside. Alexander
sinks to the floor with a groan, those few short steps draining
most of his strength, leaving him pale and panting. The tea
may have saved his life, but he'll still need time and rest to
recover.

It's impossible to leave him, but I tear myself away from
his side and rush down the passage, only pausing when I get
to a window. The familiar forest and gardens make my knees
weak with relief. *We're still in the palace.* I fly down the
stairs, shrieking for help. Staff and guests come running,
more cries going up behind them.

Ignoring the growing hysteria of the crowd, I grab the
arms of the two closest men and try to drag them to the
stairs, frantically babbling about what happened. My
incoherent ramblings seem to break through, and they run up
the steps, calling out instructions to the others.

Alexander has a little more color in his cheeks when we reach him and the knots in my chest loosen. One of the men opens the door and glances in as I avert my eyes. He quickly shuts it with a grimace. Alexander accepts their help without complaint, gritting his teeth as they haul him to his feet, his face tense. It's slow going down the stairs as the two men support Alexander on either side while I hover nearby.

People chatter around us excitedly as I direct them to help Alexander to my room, since it's closer and I'm worried about what Herr Goff might have left in Alexander's suite. I sit on the edge of the bed and cling to Alexander's hand, my stomach churning, watching him for any sign that the poison's still in his system. He closes his eyes and rests against the headboard. The mender comes striding inside, closing the door on the gawkers hovering in the hallway.

He nods his head respectfully to me, "Lady Lux, you—"

"I'm staying right here." I glare at him, leaving no room for argument.

The mender looks at Alexander, who smiles tiredly. "I'd like her to stay."

To my surprise, the mender doesn't argue. He introduces himself as Herr Usinger, then hands us damp towels to clean up while we tell him what happened. I explain Alexander was probably given velvseiess—the same poison I fell victim to five years ago—then recount an abbreviated version of the events while the mender checks Alexander's pulse, eyes, lungs, and reflexes. Alexander chimes in with details about how Herr Goff caught him off guard in his room and what happened while I was still unconscious. Herr Usinger raises his eyebrows when I explain about the cinnamon tea, but otherwise doesn't react to our story.

After he finishes his examination, he wipes off his hands

and smiles. "You're a very lucky young man." He turns to me. "Do you still have the cinnamon tea they gave you? It might help me confirm what poison was used on your beau."

My cheeks heat as Alexander grins. I gesture to the box on the vanity and say he's welcome to it. The mender advises Alexander to rest for the next few hours and he'll be back this evening to check on him, then he leaves us alone.

I lock the door and wedge the chair against it before climbing into the bed, nestling against Alexander's side. His muscles relax as he rests his head on mine, lacing our fingers together. A quiet descends and wraps around us, protecting us from the rest of the world. The normalcy and happiness of this moment is surreal after the terror we just went through.

All at once, everything that happened crashes down on me. Ice runs through me, my pulse pounding in my ears as bile rises in my throat. *I thought I'd lost him. He almost died.* If Alexander wasn't here, I'd crumble into a sobbing heap. But I can't. I need to keep myself together so he won't worry about me. After all, I was just scared. He's the one who actually got hurt. *There's nothing for me to cry about now.* I swallow hard and clench the hand he isn't holding into a fist so he won't see it shaking.

He presses a kiss against my forehead. "It's all right, sweetheart. I'm fine. I've got you."

His sweet concern breaks through my last defense. I bury my face against his shirt, tears streaming down my cheeks, my body trembling. The terror of almost losing him will haunt me for the rest of my life. Only his reassuring warmth against me convinces me he's still alive. He shudders and I wrap my arm tighter around him, hoping he's finding the same comfort in my touch that I find in his.

I don't know how long we lay together, ignoring the

outside world, trying to come to terms with what happened. Exhausted and lulled by the heat from Alexander's body, I eventually drift into a light doze, listening to his steady heartbeat.

Sometime later, I stir with a yawn. Alexander's eyes are closed, his breathing deep and even. I snuggle closer, brushing my fingers gently through his hair and tracing a finger down his jawline. He murmurs and tugs me tighter against his side, nuzzling my neck.

"You smell good," he says sleepily.

I laugh. "You like the smell of dust and sweat and Fortunes-know-what else?"

"I like you, here with me."

My heart flutters. "That doesn't mean I smell good."

"You do to me."

His hand caresses my cheek, my breath catching at the love in his dreamy eyes. Alexander presses a kiss to my lips, his touch gentle, making me feel cherished and precious. I close my eyes, savoring his touch, knowing how close I came to losing him making it all that much sweeter.

Alexander tucks a strand of hair behind my ear, a line forming between his brows. "I almost lost you again."

The man never thinks of himself. I mentally shake my head. "You seem to forget who was poisoned this time. But you won't lose me ever again, just like I won't lose you. I'll make sure of it." I brush my lips against his. "Mayhap now that we're tied for saving each other, we can call it a draw and move on to something less dangerous. Like cliff diving, or teaching Luther how to juggle fire."

"Done and done. I'm going to need a very long vacation after this party." Alexander's eyes droop, then he jerks awake.

I hesitantly sit up, biting my lip. "Do you want to sleep more? I could go."

"No." He tugs my hand until I lay down again, then he rests his head against mine with a sigh. "I'm sorry, but I'll worry if you leave right now. We don't know where the Bane is."

The Bane. Anger flares in my chest as the pieces fall into place. "But we know who it is. Lady Goethe." *I was so distracted by Lord Wentzel, I never seriously considered her.* I force myself to admit, *I didn't want it to be her.*

He stiffens. "Are you sure?"

"It all fits. She never liked you, but she's paid a lot of attention to you, including noticing you and Aliz together. And she's the one who gave me the cinnamon tea after she saw one of my spells. She must've told Herr Goff about it." I shudder. "I wonder why your reaction to the velvseiess was worse than mine?" There's no doubt that I almost died after accidentally eating those poisoned chocolates, but it took hours for the symptoms to start, and I eventually recovered without having her tea to counter its effects.

He furrows his brow. "Perhaps this was a concentrated dose? Or she wasn't as good at making it back then? I don't think we'll ever know."

I stand, my jaw clenched. "We have to tell Aliz and Luther so they can arrest her. I'm sure there'll be evidence in her room or at her estate, so it won't just be our word against hers."

He squeezes my hand, worry shining in his eyes. "Be careful. And hurry back."

I can't resist pressing a quick kiss against his lips. "I will."

There's still a crowd lingering outside my room, but

Luther and Aliz aren't there. Nobody can tell me where they are, and they keep pressing me for details about what happened. I lock the door so they can't disturb Alexander, then leave them behind. The Fortunes must finally be on my side, because it only takes a few minutes to find Luther by the entryway.

"Luther, I—" I stop at the look on his face, dread filling my stomach. "What?"

He says grimly, "Aliz is missing."

I grab his arm, my pulse thrumming. "Where's Lady Goethe's room?"

His brow furrows. "What does—"

"Trust me. We have to find her right now."

Luther catches my urgency and shouts out an order that sends a maid and footman running our way. The maid leads us to Lady Goethe's room while I briefly fill Luther in on what happened to Alexander and me, and who Lady Goethe really is. By the time we reach the second floor, Luther's face is white with rage and fear.

At the room, the maid fumbles with a key. Luther shoves her aside and rams the door with his shoulder, splintering the wood off its hinges.

Nobody's inside. Luther curses as the maid cowers in the hallway. I run over to the wardrobe and fling the doors open to find it empty. "She's taken off with Aliz." I turn to Luther. "How long ago did Aliz go missing?"

"Nobody's seen her since last night." He runs out of the room while I try to keep up. "They'll be traveling by carriage. We can catch them on the road."

"Which way did she go?"

His brow wrinkles, his face taut. "She'll be heading toward her estate in Eaglan."

My stomach knots. "Or she might have another plan."

Luther skids to a stop and glares at me. "I can't just stay here. We have to find Aliz."

"I know, but be smart about it. Send out a few spare riders in other directions in case she went somewhere else." I squeeze his hand. "I want to find her, too."

He nods, then takes off running again, shouting orders at whatever staff members are in is path. Word spreads quickly. When I reach my room the crowd in the hallway is gone, moved on to the newest crisis.

Alexander looks up, his smile turning to concern. "Did she already escape?"

"It's worse than that. She has Aliz." My muscles are tense as I grab a small pack out of the bottom of my wardrobe and start stuffing items into it. *Spare clothes. Cloak. Toothbrush. Money.*

He eyes me warily. "What are you doing?"

"I have to go after her." Food from the kitchen. A blanket? No, I'll stop at inns or sleep in my cloak.

Alexander climbs up from the bed—then falls back down with a gasp, his face gray. My heart leaps into my throat and I rush over to his side.

He waves me down with a grumble. "I'm fine. Just a moment of lightheadedness. Give me a moment and I'll go pack."

I put my hands on my hips and glare at him. "That tea saved your life, but it wasn't a miracle cure. You need to rest. Regain your strength and then follow me. I'm sure the mender will only keep you in bed for a day or two."

"You're running off into danger again. I can help." Alexander struggles to sit up.

My heart lurches and I gently press my hand to his chest

to stop him. "Not until you've recovered, which will take time." I don't want to leave him. It's tearing me up to go when he's so vulnerable and I won't be here to watch over him. But I can't leave Aliz in the hands of the Bane if there's even the slimmest chance my going will make a difference.

I take a deep breath. "I'm just going to find Aliz, nothing else. Believe me, I have no desire to see the Bane ever again." At his skeptical look, I raise my hand and say, "I promise I won't confront the Bane by myself. I'll wait for you or let Luther handle it." I lift an eyebrow. "Am I lying?"

His lips press together into a grim line. "No, but I still don't want you to go."

My heart softens and I sit next to him on the bed, taking his hand. "I don't want to go either, but Aliz needs us. We have the best chance of finding her. Nobody knows more about the Bane than us. And the Bane was fond of me." My stomach churns, her betrayal leaving a bitter taste in my mouth. "I don't know if it will help me find Aliz, but I have to try. The Bane may have let something slip that can help us find her."

His eyebrows draw together as he reluctantly nods. Alexander grips my shoulders and pulls me close, his lips crashing onto mine, desperation and urgency flowing through us. We've been through too much to be saying goodbye already, but we don't have a choice.

He cradles my face in his hands and presses his forehead against mine. "Wait for me to find you before you confront the Bane."

"I will," I promise.

"And don't forget to take your boots. You'll need them." The worry's still in his eyes, but he smiles. "Go."

My chest is heavy as fight off tears. "I love you." I kiss

him one last time, then grab my boots and dash out the door, leaving my heart with him.

22

The palace is complete chaos, with people running through the hallways and shouts echoing off the stones. Nobody pays any attention to me when I burst into the kitchen and grab bread, fruit, cheese, and a wineskin I fill with water from a pitcher.

A line of horses are outside the barn in various stages of being saddled. I hurriedly make friends with a mare by feeling her an apple, then leap into the saddle and take off down the road as the stable hands yell behind me.

When I reach the crossroads, I pause, cursing myself for never studying maps of the area. Taking my best guess, I point the horse left.

Now that the shock has worn off, I disagree with Luther that the Bane will retreat to her estate in Eaglan. Herr Goff said she wanted Alexander to follow them to rescue Aliz, and she wouldn't risk exposing her identity by luring Alexander to her home. No, she'll have something else prepared. Someplace closer. And she'll be expecting us.

As dusk falls, I stop at a large inn to exchange my

borrowed horse for a fresh one and ask if they've seen Aliz or the Bane come through recently. One of the men in the yard mentions a carriage that stopped to buy supper late last night, but he didn't see the passengers. Sending a prayer to the Fortunes that it was the Bane, I give him a coin to pass the message on to Merchwood and anyone who follows me, then continue my chase.

My body's already protesting the long hours in the saddle on top of its other recent abuses. I grit my teeth and push on. When night settles, I slow the horse to a walk until the moon rises, then speed up to a trot. I curse the slow pace even though I can't risk the horse going lame from a hole or other hidden hazard on the road. Any delay at this point could be deadly to Aliz.

The hours blur together. There are only a small number of roads in good enough shape and large enough for a carriage, which helps limit my choices. My legs went numb long ago, and every muscle in my body aches, but I can't stop. I doze in the saddle, or snatch a few hours when I stop at an inn to change horses and buy food. Sometimes there are reports of a carriage with mysterious passengers, other times I push on with the blind hope that I'm going in the right direction. Keeping my promise to Alexander, I always send word of my current location and direction back to Merchwood so he can easily follow my trail.

I'm trying to remember if it's the third or fourth day when my horse stumbles into an inn's yard at dawn. Half-asleep, I dismount, swaying on my feet, and absentmindedly ask my questions about the carriage, my attention already wandering to the bed waiting for me inside.

The man scratches his head. "Naw, I haven't seen anything like that."

A woman carrying a bucket pipes up. "Do you mean Lady Danz's carriage?"

My stomach flips and the exhaustion vanishes. "Perhaps? She would be traveling with a woman about my age." I quickly describe them both, my pulse speeding up as she nods along.

"I didn't see them, but the first one sounds like Lady Danz. Her carriage drove by a few hours ago. She lives somewhere deep in Outerwood." She gestures to the forest.

"Do you know where?" When she shakes her head, I press, "Does anyone? I need to talk to her urgently. I can pay for a guide."

The woman glances at the trees and makes a warding sign. "That wood is unnatural. Only Lady Danz goes into it. Everyone else avoids it."

I frown as my stomach twists. "Surely there must be hunters, or trackers, or woodcutters who know it?"

She shrugs nervously. "Nobody I know will set foot inside, but I'll ask around for you."

I thank her and arrange to meet again in a few hours, then drag myself inside the inn and arrange for a room. The uneasiness on the woman's face keeps flashing through my mind as I dump my bag in the corner by the bed, then gulp the last of the musty water in my wineskin, trying in vain to clear the road dust from my throat. I look longingly at the bed and sigh, then trudge out to visit the few shops in the village.

Everyone has the same story. Nobody who goes into Outerwood comes back except Lady Danz. Most say her name with fear, making a warding sign whenever she's mentioned. There are a few whispers that she's a witch and her dark powers made the wood unnatural. Others dismiss the rumors as nonsense, saying Outerwood has always been dangerous. In every case, everyone warns me away from the woods, sometimes with stories about hearing the screams and moans of the dying echoing through the trees at night.

Thoroughly unnerved, I drag my body back to the inn to see if the helpful woman has found a guide. Whatever luck the Fortunes granted me in my journey has run out. She gives me a mountain of apologies, but she couldn't find someone to lead me through the woods. Unsurprised, I thank her, my shoulders slumped.

Before I can go back inside, a group of twenty heavily armed riders comes galloping up the road and turns into the yard. When I spot Alexander among the group, my heart lifts, a warm glow forming in my chest. He's still too pale, and there's a tightness around his eyes, but he sits his horse easily and keeps a firm grip on the reins. When he only nods at me, the glow dims and my stomach knots, but I firmly push the worry away. *He must be exhausted after that long ride. And he's still dealing with the aftereffects of being poisoned.*

Luther spots me and jumps down from his mount. "Is she here?"

"No, but I don't think she's far." I update him, ending with a warning. "Lady Goethe will expect us. We need to be careful."

"Of course," he brushes me off. "We'll rest briefly, then follow the road to her house and capture her. We'll have Aliz back before dawn." Luther strides away, calling out instructions and sending a man into the inn to arrange food and rooms for the group.

I hurry over to where Alexander's unsaddling his horse, my steps slowing at the blank expression on his face. My hand clutches my mother's locket as I smile brightly. "I'm so glad to see you. Did you get my messages?"

He seems intent on looking everywhere except at me as he fiddles with a buckle. "Yes. They were very helpful."

Why is he acting so strange? If it was anyone but Alexander, I'd be worried I'd offended him somehow. I move closer, wetting my lips, then smile shyly. "I missed you." I touch his hand and he winces. I jerk back, a chill running through me. "What's wrong?"

"Nothing. I'm just tired." He rubs a hand across his face. "I'll see you in a few hours."

He walks away, leaving me staring after him, an empty pit in my stomach.

Though my body's desperate for rest, it's impossible to sleep with Alexander's odd behavior plaguing my mind. I toss and turn in the bed, going over our brief interaction, trying to figure out what changed between our goodbye at Merchwood and his arrival here, but I can't come up with any answers.

I finally admit defeat and go down to the common room. I join a few of Luther's group at a table, catching up on their journey from Merchwood and their plans to rescue Aliz. Luther may be prone to mischief, but he'd never be careless with Aliz's life. The men he brought with him are all capable and experienced, including some that fought in the wars.

I'm underwhelmed. From all their talk, you'd think the Bane's a helpless old woman instead of a wily and treacherous assassin. They're confident that they can just walk up to the Bane's home, storm in, and get Aliz back by force. There's no plan to send scouts ahead or figure out if Aliz is even inside before they break down the doors.

After the fifth smirk and chuckle at one of my questions, I'm fuming. They aren't taking me seriously! Never mind that I'm the one who tracked the Bane here and found out she's in Outerwood. You'd think that would earn me a little respect, but apparently, I'm supposed to happily step aside and stay quiet now that they're here.

The men continue to talk around me. I silently seethe as I shovel stew into my mouth. Between my exhaustion and days of inhaling road dust it's tasteless mush, but I know I'll need the energy later.

Alexander comes down the stairs and our eyes lock. He looks away and sits alone at a table across the room.

I glare at him as I scrape a limp carrot out of my bowl, my teeth clenched. And now he's avoiding me. After everything we've been through, he's running away. You'd think he'd learn his lesson from five years ago, but now he wants to throw a tantrum and not tell me why. My knuckles are white as I clench my spoon and my foot tapping furiously under the table. My pulse beats a pounding rhythm in my head as the minutes tick by.

I'm done with this. I shove my bowl aside and stomp over to his table. "We need to talk."

Alexander stares at something over my shoulder. "There's nothing to talk about."

"No? How about how you're suddenly acting like a stranger? Or how you can't even look me in the eyes?" I lean down, lowering my voice. "If you don't want me to shout at you in front of the entire inn, you'd better come outside. Now."

His eyes snap to mine and he knows I'll do it. Alexander pushes back from the table and stalks out of the inn with me right on his heels. His back is rigid as he marches around the building and past the kitchen gardens, only stopping when he reaches the low wall at the edge of the property.

Alexander folds his arms, his eyes hard. "You wanted to talk, so talk."

I open my mouth to tear into him—then close it. Instead, I study him. Alexander may always know when I'm lying, but he's not the only one with insight. I've spent countless hours with him. His habits and moods used to be as familiar to me as breathing. And right now, the tightness around his eyes and tense stance tell me he's hurting.

Putting my irritation aside, I step closer and wrap my arms around him, resting my head on his shoulder. He stiffens, then shudders and the tension drains out of him. He pulls me closer, his head resting on mine. The wind gently curls around us as the sun bathes us in its warmth.

After his muscles relax, I lean back, keeping my arms tight around him. "Please tell me what's wrong."

His green eyes fill with pain. "I—I shouldn't be with you anymore."

The stabbing pain in my chest steals my breath. It's a devastating blow that threatens to knock me to my knees, but I force myself not to react. *He said shouldn't. Not can't, or won't, or doesn't want to be. Shouldn't.* I've never pinned so many hopes on a single word, but I refuse to believe his feelings have changed unless he tells me differently. I swallow hard, trying to keep my voice even. "Why?"

He gently pulls away. It takes everything me not to stop him, not to hold him close and refuse to let go. My arms slowly fall to my side, feeling the loss of him. Alexander reaches into his coat and pulls out a piece of folded parchment, the black wax seal broken.

He thrusts it at me. "This came after you left. A message from Hartwin."

Something about the way he eyes the parchment makes me hesitate. Hartwin's busy chasing down Lord Wentzel. What information could he possibly have to make Alexander act like this?

Alexander shoves it closer. "Read it."

I put my hands behind my back, my stomach twisting. "What does it say?"

"It's the information you asked for. About me." At my confused look, he snaps, "To blackmail me."

My shoulders relax and the weight on my chest disappears. *Burn it, I'd forgotten all about that. That's all?* My lips twitch. "It doesn't look like very much. I always knew you were honorable, but I thought you'd have a little more fun than that."

Alexander glares at me. "Did you really need more? Wasn't almost killing you enough?"

I immediately sober. "I'm sorry. I shouldn't joke about it. But Alexander, I asked Hartwin to get that information on my second day at Merchwood because I was worried you'd stop me from finding the Bane. I'd honestly forgotten I asked him to do it. And I don't care what he found, or even if there's anything to find. I don't need to read it. I know you and I trust you. You always do whatever's best for everyone. That's one of the reasons I love you so much."

His arm drops, his hands clenching into fists. "You shouldn't be forced to love a murderer."

I gasp, my insides going cold. "You're not!" My heart aching for him, I reach out to Alexander, but halt when he flinches.

Alexander's shoulders slump as his eye goes blank. "I killed Herr Goff." His voice is flat.

"To save me! If you hadn't, you would've died—" I choke on the word. Swallowing down the lump in my throat, I say, "And then he would've killed me, or dragged me here for her to do it." I shudder.

"But you were only in danger because of me." Alexander grips his hair in his fists as he paces in front of me with tight, jerky steps. "All I do is hurt you. I gave you those chocolates. Then you're nearly strangled. That man kidnapped you and was going to kill you. Because of me. Because I love you."

I grab his arm, halting his steps. "That was the Bane's fault, not yours." I put a hand on his cheek and wait until he looks at me. "You know I'm not lying."

"No, but you could be lying to yourself." He eyes me, hope warring with doubt.

Burning stubborn fool. I fight off a grin. *Fortunes, I love him.* "You haven't seen me in five years. How do you know when I'm lying?"

Alexander says warily, "Because I know you."

I raise an eyebrow. "But I've changed in five years."

"You have, but you're still you."

"And you're still you," My tone leaves no room for doubt. "Trust me when I say that if you'd had any other option, you would've spared Herr Goff. But he didn't give you a choice. And you did what you had to do to save us both. Nobody can blame you for that, including you."

Some of the anguish leaves his eyes, but he's not fully convinced. Unfortunately, only time will heal that wound. As much as I wish there was a way to magically make him see it as clearly as I do, all I can do is keep reminding him of the truth until he believes it too.

I sway on my feet, the world going gray and dim. Alexander grabs my shoulders to steady me. I shake my head, the moment of lightheadedness passing.

"Sorry, I just need to sit for a moment."

"You need more than a moment," he says firmly. "You need to rest for at least a day or two."

I wrinkle my nose and grin. "Are you using my words against me?"

"It was good advice then, and it's good advice now."

He's not wrong. I'll be more burden than help if I fall asleep in the middle of Aliz's rescue. "Two hours," I counter. "A day's too long."

"Three, if you actually sleep," Alexander returns. "That's my final offer."

"Done and done." I chuckle. "I don't think I can stay awake if I tried."

Alexander keeps an arm around my waist as he helps me inside and up the stairway. I could probably make it on my own, but it's sweet that he wants to fuss over me and I've missed him the past few days.

When I get to my room, I press up on my toes and kiss him, loving the way his heart beats faster, just like mine. I keep my eyes locked on him as I close the door, a ridiculous smile on my face, feeling like I could float away. Not bothering to undress, I kick off my boots and collapse on the bed. I glance at the door and frown. *No footsteps?*

I drag myself to the door and open it, unsurprised to find Alexander leaning against the wall. "Standing guard?"

He frowns. "You should be sleeping."

"So should you."

"I'd rather make sure someone isn't going to kidnap you, or poison you, or have some other disaster happen to you." He groans with a hint of his old humor. "Every time I leave you alone, trouble finds you."

I wink at him with a mischievous smile. "Then you'd better keep a close eye on me." I tilt my head toward the room. "Come in. The bed's plenty big enough for both of us."

His head draws back, his eyes wide. "Carina! I can't stay in your room. Think of the gossip."

"I've learned I don't care much what the telltales say about me. And it won't be the first time we've slept in the same bed."

To my everlasting amusement, he blushes, the tips of his ears flaming red. "We were children."

"That's odd. On my last day at Merchwood, I seem to recall laying in a bed with someone snoring in my ear." I laugh as he splutters. "I can't sleep if you're standing outside my door. So. Either come in, or leave." I fold my arms and quirk an eyebrow at him.

Alexander glances around the empty hallway, then ducks into my room with a curse. Grinning, I lock the door, then gleefully crawl back into bed as he stands awkwardly in the corner of the room.

I yawn as I wrap my arms around the pillow. "You can sleep on the floor, or you can sleep in the bed. Your choice. See you in a few hours." My eyes slide closed and I drop into unconsciousness with a happy sigh.

Voices in the hallway jolt me awake. I look out the window, relieved that the sun's just slipping below the horizon. My hand reaches out, but the other side of the bed is empty. My stomach twists, thinking he left, until I spot his hand resting on the edge of the bed.

Alexander's stretched out on the floor on his back, his other arm flung over his head. I cover his hand with mine. When he smiles in his sleep, a warmth blooms in my chest. Sleep has softened the lines on his face, but the dark shadows under his eyes and pale skin confirm he's still recovering from the poison.

Alexander stirs, squinting at the soft light streaming in from the window.

I grin down at him. "I see you decided the floor was more comfortable than the bed."

He stretches with a groan. "It was in self-defense. I thought if I slept here, it was less likely that your brother would hunt me down and strangle me."

Since when does he care what Cristoph thinks? "Aww, don't be scared. I'll protect you from him. Besides, he has no idea that we're here."

Alexander scrubs a hand across his face as he yawns. "You may not worry about him, but I'd rather not give him a reason to hate me since he's technically your guardian." Before I can delve into this sudden concern about my brother's feelings toward him, Alexander climbs to his feet and glances out the window. "Luther's probably left by now. It'll be hard to find them in the woods."

My stomach knots as I sit up in the bed. "Do you want to wait for them to come back?"

He shakes his head. "Aliz is my friend too, and I want to help her. I'd rather you stay here, but I know that's not an option."

My shoulders relax. I can't blame him for wishing I'd stay out of danger, but knowing he won't try to convince me makes me love him impossibly more. "Good. Then let's go. We have an assassin to stop."

As eager as I am to set out immediately, we pause to put together a pack with some supplies and a rough map of the area that the innkeeper drew at Alexander's request. Outerwood is a large blank spot taunting us from the center of parchment, surrounded by a smattering of small villages. It seems impossible that we'll find wherever the Bane's holding Aliz with so much ground to search.

Shouts come from the yard. The inn's door bursts open and Luther's group staggers into the common room. My heart sinks at the destruction wrought from a few hours in Outerwood. There's only ten of the original twenty, and they're in terrible shape. Every one of them is nursing injuries and two of them of them are being carried. Luther's leaning on a man's shoulder as he limps inside, a bloodied cloth held to a nasty cut on his head.

We rush over to him, my stomach twisting. "What happened? Were you attacked?"

Luther drops on a bench by the table with a curse. "It's the forest. The whole thing's a death trap. We'd followed the road for less than a mile when it started. First, the ground fell away beneath our feet into a pit of spikes. That's how we lost Oskar and Marzell. Then Volker fell in the bog with its creeping vines that tangle your feet and drag you under. And all the time there were those burning birds always circling overhead and taunting with their cries. Sounded like human screams. It's enough to make a person go mad. But I thought we'd make it until the fog came." He shudders. "Crept over us unnoticed until it was almost too late. Poisonous. Thank the Fortunes Engel was scouting ahead. He managed to shout out a warning and saved us. We barely escaped before the fires started."

A man behind him with a charred shirtsleeve and angry red burns on his neck grunts. "Combustible gas pockets. It builds up in the ground until something sets it off. Probably our torches. But it was too burning dark to see in there without them."

Luther buries his head in his hands. The remaining men slouch off to attend to their injuries or disappear into the corners. Nobody will meet my eyes, keeping their backs turned to us, their shoulders hunched. There's no rallying cry or mutterings about going back into the forest.

I tug Alexander away from Luther and lower my voice. "They've all given up, and Luther's too injured to go back into Outerwood."

He nods gravely. "Are you still determined to go? You've seen what can happen."

I lift my chin, my chest tight. "Yes. Are you?"

Alexander gives me a grim smile. "Where you go, I go. But I don't think we can capture the Bane without more people. She's crafty, and she'll have the advantage."

I hate the Bane, but I love Aliz more. "Getting Aliz

home is the only thing that matters. We find her and leave. Hartwin can deal with the Bane later."

Alexander looks intently into my eyes, then presses a kiss to my forehead. He grabs our supplies and we slip out of the inn unnoticed.

The forest looks even more ominous at night. I grip his hand as we walk down the road, taking the turn that leads into Outerwood. Calling it a lane is generous given the drooping branches that brush against the ground and the knee-high weeds blanketing the route. The moon hasn't risen yet and the feeble lantern only illuminates a few feet in front of us, making me feel like we're being swallowed by the darkness.

Alexander stops after a few minutes and lowers the lantern to the ground.

I twist the end of my braid around my hand, keeping a wary eye on the shadowy trees and anything hiding in them. "What are you doing?"

"Looking for any signs that a carriage or horse came this way. The Bane wouldn't go through all those hazards Luther talked about, so there must be a safer path."

Impressed, I crouch down next to him and scrutinize the path. I'm not sure what I'm looking for, but I hope something will pop out. Unfortunately, all the dirt looks the same, and there's no signpost saying 'This way to the Bane's hideout' around. "Wouldn't Luther have checked for that?"

"Not if they were in a hurry." Alexander points to the side of the road where the soil's softer. "There. See that hoofprint by the tree? She must've hidden the carriage somewhere and continued on horseback."

I bite my lip as I stand, my chest in knots. What did she do to Aliz to make her easier to carry on horseback?

Alexander squeezes my hand. "We'll find her."

"I'm putting us in danger again." Tears sting my eyes and I swallow hard. "I'm sorry. But I don't know what else to do! We can't abandon Aliz. But I would die if anything happened to you."

He wraps an arm around me, pulling me tight against his side. "We won't leave her with the Bane."

I grip his shirt and look up at him beseechingly. "Promise me you won't die."

He chuckles. "I promise. Coming close once was more than enough."

Some of the knots in my chest loosen and I manage a wobbly smile. "Aren't you going to make me promise too?"

"No. Because I won't let you." He kisses my temple. "Let's keep going. And keep an eye out for those traps."

We follow the horse's path, Alexander taking the lead and holding the lantern low so he can see if the trail veers off anywhere. He moves carefully, testing each step to avoid triggering another trap. When we pass the pit Luther mentioned, I keep my eyes firmly averted, my heart pounding. The trail soon veers away from the road and deeper into the trees, leaving every trace of civilization behind in the dark.

After an hour, Alexander curses. "The ground's too hard here. I can't see any more hoofprints." He glances over his shoulder with a stern, "Don't move," then creeps forward, slowly swinging the lantern from side-to-side.

The moonlight casts strange shadows in the trees, tricking me into seeing twisted creatures behind every trunk, their glowing eyes watching us as they prepare to attack. Though the night air is warm, goosebumps break out over my skin and I shiver.

A soft breeze caresses me, and my shoulders relax as a familiar scent tickles my nose.

My brow furrows. "Do you smell that? Cinnamon."

He calls back, "Cinnamon trees can't grow here. It's not warm enough."

"And yet, cinnamon." I breathe deeply, trying to locate the source. Somewhere off to the left and behind us. I turn, squinting into the darkness. A glint of white. Why does that seem familiar? My mind nags at me until I remember what Herr Goff told me about the Roma lining their roads with white stones so they could see them in the moonlight.

My pulse speeds up and I grin as the first ray of hope breaks through the gloom. "It's this way."

We creep through the forest, following the white stones glowing in the moonlight. The rocks are a little smaller than my fist and placed about fifteen feet apart. The path isn't perfect, with some scattered or covered with foliage, forcing us to frequently halt and scan the area until we can spot the next marker.

At one stop, Alexander reaches out to push a bush aside and I yank his hand back, my heart leaping into my throat.

"Don't touch that! It's nightshade."

He raises his eyebrows. "Thinking of planting a garden?"

I grimace, my lips twisting. "You might've noticed I became a bit obsessed with the Bane over the past few years, including all the poisons she's used. Nightshade was one of them. You could get sick if you touch it."

"Ah." His fist clenches, but he keeps his tone light. "Please feel free to stop me from stumbling into any other dangerous plants." Alexander points to the right. "There's another stone."

We spend another hour zigzagging through the forest. I spot several more lethal plants along the way: foxglove, hemlock, wood spurge, and the infamous Black Bryony. A fog crawls through the trees and brushes along the edge our trail, making the hair on the back of my neck stand up. We keep a wary eye on it, but it stays low to the ground and doesn't cross our path. We hurry our steps, noting the lightening eastern sky. Dawn's barely breaking the horizon as we reach a large meadow.

I rub my eyes, convinced I must be hallucinating. "That can't be real."

24

I expected the Bane's hideout to be a cave, or maybe a cottage that's half-falling down from neglect. Instead, it looks exactly like a giant gingerbread house.

Sitting in the middle of the meadow is a three-story building dripping with bright trim and delicate wooden lacework. The dark brown paneling is covered in lines, with random patterns of triangles, dots, and squares painted in every shade of yellow and green. Columns are spiraling rainbows and the pastel window panes glint in the light. Even the path leading up to the bright orange door is made of alternating red, purple, and pink cobblestones.

Alexander and I huddle in the forest's shadows as we study it, making sure we're hidden from the windows. The clashing colors and chaotic patterns make me queasy as I try to take them all in.

I make a face. "If I didn't already know she's insane, the house would prove it. Where do you think Aliz is being held?"

"If she's in there, probably the basement. Or the Bane

could be keeping her with her as a hostage."

If? My stomach knots as my pulse speeds up. I'd never considered the possibility that Aliz could be somewhere else. "Do you think she's here?" I bite my lip, unsure what answer I'm hoping for.

He thinks it over, then nods. "Probably. The Bane wouldn't risk having her somewhere where she couldn't easily check on her." He lifts a shoulder. "But if she has another partner, Aliz might be with them."

I shake my head. "Having anyone else besides Herr Goff would be too big of a risk."

"But we can't know that." Alexander holds up his hand before I can argue. "You're most likely right, but it's safer to assume there's someone else inside, even if they're just staff who don't know what's going on. We need to be careful if we're all going to come out—" Alexander clears his throat.

Come out alive. I square my shoulders, pushing aside my fears. "We're not splitting up."

"Agreed. Let's see if there's another way in. Start on the bottom and work our way up?"

I give a terse nod. Before he can move, I grab his shirt and press my lips against his, melting against him. He crushes me against his chest, our desperation and fear adding an urgency to our kiss. Every nerve is on fire and all I can think of is how much I love him and couldn't bear to lose him again. We cling to each other a minute longer, then reluctantly pull apart.

Alexander tucks a loose strand of hair behind my ear, his hand softly trailing down my cheek. "Stay close."

We slip through the trees and circle the house, examining it for any sign of a cellar door or other entrance where we might sneak in unnoticed. There are plenty of windows, but none look like they open. No side doors or panels, not even a crawlspace.

We exchange a grim look. I tilt my head toward the front door and raise my eyebrows. He grimaces, then creeps to the entrance with me close on his heels. I pull out the dagger Alexander gave me, my hand shaking. Alexander holds his sword at the ready. The door swings open silently, confirming the decor inside the house matches the outside. A large seating area with a cozy-looking settee next to the empty fireplace is in front of us. Off to the right and through an archway is a bright kitchen, and a formal dining room with a yellow table and eight orange chairs sits to the left. Nothing about the normal, though boldly colorful, home would hint there's a dungeon or cell in the manor. *But the Bane wouldn't bring Aliz here without being prepared.*

Alexander squeezes my hand, then slips into the kitchen. If I ignore the eye-watering decorations, it reminds me of Wittrow, with its long counters against two walls and the ovens built into the third. There are cannisters and jars scattered across the surfaces and on shelves. Dried herbs hang from the ceiling, but there's no fresh produce in sight or lingering aromas that would hint at any recent meals.

What appears to be the cellar door is set into an angled section of the floor next to the longest counter, a large nested iron ring in the center. Alexander wraps his hand around the ring and cocks his head. I brace my feet, then nod.

He yanks the door open and jumps back.

Nothing.

Dank, chilly air drifts out of the opening. Alexander ducks his head inside. I bite the inside of my cheek, my heart pounding. He holds up a hand to me, then cautiously starts down the perilously steep stairs set against the stone wall.

A few feet down, he crouches, listening, peering into the darkness. I inch forward, hovering on the top stair, my heart pounding.

Alexander whirls around, his eyes wide. "Back! Back!"

He shoves me, sending me sprawling on the floor. A panel slides shut across the entrance, sealing him inside.

My heart stops and ice fills my veins. I scream, "Alexander!" and pound my fists and dagger on the wood, frantically to break through, but the heavy cover doesn't move. "Alexander!"

I hold my breath, pressing my ear against the door. Silence.

A roaring fills my mind. I fly around the kitchen, knocking jars off the counter and dumping contents out of drawers, searching for some kind of trigger to release the lock. Flour dust fills the air. Beans spill across the floor. Choking on tears, I half-crawl into the ovens, feeling for a hidden lever or switch. Bile burns the back of my throat. I scrape every corner, desperate, needing to find a way to get to Alexander.

As the precious minutes tick off, my frenzy eventually slows until I finally drop to the floor, my shoulders slumped and chest hollow.

Wrapping my arms around my legs, I grip my locket and take a deep breath. My dagger didn't damage the wood, so it must be something extremely strong. I haven't seen anything like an axe that can break through it. But there must be a way to get Alexander out. I grit my teeth. The Bane will know. She couldn't have overpowered Alexander, so she must be somewhere else in the house. And I might be able to find something to open that panel while I'm searching for her.

I dig through the mess on the floor until I find another knife and tuck it into my waistband, then creep out of the kitchen. There's no sign of anyone on the first floor, just a few more tidy rooms full of garish decorations. A second-floor bedroom shows the first signs of life, with a steaming teapot left next to an open book on the bedside table, and a pair of muddy boots still drying by the door. My hand trembles as I hold the dagger out in front of me. I slink along the wall toward the open door at the end of the hallway.

The parlor is richly appointed in surprisingly subdued shades of blue that seem dull after the candy-colored explosion throughout the rest of the home. A rug the color of the night sky covers most of the floor, while the walls are papered in light blue fabric that peeks between large tapestries of white birds in flight against a sapphire sky. The only furniture is a pair of upholstered chairs and a low table set off to the side.

I almost miss the small door tucked in the corner.

25

The Bane's leaning over a worktable, a long leather smock covering her dress. Her cloak's thrown over a corner of the table, the rest of the surface littered with a variety of small bottles and boxes. Thousands more line the floor-to-ceiling shelves on all four of the windowless walls, the only light coming from two lanterns hanging above the table.

Without looking, she cheerfully calls out, "Close the door, dear, and give me a moment. This mixture can be tricky."

It's hard not to gape at her. Ever since I figured out that she's the Bane, every moment we spent together, every word spoken, has taken on a different meaning. But she's acting like we're still friends. That everything she's done—everything she's done to *me*, that she was going to do to Alexander and Aliz—doesn't matter.

My chest tight, I force my mind to focus on the present instead of the past. Alexander's trapped. I could probably get him out eventually, but only the Fortunes know where Aliz is and if she's hurt. I need to capture the Bane alive so she can tell us how to save Aliz.

Keeping the dagger up, I close the door and press my back against it, ensuring she can't get past me. My stomach's jittery and my breath is coming too fast. If it comes down to a fight, I'm not sure who will win. The Bane's crafty and a survivor. I don't know how much of what I've seen over the past few weeks is real, and how much she was playing the harmless older woman to keep suspicion from falling on her. But the kitchen knife in my waistband is a reassuring reminder that I have a few surprises of my own.

She turns around with a smile, wiping her hands on a stained cloth. "How do you like my home? I was cleaning most of the day to get it fit for company. Dust, dust, dust everywhere. It's too much work for one old woman to keep up. I really should've abandoned this place years ago, but it's my favorite."

"Where's Aliz?" I hate how my voice shakes.

The Bane lifts an eyebrow and tuts. "No concern about Lord von Bron? Do you really think I'm foolish enough to trap any intruders instead of simply getting rid of them?"

My heart stops. I thought Alexander would be safe until I could get him out, but what if I'm wrong? I grip the dagger tighter, my palm slick with sweat. "I'm here alone."

She gives me a disappointed look. "Let's not lie to each other, dear. I know all about *Kangan* Brecht's attempt to rescue his sister, and that you came here with von Bron. Very clever of you to avoid my traps."

"Let's not lie?" I nearly choke on the words, rage filling me, drowning the terror. "You've done nothing but lie to me since we met. You're not a sweet, caring woman who lives on her country estate. You kill people for money."

The Bane props her hip on the table, her tone mild. "I told you the truth. I do spend most of my days at my estate in Eaglan, though I take the occasional assassination job when the price is right. As for being a killer…" she shrugs, unconcerned. "It depends on who you ask. I learned a long time ago that people will excuse a murder as long as they think it's justified."

My stomach churns remembering how quickly I dismissed Alexander's guilt over killing Herr Goff. *But that's different!* "You're insane."

Her smile widens, sending chills down my spine. "Aren't we all a bit mad? And before I forget, I'm sorry I had to rush off without saying goodbye. Very rude of me, I know. I was planning to explain everything after."

I screech, "You thought I'd want to talk to you after you killed Alexander and Aliz?"

She frowns. "I was only going to kill von Bron."

"That doesn't make it better."

"Of course it does. As much as I dislike *Kangan* Brecht and *Rirzan* Brecht, killing either of them would be unnecessary. I only took *Rirzan* Brecht because I needed her for my plan." The Bane tilts her head to the side, a small smile on her lips. "Although I'll confess that I'm happy it's her, and I didn't have to involve you or some other innocent girl in my plans."

A piece of the puzzle snaps into place. "You took her to lure Alexander out of Merchwood. That's what the note was going to say. That you have Aliz and he needs to come alone or you'd kill her." *Because the Bane thinks Alexander loves Aliz.* I snap my mouth shut, too late realizing that my thoughtless comment confirms Herr Goff never left the note, so the only way we could know about it is if Herr Goff told us.

The Bane chuckles at my expression. "That's all right. I know Edgar told you everything, otherwise you wouldn't have been able to find my home or avoid my traps. Was he captured?"

We didn't need his help to find you. We did that on our own. It's annoying that even the Bane underestimates me. I consider lying to her in case news of his death sets her off, but find I'm past caring. The reckless part of me almost wishes she'd attack me instead of acting like everything's perfectly normal. "He's dead."

The Bane sighs deeply. "My nephew always was a disappointment. I never wanted an apprentice, since there's always a chance they'll betray you, but I had to take Edgar in when his parents died. And after he grew up, he needed a career. At least it worked out in the end. Now I can go into my retirement with no loose ends."

The callous way she dismisses her nephew's death is even more chilling than knowing she's an infamous assassin. I straighten and lift an eyebrow, hoping she can't sense how much she unnerves me. "His plan sounded better than yours. Why kidnap Aliz to get Alexander to leave Merchwood? He was right. You should've just taken Alexander and left Aliz alone."

"Is that what he told you? He really had no idea the details and art that go into planning a murder." The Bane pinches the bridge of her nose, her eyebrows drawing close together. "Fortunes, it's a good thing he never took over. If I left it to him, he'd just run in with a sword and stab everyone." She shakes her head, then looks at me, her eyes bright. "I'm actually quite proud of this one. I worked on it for over a year. Since it's my last act as the Bane and it's personal to me, I wanted to make it special."

My lips curl back, baring my teeth. "How can it be personal? Alexander hasn't done anything to you. He never even met you until the party!"

"No, but his father has." The Bane frowns to herself, then refocuses on me. "I'm sorry you were hurt during my first attempt to punish him, dear. I didn't anticipate that you'd get caught in my trap."

She's acting like she spilled tea on my gown. A sour taste fills my mouth, as I clutch my locket. "You almost killed me. You killed my mother!"

The first hint of anger flashes across her face. "As I said, I didn't intend to harm you. Besides, you got the slower-acting version, and I sent the antidote to your home as soon as I heard. You both should've made a full recovery in a few days. It's not my fault if the menders and your family didn't give it to you."

Fury whispers in my ear to kill her, but I grit my teeth, resisting. I need to keep her talking about Alexander and Aliz. Hopefully she'll let something slip that'll help me free them. "If you're so set on revenge, why not kill Alexander's father? Why hurt Alexander?"

She looks at me in surprise. "Because I love Philipp. I could never harm him."

I blink. *Love?* My stomach twists. *Impossible.*

Her lips press into a thin line. "But I need him to feel the same pain and loss that I did. I knew the Sunselt party would be the perfect opportunity to act. I always get an invitation, and it would be easy to blend into the crowd. Nobody would pay attention to the eccentric old lady from an unimportant estate. Von Bron had been toying with the idea of courting *Rirzan* Brecht for almost a year, and it looked like he was finally ready to get serious about it. I was actually hoping they'd be engaged by the time I took *Rirzan* Brecht, but it didn't matter as long as he was in love with her."

I'm surprised by the flash of jealousy at hearing how long Alexander was interested in Aliz. I push it aside. I can't blame him for trying to move on and live his life. He thought he'd never see me again. Besides, nothing happened between them. They both told me that.

"After von Bron got the note with my instructions, he'd run off through the providence until he reached the spot where Edgar would ambush him. That way he'd disappear without a trace, far away from here. You see, I didn't want von Bron to come here in case he was followed. I was also trying to keep my identity a secret so I could retire to Eaglan, but it seems like that was too much to hope for."

The Bane takes the small jar off the table and walks to the wall of shelves, her back turned to me. My hand shakes, and my body tenses. *I can't attack her. I need her to tell me where Aliz is. Is this a trick to try and get me to drop my guard? Or does she think I'm so pitiful that she can ignore me?*

Before I can make up my mind on what to do, she puts the jar on the shelf and faces me. "You asked why I would take *Rirzan* Brecht instead of von Bron. That's a rather genius move on my part if I do say so myself." She beams. "It serves several purposes, all designed with Philipp in mind. People would see von Bron leave Merchwood alone and stay at several inns along on the way before we took him. That way Philipp would always know his son went willingly and wasn't kidnapped. He'll also know von Bron could've gone home to his family, or asked for help at any point, but he didn't. Philipp will be angry at his son for not saving himself, and then feel guilty about being angry. Very clever, don't you agree?"

I grit my teeth, staying silent.

She's unfazed by my lack of response, cheerfully proceeding with her story. "But that's only the beginning. Once I had von Bron and *Rirzan* Brecht here, I'd take turns torturing them in front of each other." She winces. "It's not my favorite part of this line of work, but unfortunately it's necessary sometimes. *Rirzan* Brecht has to suffer, and she has to know exactly what happened to von Bron for maximum impact."

Bile rises up my throat and I try not to gag. I want to cover my ears and scream to drown out her words. *How can she talk so calmly about such horrible things?*

"Then I'd pretend we're moving to a new location because *Kangan* Brecht's too close to finding us. I'd let *Rirzan* Brecht escape without making it obvious that I'm letting her leave. She'll go home, hurt, scared, and tell everyone what happened, including Philipp. He'll know exactly how his son suffered. But what he won't know is if von Bron's still alive and in agony somewhere, or if he's dead. And he'll have that question hanging over his head for the rest of his life, driving him mad, stealing all his joy and happiness until the day he dies."

I clap a hand over my mouth, my gut tightening. What she has planned for Alexander's parents sounds like a living nightmare. How could she ever think I'd approve of any of this? It's monstrous. Inhuman.

The Bane grins. "By comparison, the other misery he'll go through is hardly worth mentioning, but it'll be there too. How *Rirzan* Brecht's kidnapping and torture will overshadow von Bron's disappearance, proving how little people care about the von Brons, making Philipp feel even more alone in his torment. How his family and businesses will suffer because everyone will cut him off, since they'll know *Rirzan* Brecht was only taken because of her relationship with von Bron."

The joy she's taking from her horrible plan is sickening. I don't know how I could've ever though this woman was my friend. The part she played at the party was certainly convincing, but I can't believe I missed the evil lurking below the surface.

She frowns at me. "I wore a mask to hide my identity when I took *Rirzan* Brecht, so Philipp would never know who was behind his son's abduction, but I guess that secret's out. It's too bad. I even had plans for establishing my alibi back at Merchwood while my nephew managed *Rirzan* Brecht's escape. And he'd kill another staff member and hide his body, so the suspicion would fall on him instead of us. But it's no matter if people know it was me." She taps her lips thoughtfully. "It might even be better since Philipp will know it's his fault his son's dead. And this chapter of my life will be closed and I can disappear somewhere. The continent's large and I've picked up enough tricks and contacts over the years that they'll never be able to find me."

"Why?" I choke out. "What did Alexander's father do to deserve this?"

She tilts her head to the side. "He didn't love me."

I wait, but she doesn't say anything else. Blood pounds in my ears as my chest in knots. "That's it? He didn't love you, so you have to destroy his life and family?"

"Of course. You know what it's like to be rejected and abandoned by the man you love. How it eats you up inside until you feel hollow and worthless. That's why I thought

you'd be happier about von Bron's death. We're kindred
spirits."

"But—but Alexander's parents have been happily
married for years." I bite my lip, dread filling my stomach,
almost afraid to ask because I don't want to know the
answer. "Are you saying you had an affair with his father?"

The Bane's head jerks back, a disgusted look on her
face. "Fortunes, no! I'd never accept that. We met when we
were young and freshly introduced to society. The moment I
set eyes on Philipp, I knew I'd marry him. It was true love.
Until that *woman*—" she spits out the word. "She wrecked
everything. I tried to tell Philipp that he was making a
mistake, but he wouldn't listen. He abandoned me to marry
her, just like von Bron left you when you were ill."

It's sickening that she thinks our situations are the same.
"He didn't abandon you. He made a choice, just like you
have a choice. You can't punish him because he didn't love
you."

"Philipp betrayed me. Betrayed us. I can't forgive that."
She waves a hand through the air. "Since I wouldn't marry
anyone else, I had to find a way to make a living and fund
my estate. Luckily, people are willing to pay handsomely for
murder. It was surprisingly simple to take my plant
knowledge and turn it into a lucrative business. And now it'll
help me get revenge for Philipp abandoning me all those
years ago." The Bane shakes her head. "We were both
foolish enough to love von Brons, and we paid the price.
Now they have to pay theirs."

When she steps toward me, I block the door, my hands
shaking so badly I almost drop the dagger, my heart
thundering "I won't let you hurt Alexander and Aliz." I ball
my other hand into a fist, fighting the urge to touch the other

knife hidden in my back waistband, afraid to call her attention to it.

She lifts her eyebrows. "There's no need to be dramatic, dear."

I snarl, "I'm not your *dear*."

The Bane sighs. "I understand, but I wish it didn't have to end this way."

She flings a green bottle at me. I duck, the container shattering against the door, showering me with glass and a foul-smelling liquid. Two more jars fly at me and I dive to the side. The knife in my waistband clatters to the floor, out of reach. I scramble up, locking my eyes on her.

The Bane has a wicked-looking dagger in her hand. She looks a lot more confident wielding her blade than I feel with my small knife. "We could end this right now. I'll go take care of my errands, and you can leave. Tell *Kangan* Brecht that you and von Bron got separated in the forest, and nobody will be the wiser."

I stall, frantically trying to think of a way to get an advantage over her. "So you can kill me later? That doesn't sound very smart." *Should I run straight at her? How can I get that knife away from her?*

She tilts her head to the side, her brow furrowed. "Why would I do that? My identity's already exposed. No, once I have my justice, I'll retire in peace. You'll never see or hear from me again."

The Bane sounds sincere. I consider pretending to accept her offer and then follow her to where she's keeping Aliz and Alexander. But it's too risky. If she caught me or gave me the slip, they'd die. *I have to finish this here.*

I grab a large bottle off the shelf and fling it at her.

She doesn't flinch. It goes wide and smashes against the

wall. I curse and throw another. She dodges it easily, then lunges at me. Everything turns into a blur as I move purely on instinct and fear. Her blade slices my arm, leaving a trail of fire, as I blindly stab out with my dagger. Our screams mix. Knives and pain and blood. The dagger flies from my hand. I slam into her, clawing, scratching, biting. We stagger across the floor.

My side smashes into the table with a loud *crack*. White-hot pain flares in my ribs. I crumble to the ground with a groan.

The Bane steps over me and opens the door. "You'll be all right until I return. Don't touch anything."

I push myself up and lunge at her with an incoherent scream. My fingers grip the hem of her dress, tripping her, sending her crashing to the ground. I try to pin her—but she's too quick, rolling over and grabbing my hands. We grapple on the floor, rolling across the stone. She shoves me away with surprising strength.

We both climb slowly to our feet, panting. I press a hand to my throbbing side, gritting my teeth against the pain, tears stinging my eyes. I keep my gaze locked on her as I inch to the left, putting myself between her and the exit.

The mask has finally dropped. The Bane stares at me with chilling gray eyes, her face disturbingly expressionless as she walks over to the table and reaches up. "I can see you're going to be a problem."

She hurls a lantern at me. I barely duck in time. It whizzes over my head into the next room and shatters. The Bane charges me, the kitchen knife pointed straight at my heart. I grab her hand with both of mine. We wrestle, shoulders hitting the wall, feet tripping and sliding. She slips. Her grip loosens and I wrench the knife from her.

And drive the blade into her neck.

Her eyes widen and she clutches my arms with a bruising force. I stare in horror as her mouth opens, but no sound comes out. The hot scent of iron fills the air as I fight to push her off. She slides to the ground, dragging me down with her in her vice-like hold. Her grip loosens and I shove her away. She slumps to her side, then falls back, a wet rattle coming from her ruined throat. Her blank eyes stare unseeing at the ceiling.

I scramble away until my back hits a wall, bile rushing up my throat, my stomach writhing. I cover my mouth with both hands and force my eyes away from her, focusing intently on the corner of a stone as tears stream down my face. Uncontrollable shudders sweep through me as my breath hitches. I wanted her dead, but I didn't want this. I don't know how long I sit there staring, shivering with horror, until my mind slowly comes back to reality.

She made me do it. She wasn't going to stop.

The Bane's words echo in my head: People will excuse a murder if they think it's justified.

No—I won't let her haunt me anymore. I shove her words away and take a deep breath, then gasp at the sharp, stabbing pain in my ribs. I didn't realize how many injuries I have from our fight.

My body's one giant bruise with flares of burning pain. The ribs seem to be the most serious, but I'm covered in cuts and scrapes. My legs have gone worryingly numb, though I still can move them with effort. Nothing life threatening from what I can determine, but I'd better see a mender sooner rather than later.

I rip strips from the hem of my skirt and clumsily bind up the worst cuts, my sluggish mind trying to call my attention to something in the room behind me.

An odd roaring fills the air. I cough, my throat stinging. *Smoke*. I drag myself to the door, my eyes widening in horror.

The house is on fire.

26

The floor above me collapses, raining down a shower of fire and wood. I dive to the side and roll until I hit the wall, my ribs shrieking. Small, popping explosions sound behind me. The floor shudders.

A loud grinding makes me look up. A huge iron chest is precariously balanced on the edge of the ruined floor above, slowly sliding down the remains of the floorboards. I cover my head with a shriek. The chest drops, crashing through the floor next to me, sending sprays of splinters and embers through the air. My sleeve flares up, searing my arm. I scream and pound the flames out with my hand, tears pricking my eyes at the scorching pain.

Blazing lines of fire climb up the walls and tapestries, hungrily devouring anything in its path. I crawl along the remains of the floorboards, gasping in the oily black fumes. Distant crashes and explosions sound throughout the house. The floor between me and the hallway door has disappeared, replaced with a gaping hole and a wall of fire. I frantically squint through the smoke, trying to find any way out. The

Bane's small workroom is a dead end, and there are no windows on this side of the room. My stomach drops.

I'm trapped.

"Carina," Alexander shouts, panicked. "Where are you? Carina!"

"Over here," I cough, trying to be heard over the crackling flames.

Pounding footsteps sound on the far side of the room, then Alexander staggers in, clutching his bleeding side. He curses and jerks to a stop before reaching the hole that used to be the floor. "Carina!"

I grit my teeth and force myself up, using the wall as leverage, my stomach lurching. His shoulders sag with relief, his eyes running over me frantically.

I hold up an arm to shield my face from the intense heat. "Where's Aliz?"

"Right behind me."

She limps into the room, her arm held at an awkward angle. "Carina, thank the Fortunes you're all right!"

I cough again, trying not to pass out from the pain in my ribs. The wall of fire swells out toward me and I cringe back. "Alexander, you have to get her out of here. The roof's going to come down." An ominous cracking noise overhead reinforces my warning.

"Not without you." He moves toward the hole, eyeing the wide gap between us.

My stomach fills with dread and my heart goes cold. *He'll never make it.* "There's a way out this way." I point to the workroom, the partially closed door blocking his view of the interior. "Go, I'll meet you outside." I will him to believe the lie with every fiber of my being, forcing myself to believe it too so he won't know I'm trapped. He'll never forgive me, but I won't let him die with me when I can save him.

He hesitates, indecision warring on his face.

"Hurry. You don't have much time. Aliz needs you." Gritting my teeth, I limp toward the room, putting all my focus and energy on making it to the workroom door.

He stays stubbornly for a moment longer, then goes to Aliz and helps her out of the room, shooting worried glances at me over his shoulder. It tears my heart up not to look at him and memorize his face one last time, but he'd know I was lying if I did and he'd die here with me. I swallow hard, the heat drying my tears before they can fall. My damaged hand grasps my mother's locket. I keep forcing my body toward the door even as every muscle cries out in agony and bile burns my throat.

After I'm sure they're gone, I collapse to my knees, retching. My muscles feel like they're full of lead and it's hard to think past the grinding pain in my ribs. It would be so easy to lie down and close my eyes—but I won't. I refuse to be the Bane's last victim.

There has to be a way out. Something. Anything.

The smoke and fire make it hard to see. My eyes sting as I squint at what remains of the floor. Shadows dance through the haze, and it's impossible to tell what's real and what's shadow.

Is that...? There's a floorboard still in place along the nearest wall. Half of it's missing, but it offers a path from my side of the room to the door. But first, I need to get through the wall of fire guarding it without getting burned alive.

I drag myself across the floor, shoving open the door to the Bane's workroom. The fire has inched its way in here, with shards from exploded bottles littering the floor and fingers of flames crawling along the shelves. There's no container large enough to hold enough liquid to put a dent in the fire, not that I could lift it if it did. I also don't know if the concoctions in here will kill the fire or feed it, which leaves me with only one choice.

I reluctantly move to the Bane's body and numbly pull out the knife, my damaged hands clumsy. Averting my eyes as much as possible, I remove her smock, gagging, my vision going gray from the agonizing pain in my ribs. Then I drag the cloak off the table and crawl as fast as my injuries will allow back into the main room. I hurriedly wrap myself in the double layer of fabric, making sure none of my skin's exposed, thanking the Fortunes I have my boots instead of slippers.

I look through the curtain of fire lining my side of the hole, squinting to find the slim board that's my goal. My pulse pounds in my ears as my stomach lurches. *This is insane. It'll never work. There has to be another way. I can't. I can't.*

Two running steps and I jump.

The low hood covers my face as I pass through the flames, the fire roaring around me, trying to drag me into its depths. I smash against the wall, screaming as my damaged bones grind together. My fingernails scrape the plaster, trying to find a handhold. I overbalance, teetering precariously over the gaping hole.

The floor below is an inferno, with flames greedily reaching up toward me. My fingers find a crack and I seize it, clinging to it with every ounce of my will. My balance steadies and I thump my forehead on the wall, my body sagging against the surface. But the crackling air and roaring heat tell me I'm running out of time.

Using one hand, I clumsily unbutton the smoldering cloak and let it drop into the flames below. I gulp and press myself against the wall, gritting my teeth against the stabbing pain in my ribs. Slowly, I slide my foot down the floorboard, wincing as the wood wobbles beneath me. I keep my eyes fixed on the edge of the sturdy flooring ten feet away, praying to the Fortunes that my ledge holds a bit longer. The board shivers as I hold my breath and inch along it. Every tremble threatens to drop me into the fire below. Every nerve's on edge.

The wood cracks. The section under my foot falls away and I stumble forward, my toes balanced on the thin sliver of floorboard sticking stubbornly to the wall. The piece shudders and there's a loud *snap*!

I fling myself forward as the board drops into the flames. My desperate leap lands me mostly on the solid floor, my left leg dangling over the edge. I quickly pull my leg up with a wrench, grinding my teeth against the agony in my chest, then breathe a sigh of relief when the floor holds. With no time to lose, I struggle up to my hands and knees and crawl towards the doorway, willing my shaking muscles to carry me just a bit farther.

My heart speeds up, racing, trying to break free of my chest. Sweat breaks out over my skin and instantly evaporates in the heat. My already mangled lungs wheeze for air. "No!" Black spots dance in front of my eyes, growing larger with every strangled breath. "No," I growl, clinging to consciousness.

I collapse, all my strength gone, as my heart pounds in a frenzied gallop. My cheek presses against the hot wood. I gasp in the scorching air. My hands shake as I reach forward blindly, trying to drag myself to the door. The room fades to black. My fingertips scrape at the floor, then still.

Strong arms scoop me up.

Alexander mutters, "Stubborn girl." He swiftly presses a kiss to my forehead as he lurches down the stairs.

We burst out through the front door, greedily sucking in the fresh air between coughs. Alexander staggers to where Aliz's standing and gently sets me on the ground. He lurches a few steps away and collapses into an unconscious pile.

"Alexander!" I feebly crawl closer to him, my stomach in knots, my heart in my throat.

Aliz drops to her knees next to him. "Burning fool threatened to tie me to a tree if I wouldn't wait here, even though he was the one could barely walk." She uses her good arm to peel his bloody shirt away from his side and swears as she presses a wadded cloth against it.

"Is he going to be all right?" *Please, please, please be all right. Please. I can't lose him. I can't.*

"Yes, yes. Stop moving, you're just going to hurt yourself. Look, the bleeding's almost stopped."

The tension runs out of my body and takes all my strength with it. I slowly wiggle out of the gory smock, then curl up in a ball on my side to relieve the pressure on my ribs and force a grin. "I didn't know you could swear."

"And I didn't know how idiotic you both could be. You deserve each other." She shakes her head and smiles tiredly as she awkwardly ties a bandage around his waist. "Thanks for saving me."

"I had to. You're my only friend, since the other one turned out to be the Bane."

She grimaces. "I still can't believe it. All that time, right under our noses. I never suspected a thing."

"Nobody did." I snicker, imaging how the gossipmongers will be salivating over this story for years. "The Merchwood Sunselt party was already legendary, but you'll never be able to top this."

Alexander groans, his fingers twitching. I take his hand and squeeze it, ignoring the pain in my palms. I move closer to him and brush back his hair as Aliz wisely slips away, giving us some privacy.

His eyes flutter open. "Carina?"

"I'm here." I press my hand against his cheek, tears stinging my eyes.

His grip on my hand tightens. "Are you all right? Where are you hurt?"

"I'll be fine. My ribs are the worst of it." I gently chide him, "What were you thinking? You could've been killed coming back for me."

He leans into my palm and closes his eyes with a relieved sigh. "I told you I wouldn't let you die. I knew you needed my help, but were too stubborn to ask for it."

"Not as stubborn as you," I wheeze. "I said I could get out."

"And I always know when you're lying. But I also knew you'd argue with me until Aliz was safe." He sit ups with a groan, then carefully tucks me against his side. "I think I need a trip to the Anglish countryside to recover from this party."

I lean my head against his shoulder. "I can show you the perfect spot. It's the least I can do since you're always rescuing me."

"And I'll be happy to keep doing it." He winces and touches his bandage. "But give me a week or two to recover first."

He's not the only one who needs to heal. "Let's agree that we're not going to chase down murderers, or fall out of trees, or jump out of any windows for at least two months. And no running into burning buildings for six months."

"Done and done." His lips brush against my hair. "I'm sure we'll find a way to pass the time."

Alexander puts up the oars and leans back on the rowboat's bench. "Do you think we'll sink again?"

I glance across the empty lake and shrug. "I'd say there's no chance, since Luther isn't here, but the Fortunes love to surprise us."

He chuckles as he rolls up his sleeves, offering me a tantalizing view of his muscled forearms. "Did Aliz decide when she's coming out to visit us?"

"Not for another month. She's waiting until the storm season's over so Luther won't fret about her getting stranded somewhere if the roads flood. He's being annoyingly overprotective." I nudge his leg with my toe. "Like someone else I know."

Alexander's lips twitch. "I've never been overprotective of Aliz."

I crinkle my nose at him. "Of course not. You don't have time, since you've been hovering over me since we left Merchwood, making sure I don't climb any interesting trees."

Alexander raises his eyebrows. "Do I ever stop you?"

I playfully fold my arms and narrow my eyes. "No, but you distract me every time I start to."

He smirks. "You don't seem to mind."

True. My cheeks heat and I giggle at the memory of his last diversion. "I only let you get away with it because my ribs aren't fully healed."

"And when they are, I'll be ready to catch you when you fall again." His grin is full of mischief. "But I'll still try to distract you first, because I'll use any excuse to put my arms around you."

I laugh. "I don't think you need an excuse."

"In that case." He slides over to my side of the boat, carefully tucking me against his side, always more cautious of my injuries than I am.

I snuggle against him with a happy sigh. I know that we'll bicker, and argue, and we'll even fight. But in the end, we'll always find our way through things together. Our time apart may have been unnecessary, but it hopefully taught us to talk through our issues instead of ignoring them or letting them drive us apart. I can't pretend that we won't make any foolish mistakes again, because I'm sure we will, but I have faith in us. Having lost each other once, we won't let it happen again. We'll face whatever the Fortunes throw at us together.

A gentle wave rocks the boat as I trace random patterns on the back of his hand. "We should go back to Wittrow for Wintertide. It'd be nice to be home for the celebrations."

"Your wish is my command, love. My parents will be thrilled. They're already asking when we're coming back."

"Cristoph, too. It's harder for him to get away from the estate these days, and I know he misses us."

Alexander toys with a strand of my hair. "It'll be good to see everyone again. But I have to confess, I enjoy having you all to myself for a while."

"You're always jealous about sharing my attention with other people," I tease.

"I can't help it. I'm selfish when it comes to you." He kisses the tip of my nose. "And we're making up for lost time."

"It has been fun getting to know grown-up Alexander." I adopt a mock serious expression. "He's so much more solemn and responsible than the young Alexander who helped me steal sweets and break into the attic."

He narrows his eyes, then nips my neck, making me yelp. "Not that solemn or responsible. After all, I'm out here wandering in the wilderness with you."

"I'd hardly consider a fully staffed inn roughing it. And didn't we come out here so you could go fishing? Or is that another excuse to keep me out of trees?" I give him a playful shove.

He moves back to his seat with a good-natured grumble. Alexander picks up the fishing pole and pulls a wiggling worm out of the bucket behind him. I scrunch my face as he puts it on the hook, then casts the line out into a shadowy patch of water near the bank.

He laughs as he sets the pole in its holder. "The worm bothers you?"

"I'm a lady. We're delicate creatures."

"Delicate is not a word I would use to describe you. Kind. Loyal. Precious. Beautiful, and a thousand other things come to mind. But delicate?" Alexander shakes his head. "Anyone who can jump through fire and climb trees is made of sterner stuff." He captures my hand and presses a kiss to my scarred palm.

Fortunes, I love this man. "Be sure to tell Cristoph that the next time we see him. He's still convinced I'll faint from shock if someone raises their voice around me."

He shakes his head, amused. "Even after that earful you gave him?"

"The man refuses to admit I can take care of myself."

"And where does your brother think you are right now?"

I grin mischievously. "Still in the Anglish countryside. If he doesn't know, he can't get mad."

He laughs. "One of these days, he'll find out the truth."

I shrug a shoulder. "And do what? He's my guardian in name only. He may feel like he has to protect me, but I've never let him tell me what to do before, and I'm not going to start now." I look up at him through my lashes. "Now you, on the other hand. You're a different matter"

He raises his eyebrows in mock surprise. "You'll follow my orders?"

"Of course not." I slip over to his side of the boat, my fingers lightly trailing up his arm, and he sucks in a breath. "But I think it's only fair that I consider your opinion from time to time. After all, it's always handy to have someone around who knows how to pick a lock. And you're brilliant. Loyal. Handsome. Kind." I press my lips to the corner of his jaw, tasting the sweet saltiness of his skin. "Charming. Humble." Another kiss below his ear. "Funny." A lingering kiss at the corner of his lips.

Alexander's arm tightens around my waist. "I thought I was supposed to be fishing." His voice is hoarse.

"Are you?" My finger traces his lips, then skims down his throat. His freshly shaven skin is enticingly soft, and I let my fingers wander, enchanted by the feel.

He clears his throat. "I've been thinking. Locklan's border is only a few hours from here."

"Hmm?" I run the back of my hand lightly along his jaw, mesmerized by the way his pulse jumps at my touch.

"We wouldn't need Cristoph's permission to get married there."

My heart skips a beat.

"Or we could go back to Wittrow, so your brother and my parents can be there. I'm sure Aliz and Luther would come." Alexander brushes his lips across my knuckles. "And we'll invite Ziggy and Lotta and anyone else you'd like. We could have the ceremony at our lake." His eyes dance with humor. "But we'll have to make sure Luther stays away from the boats."

My stomach fills with butterflies as I lift an eyebrow, trying not smile. "You're being rather presumptuous with all this planning."

Alexander puts his hands on either side of me and leans close, playfully narrowing his eyes. "Do you want to marry me?"

Obviously. I've known I was going to marry Alexander since I was six. I tilt my nose in the air and give him a haughty look. "No."

He grins and the heat in his eyes blazes. "Liar."

His thumb traces my cheek and my eyes slide closed. Alexander presses a gentle kiss to my eyelids, my cheeks, the corners of my mouth, igniting tiny fires on my skin everywhere his lips touch. He takes his time, savoring every touch, until I gasp at the intimacy of it, convinced I'll burst into flames at any moment. He whispers my name before tasting my lips with his. I wrap my arms around him, feeling his heart pounding in his chest. Despite his claim that I'm not delicate, he's oh so gentle when he pulls me into his lap. The sweet love in his kiss is mixed with hunger and need and promises. I lose myself in his touch, feeling at home in his arms, his body warm and solid against mine.

When we finally break apart, we're both gasping. I nuzzle his neck, breathing in the scent of his warmed skin.

Alexander cups my cheek, a tender smile on his face. "Carina, I've loved you since the moment I saw you. I foolishly lost you once, but I'll never make that mistake again. I want to spend every moment with you. I don't know what adventures and fires the Fortunes have planned for us, but I know I want to go through them with you."

He pulls out a familiar gold ring with an emerald surrounded by diamonds. My breath catches as tears fill my eyes, a warm glow bursting in my chest.

He ducks his chin, the tips of his ears turning red. "I asked Cristoph for it before we left." Seeing the tears streaming down my cheeks, he worriedly adds, "But my mother would love for you to wear hers if you'd prefer. Or I can buy you a new one. We can go into town and you can pick out—"

"No," I sniffle, giving him a watery smile. I swallow around the lump in my throat as I squeeze his hand. "This is perfect. Absolutely perfect."

He takes my hand and slips the ring on my finger. "Will you marry me?"

It's adorable how nervous he is, even though he knows what my answer has to be. "Yes, yes, yes." I wrap my arms around his neck, staring deep into his eyes, my heart swelling with happiness. "What took you so long?"

Alexander smiles, an immeasurable love shining in those green depths. "I had to wait until we grew up."

"As long as we're never too grown up to have adventures together."

"Never," he whispers before his lips capture mine.

***

Want more Carina and Alexander (plus a chance to meet the infamous Cristoph)? Sign up for my newsletter to get an exclusive BONUS SHORT STORY for more flirting and steamy kisses:

www.amandakayebooks.com/trails-blades-subscribe/

NOTE FROM THE AUTHOR:

Word of mouth is crucial for any new author. If you enjoyed the book, please leave a review on Amazon, Goodreads, or your favorite review site. Even a few words make a huge difference and are greatly appreciated!

Thank You!

Amanda Kaye

ALSO BY AMANDA KAYE

To hear about the next exciting release from
Amanda Kaye, sign up for her newsletter at:
AmandaKayeBooks.com/subscribe-now/

<u>Blades Series</u>
Cinders & Blades (short story)
Briars & Blades
Wolves & Blades
Beasts & Blades
Sirens & Blades
Trails & Blades

<u>Other Short Stories</u>
An Oath of Fire
Slithers & Swords
Restless Tides

ABOUT THE AUTHOR

Amanda Kaye loves plotting new ways to torture her characters and throw them into danger. Nothing makes her happier than reading an amazing book with an awesome character arc; her favorite authors include Mercedes Lackey, Robin McKinley, and Patricia Briggs. She can always find an excuse to buy sparkly nail polishes and chocolate chip cupcakes. Amanda lives in sunny California with her two mini-monsters masquerading as kittens.

Her stories remind you that there's always a silver lining no matter how dark the night. She'd love to chat with you about your favorite books at:

www.amandakayebooks.com/subscribe-now/

9 781737 360643